We Have Something to Say!

We Have Something to Say!

SONIA MYERS

atmosphere press

For Coral

"With every drop of water you drink,
every breath you take,
you're connected to the sea.
No matter where on Earth you live."
                    - Sylvia Earle

Part I:
The Blue Ocean

THE SPINNING EARTH

Picture this: The state of California, and along the edge a bumpy coastline where the continent meets the ocean. On that coastline, the land opens up and is filled with water from the ocean. This is the San Francisco Bay. Further in, you can see where the land was separated and is now surrounded by water on three sides. We call that the peninsula. Now imagine you could take your index finger and your thumb and zoom in on that peninsula to see a large school, and in that school was an inconsequential, short, curly-haired girl who was perfectly content being ignored.

Oh wait, that's me.

"Pull out your evidence journals, please," Ms. Morgan announced. She is our science teacher, though I wish I had her for every class.

We all reached into our backpacks and pulled out what everyone calls our science notebooks, except when Ms. Morgan is around, and then we call them our evidence journals. The first day she showed up she handed us these sturdy spiral notebooks. They were white with a hard cover and an abundance of thick blank pages. The journal was much bigger than our other notebooks. In fact, it is probably the nicest notebook we have ever received from a teacher. That was Ms. Morgan. She has a way of making us feel as if what we had to say was important.

Ms. Morgan had told us, "This is your evidence journal. Every scientist has a journal to write down notes, observations, and plans." She then showed us pages from Jane Goodall's notebook. It was filled with sketches, notes and labels. "I won't tell you what to write in your evidence journal. This is yours to explore. Write down what is of interest to you. Have fun with it. Use color, or don't use color!" She threw up her hands like she truly didn't care what we put in between the hard covers, but we all knew she was desperate for us to become explorers.

Our first assignment was to decorate the front cover of our evidence journal however we wanted, and have it ready by the following week.

Ms. Morgan drank a lot of free-trade coffee, she called it, and talked a lot about choices. She smiled a lot and laughed at our jokes. I'm not sure if she actually thought we were funny, but she made us feel special. Some of her students called her a VSCO girl because she wore Birkenstocks and she drank from a huge water bottle (it wasn't a Hydro flask though, I looked). Some students gave her scrunchies as a holiday gift last year and she actually put them around her wrist.

Ms. Morgan wasn't afraid to talk about environmental changes and how we could be a part of positive human impact. I listened and wondered, *How can I make a difference*? The problems she described were too big. I didn't say it out loud however, because then Ms. Morgan would go on and on about how important we are and how even the smallest act could have a big impact.

Ms. Morgan interrupted our transitional chatter and asked, "What are we looking at here?"

Our eyes moved up from our desks at what was a large picture of the Earth projected on the white board.

Observations soon flooded the room:

"The earth."

"The world."

"The world from outer space."

Then came a slide of two Earths side by side, one from 1972 and the other from 2015.

"What are your observations?" she asked us.

None of us said anything. She walked around our desks, then asked, "What do you notice?"

Lola finally mustered up the courage, "Well, the one in 2015 looks more blue," she said.

"Yes, sure," said Ms. Morgan. Then she called on Arjun.

"There are more clouds on the left?" he said with a bit of uncertainty.

"Great observation," said Ms. Morgan. Then she called on Brian.

"They kind of look the same to me. Sorry."

I think a lot of us agreed with Brian. I wondered what she wanted us to say. I didn't raise my hand very much during Science, or Math for that matter. I'm more of the

5

writer type, I think? I didn't want Ms. Morgan to call on me, so I made myself scarce and averted my eyes from the board to look down at my notebook. I had decorated it with puppy stickers and tape of different patterns. I wrote across it:

PROPERTY OF JENNY BARAJAS
HANDS OFF!

I glanced at Celia's notebook, who sat next to me. She had a printed-out sheet of the periodic table of elements. Jaime on the other hand had a really good drawing of Albert Einstein with $E=mc^2$ written all over.

Ms. Morgan flipped to the next slide. It read, Earth's Major Systems: Hydrosphere, Atmosphere, Geosphere, Biosphere. There was a lot of chatter now. People were saying things like:

"I know the hydrosphere, that's water."

"The atmosphere is oxygen."

"Oh-TWO!"

"I'm glad you are all excited!" said Ms. Morgan. "Now raise your hands. Tell me, what do you know about these systems?"

Celia was called on. "I think the biosphere is all the living stuff, like animals."

"Yes, great!" said Ms. Morgan.

Then it was Lola's turn, "The geosphere. Wait, did I say that right?'

"Mm-hmm," murmured Ms. Morgan.

"The geosphere is the inside of the Earth, like the core where it is really hot."

"Yes! Well, mostly. We will talk about the inner and

outer core in a little bit."

It was odd how Ms. Morgan got so excited at the dumbest answers. Of course I didn't know much, but it didn't seem that what Lola said was so profound.

Ms. Morgan gathered a few more comments from others and then showed us the next slide. It was the same picture as the first Earth from outer space. The class got chatty about how we already saw that picture, and then Jaime yelled, "You're going the wrong way!"

"Hold on, hold on," said Ms. Morgan. She clicked on a really small link below the Earth which sent her to the NASA website. The Earth was now live and was turning ever so slowly. We got quiet and watched. There was Africa, and you could clearly see the green in the middle of the continent. The tip of South America showed up. Then we saw the United States and Mexico. Clouds covered the spinning Earth, and water filled in every other part. It seemed the Pacific Ocean was going on forever. At a certain point it was all you could see. No land, until Australia came around, and then Asia, then Europe. The video was 2 minutes and 24 seconds long.

I don't know why, but I was captivated. The Pacific Ocean really stuck in my mind. Was it actually that big? The blue of the ocean appeared as deep as I perceived forever to feel.

"This is a series of photos that were taken and put together to form this video you are watching. What do you think?" Ms. Morgan asked us. It seemed like everyone's hand shot up. "Yes!" she yelled. "I love that you are all so eager!" She kind of jumped up and down in her Birkenstocks.

"That was really cool!"

7

"Can we watch it again, please?"

"Is that what it really looks like?"

She let us shout out and she sort of answered everyone's questions individually, and all at once. Then she asked us, "How do you think Earth's four systems come into play?"

"I think that all the systems have to work together to literally make the world go 'round," Arjun laughed.

"The world goes around because of gravity and its orbit around the sun," blurted Joshua with his arms in the air. Joshua was constantly frustrated at our lack of knowledge. I think he knows just enough to get him in trouble. He tends to have more issues at the lunch table, which makes him more arrogant in class.

"Thank you, Joshua," said Ms. Morgan. "And, thank you Arjun. Your observation is brilliant!" She continued. "No one is wrong. As long as you ask questions, and make observations you're all correct. Arjun is correct in that all the systems work together, and when they do we have a healthy planet, and a beautiful place to live."

She smiled, and we listened.

TRAFFIC

When school is finally out, I head to the parking lot and look for Dad. While he is always on time, rain or shine, he finds a new spot to park every day. Some days this can be very irritating.

After I have buckled up and settled in, he generally asks me how my day went, and I usually answer, *"Good."* Today was no different.

"Just good?" he prodded, asking for more details.

"Yeah."

Dad is a thinker. He spends so much of his time analyzing footage on a screen that he forgets what the real world is all about and how to converse. When he asks how my day went I understand it is the go-to phrase to use, the easy question to ask. There are days when I know that he cares, but most of the time I know he is thinking about the next edit.

We sat in silence for a while. I picked at the little piece of plastic that was hanging from the lock. Then I said, "Our science teacher is kind of funny."

"Oh yeah," Dad said. "What did he say?"

"He's a she."

"Oops, sorry." I could tell he was embarrassed.

"She doesn't really say things that are funny. It's more that she gets so excited. She thinks everyone in class is *brilliant*."

"That's cool," said Dad.

"Yeah, it's *cool,* but I'm nervous she is going to call on me. When it comes to science class I really have no idea what is going on or what is being talked about."

"That's not true," Dad said. He patted my knee with his show of encouragement.

All I could do was stare right back at him. He knew science wasn't my strong suit, and I knew he was just being kind.

People call my dad Peter, but Mom calls him Pedro. He makes movies. Not the kind you buy a ticket for at a movie theatre. No. He documents, which means he films real life. No scripts or planned scenes, except maybe the interviews. He is always working on some project, and always wants to show me some of the clips, but I have no interest. I tell him, "Wow, so cool!" But most of the time I would rather build a world in Minecraft or ride bikes with Jolene.

Jolene is my very best friend. We are neighbors, and so we ride our bicycles around all the time and buy serious junk food from the little store down the road. I mostly buy Whoppers and Doritos and eat them before my parents can see me, and I get rid of the plastic wrappers in the big garbage can outside.

Just last week when Jolene and I came back from our ride Mom noticed the Whoppers.

"Jenny!" she yelled. I had been thinking I was being sneaky. When she yelled the second time the Whoppers flew out of my hands and scattered about the floor. As I was collecting them she kept going, "Again? All that sugar is going to rot your teeth."

"Mom, I'm fine," I said, trying to reassure her, as well as making sure to regain my Whoppers without her noticing my desperation for each and every one. "Mom, it's okay." Though, I don't think she was buying it.

"Just don't make it a habit. It will be tough to break later."

Mom always seems tired—*exhausted,* in her own words. She doesn't like her job, but she doesn't really hate it either. At dinner the conversation is always about her work, which is at a bank opening up accounts, and she goes on about the people she works with and the anonymous customers she helps throughout the day. She has worked there for my whole life, and I think longer. The name plate at her desk, "Sofia Barajas," really needs to be replaced. Once when I was little, and ate as many lollipops as I could grab from the bowl by the tellers, I grabbed her name plate and smeared sugary fingers around each letter as I waited for Mom to finish up (it was one of those days where Mom and Dad's schedules collided like a meteor shower and felt like the world was coming to an end, but really Dad just had to drop me off at the bank and I had to sit there while Mom worked the last 30 minutes, and then we went home). I think some of the lollipop from all those years ago is still on her name plate. Mom seemed stressed that I was there that day, but everyone else at the bank appeared overjoyed with my presence.

Living here in the Bay Area is filled with salty coastal air and yet thick with highways and freeways. Apparently it is one of the most influential places in the world. That must mean it's a good place to live? We have things like Google, Apple, Facebook, and Salesforce (I'm not exactly sure what Salesforce does, but people say it is worldwide). Not to mention a ton of bridges connecting to other cities, and then there is the Pacific Ocean. I must also mention we have seven million people living here!

Mom complains about traffic. She says things like, "I will spend 500 hours in traffic this year." I imagined pulling all those hours, back-to-back, like a chain. With 24 hours in a day, and 168 hours in a week, Mom would spend three weeks in her car stuffed on a freeway with thousands of other cars. That sounded like a nightmare, one in which I was not privy to become the star actress. I don't want to be an adult if I have to give away three weeks out of my life in traffic.

Overall, I would say it's a pretty normal life. We eat as a family because Mom says it is important to sit together and eat a warm meal and talk about our day, even though she is the one doing the talking, and then my older sister Jackie inevitably takes over the conversation with stories no one cares to hear. Jackie is another story altogether. So, instead of talking about my day, I try to be invisible. No one seems to notice.

WORLD WILDLIFE FUND

When I got home I immediately grabbed my bike and went out with Jolene. Jolene and I don't go to the same school. Her mom, Eve, is at teacher at a private school, where Jolene attends. They are always doing fun projects, and going on field trips, and making robots, or at least that is what Jolene talks about.

"Want to go to the store?" Jolene asked me.

"Sure," I said. "I think I have some change."

Change was something that was scarce, and we were often desperate for a handful of quarters. If I had money from a birthday or something like that, I paid. Jolene did the same thing. Unfortunately, birthdays only come once a year. One time we were so desperate for money we got creative. We took two of my dad's undershirts, turned them inside out, and wrote W-A across the chest, for Wildlife Association. We decorated a coffee can, and went door-to-door asking our neighbors for donations. We collected nearly $15 and spent every last cent on candy. Eventually Mom found out, because my candy stash seemed endless. I had to come clean. Mom then called Eve and the two of us got in the most trouble we had ever been in. We were of course grounded and couldn't ride for two weeks. Eve told us we had to earn some money to make a real donation. Jolene and I held a lemonade stand for an entire weekend and made $33, after we paid Eve back for the ingredients. That night Jolene and I sat down with all our parents and handed over the $33 and watched Mom write a check to the World Wildlife Fund.

"I don't ever want to see this behavior again," Mom said. She was frustrated and embarrassed. I think she was only slightly relieved that at least Jolene was a part of it as well. Jolene and I felt really bad. It was pretty much the worst idea ever, and we learned our lesson.

"Jolene, have you ever seen a picture of the Earth from space?"

"Yeah," she said. She was busy eating her Twix bar.

"What about one that spins?" I asked.

"Like a video?"

"Yeah."

"Sure."

"The Pacific Ocean is really big," I said. Jolene didn't seem to care. She was slowly separating the chocolate from the caramel and cookie. I felt like a big nerd for bringing it up, so I changed the subject. "Want to go on the swing tour?"

"Sure."

The swing tour was a quick ride on all the rope swings around the neighborhood. It gave us something to do when we were bored and didn't want to go home and do homework. Homework wasn't awful, but it wasn't something I looked forward to. I would rather do it after dinner when the sun was down and I had absolutely nothing else to do.

Jolene at least had a younger brother to play with. She says she hates him, but whenever I go to her house, they're always busy playing together. Of course she immediately ditches him when she sees me.

I have an older sister. She's a lot older than me. She's graduating from high school this year. My parents decided to have a decent-sized gap between kids. Though, I don't know if that was actually their plan. Jackie doesn't really seem to be interested in anything that has to do with me, so it's kind of like being an only child.

Jackie is what my parents think of as *passionate*. She is involved in everything, and once she got a car we barely saw her. She is the editor for the school newspaper and is the President of the school, and is on every committee to save something. She is a strict vegetarian and has traveled some place every summer with a school group to study and learn more. About what? She doesn't tell me about any of her work. The only time she is at home, she is just writing or yelling about some injustice happening in the world. At least that is how it feels.

That was one thing we had in common. We both like to write. She writes about changing the world, and I like to write about friendship and my latest dream. Mom says Jackie has been writing ever since she could hold a pencil. She had a poem published when she was seven. I said, "I like to write too."

"I know honey," Mom said, giving me a hug. "It's just different. Jackie is very passionate."

"Sofia," Dad said. "Jenny is a good writer as well. She just hasn't found what she wants to write about."

"I have," I declared. "I like to write about my friends and funny stuff. Jackie writes about *boring* stuff."

From the other side of the house, inside her closed bedroom, with music on, Jackie yelled, "This stuff isn't boring, dork!"

She never cared about anything I had to say, except when I said she was boring.

THE HYDROSPHERE

"Now that we have some base knowledge on all four systems, let's dive deeper," said Ms. Morgan.

She had her thermos of coffee, and her hair was down in big curls that crowded her face every time she said a word. Her shirt today was bright green, with "L" then the circular Earth, then "V", and then "E." She was often wearing t-shirts with a message. My favorite one of her t-shirts says, "There is no planet B."

"Today you are all going to break up into groups and do a bit of research on one of the four systems," said Ms. Morgan. "I have already picked your groups, so no need to start finding a partner, and I created a web quest so no need to fret about where or what to research."

There was the usual grumble of not being able to pick who we wanted to work with. I thought having her pick the groups was much easier. We didn't have to think and no one's feelings got hurt.

Jaime raised his hand at this point.

"Yes, Jamie?"

"Ms. Morgan it's *hi-meh,* not j*ay-mee,*" he said.

"Oh, I'm so sorry, Jaime. I can't believe I said that again. Please forgive me," said Ms. Morgan. You could see she was genuinely embarrassed. I would be too, though she has mispronounced his name so many times. "I know I told you about my friend named *Jamie,* right?" She said, "I get confused."

We had all heard it before, but we liked her, so it seemed different than the other teachers who mispronounced someone's name and seemed to move on without notice.

"Was there anything you wanted to add?" she asked.

"I had a question," he said. "What's a *web quest*?"

This is where I am completely different from the students in my class. I had no idea what a web quest was either, but I was not going to admit I didn't know. Even though Jaime acted like a know-it-all sometimes, and that can be annoying, I was glad he asked.

"Has anyone ever heard of a web quest?" Ms. Morgan asked us.

I looked around and saw most people shaking their heads.

"Well," she started. "A web quest is a list of websites, that I already found, centered around a topic where you can gain a lot of information without having to weed through all the other sites."

A few nodded their heads.

"Okay, here we go. First group is the hydrosphere,"

she announced. We shot hopeful looks to one another, hoping we would be grouped with our friends. "Celia, *Jaime,*" she smiled at him. "Brian, Jenny, and Lola."

"Yes!" I yelled, putting my hands into fists and dropping them down my elbows.

Celia and Jaime looked at me with surprise.

"Since when did you get excited about science?" asked Celia.

"I just wanted to be in the hydrosphere group," I said.

The Pacific Ocean was officially ingrained in my mind since the video of the spinning Earth. Its immensity was a mystery to me. I had looked it up that day and discovered the Pacific Ocean takes up about 30 percent of the Earth's surface. That means that almost a third of our planet is the Pacific Ocean. You cannot deny that is big!

"Is it because it sounds like *Hydro flask.*" Jaime laughed at me. He got Celia to laugh at me too.

"No," I said. My face was flushed and running at a high temperature. Could they see my cheeks turning red?

Ms. Morgan announced the rest of the groups. We grabbed our laptops and with the list of websites Ms. Morgan arranged for us to look through, we got started.

"Take 20 minutes to gather as much information as you possibly can on your system," Ms. Morgan said. "After those 20 minutes, you will break up into different groups and teach the others about your system. You'll listen to others and take notes on their systems too. OK, got it? Go!"

"I'll go to the first site," barked Celia. "Lola go to the second one."

I wasn't fully listening to Celia anymore, because I was suddenly very aware that I was going to have to present my "research" to others in the class, and I cannot think of something more horrifying than people actually needing information from me. Plus I was still thinking about what Celia and Jaime had said about me. Just because I didn't have Albert Einstein on my journal didn't make me a VSCO girl.

I explored the websites on my own. The hydrosphere was mostly the water cycle, something we first learned about in first or second grade. Typing in the url was difficult all on its own. I kept leaving out a letter or a number. Eventually I got to a National Geographic article. As I read through it I could actually understand what it said, and it was so interesting. My pencil started to move across the page as I was quickly jotting down notes. Pretty soon the 20 minutes were up and surprisingly I had an entire page of information.

"Whoa!" Brian shouted. "Jenny, you wrote too much." He looked at the others in our group with worry. "I don't have that much."

"It's not too much," Lola said to me. "You just wrote a lot."

"Well," I started to say, but Ms. Morgan began assigning us to new groups. We were instructed to move around the classroom and find a new seat.

"Each of you will have two minutes to tell the others what you just learned," said Ms. Morgan. "Let's start with the geosphere."

I listened about continental drift, tectonic plates, and the layers of the Earth below the crust. All I could think about was how the ocean floor felt with all that movement below.

"Good work geosphere," said Ms. Morgan. "Let's move on to the biosphere."

I heard about the first single-celled organism and how humans really came so much later. We haven't been around for very long compared to the 4.5 billion-year-old Earth.

"You are all doing a wonderful job," said Ms. Morgan. "I'm learning new stuff too. Now on to the atmosphere."

There was some interesting stuff, like Ms. Morgan had said. Again, while Joshua droned on, all I could think about was if we polluted our air with too much carbon, it would get mixed in with the clouds and then rain down on us. It was doubly bad then, right?

"On to the hydrosphere!" Ms. Morgan instructed us.

I hated being on the spot, but I had little choice. Everyone had taken their turn. Now the attention was on me, and everyone in my little group was either staring directly at me, or they were staring at their notebooks ready to write what I had to say. I imagined I would get it all wrong, someone will correct me, and again I will feel like the dumbest person in the room.

I took a moment to clear my throat, then began. "Well, the hydrosphere is one of the coolest spheres, because water makes up 75 percent of our planet. That's why Earth is called the blue planet. Less than 3 percent of the Earth's water is fresh, and mostly frozen. A small amount of freshwater is found underground in aquifers, and only a really really small amount is easily accessible. Water is what made life on the planet possible. When water vapor, that's steam, got cold enough it rained and then filled up empty holes and formed oceans, and that's where life started."

"Good work, everyone!" announced Ms. Morgan.

Phew! It was over before it began. I needed a sip of

water after all of that.

I hadn't realized but Ms. Morgan was listening to me the whole time. "Jenny, that was brilliant," she told me. "Well done."

"Oh," I said, shifting in my seat. "There is still a lot more."

"I can see from your notes. That's all the time we have for now, but we are going to be talking about the ocean soon enough. Keep those notes."

She walked off to the front of the class and gathered everyone's attention.

"Well that was impressive," she told us. "You all did great research. That's a large part of being a scientist. It is not always an experiment. Oftentimes it is how to find information, and then what to do with this new information once you found it. That's when you discover solutions to problems. You are on your way to becoming solutionaries!"

FOOD WASTE AND GIRLS' EDUCATION

That night at dinner I couldn't help but think about how Ms. Morgan said I was brilliant. I know she thinks we are all brilliant, but now I was somehow part of that group. It felt good. Better than having to listen to Jackie go on and on about her latest cause.

"Food waste is a huge contributor to carbon emissions in our air," she said. "Almost a third of the food produced is wasted or lost. It's crazy because there are people who are starving all over the world, or are food insecure, like close to 12 percent of the global population, and there is enough food to feed everyone. Seriously, 40 percent of food is wasted in the United States."

Jackie never tired of letting us know about the injustices of the world. The question that often ran through my mind is what does she do with all that information besides being angry and spouting off facts wherever there was an audience. What was the point? Jackie joined every club at school that would have her, but what would a club help her with when she graduated high school and moved on. I hope that whoever she meets at college will flick her off like a pesky flea.

"Where did you hear that?" I asked Jackie.

"Hear what?" she said.

"Hear about food insecurity and carbon emissions," I responded.

"I read it, duh." She flipped her broccoli to the side of the plate then stabbed it with her fork.

"Where?"

When Jackie finally stopped chewing and put her fork down, she said, "Why do you care?"

I didn't know what to say. Did I care? I think so?

"Never mind," I said.

We went on eating our dinner.

"It was from a book called *Drawdown,*" Jackie eventually said. She couldn't help herself. "It was published in 2017, and it ranks all the possible solutions to greenhouse gases, from one, being the solution that can reduce the most greenhouse gases, to 100. I came across it in this youth seminar last year with the county of education."

"That's interesting," Dad said. He continued mixing the food on his plate onto his fork for one flavorful bite.

"Honestly, if you have an ounce of care in your body, you'll look through it," said Jackie raising her eyebrows, but not bothering to look my way.

Mom then started in on someone at the bank, but then Jackie interrupted. "Want to know something even crazier?" she said. "The number six solution with the highest reduction of greenhouse gases is, oh wait." She smiled at all of us. "Try to guess."

We stopped putting food in our mouths. We stared at Jackie and each other without a clue in the world.

"Electric cars?" said Mom. I could see Mom was nervous just guessing.

"Nope. It's women's education."

"Really?" said Dad. "That's interesting."

"Yeah, crazy, right?" said Jackie. "Basically the less education girls receive, the higher the rate of children they birth, which causes overpopulation, which is essentially a strain on the planet's resources."

For once Jackie actually had me thinking. Do most girls in the world not have access to education? Does education really make a difference? While this was intriguing, I was not going to let on that I had the slightest bit of interest. It would give Jackie too much satisfaction.

After Jackie exhausted herself on food waste, and the inequities of the educational system Mom started up again about some customer who rudely corrected her grammar at the bank today.

"It's so boorish when people think they are better than you," said Jackie to Mom. "Especially when they don't even know you."

Mom looked at Jackie and nodded.

"You do that all the time," I told Jackie. Then I swallowed hard.

"Excuse me?" said Jackie.

Jackie can be very scary. However, every now and again I feel the need to give it to her, just a little. I'm a little sister. "You're always telling people what they *should* believe in."

The room stopped. Mom, Dad, and Jackie stared in my direction. It was like teaching the hydrosphere all over again. All eyes on me, waiting, wondering. I was nervous, because I know that I cannot compete with Jackie. It's not just her knowledge, but her ferocity, and stop-at-nothing approach when it comes to debate.

"On issues that matter," said Jackie. "Not something that is just going to hurt that person's feelings over something inconsequential and meaningless."

I waited for time to pass, hoping maybe the conversation would go in a different direction, but before I knew it I was opening my mouth again, "How do you know? You might have hurt their feelings," I said.

"They may feel *guilty*. I'm helping them to be more aware."

"Actually," I said. "You're just mean."

"Okay, okay," said Dad. He held his arms out to silence our argument. "I think we are misunderstanding one another." Dad turned to me, "Jenny, what Jackie is speaking about is bringing up uncomfortable topics that people may not want to discuss."

"My science teacher tells us a bunch of stuff that is hard to understand, but she doesn't attack us." Then I looked at Jackie with hard eyes.

"You wouldn't understand Jenny. All you care about is getting distracted by some trivial commercial product that pollutes our world," she said.

I narrowed my eyes into thin slivers, and stared right through Jackie. Jackie the Jerk.

She is right, though. I do get sucked into lifestyle choices that I know are shallow. Even if I were to bring up something with more depth, no one would listen to me, anyhow. Even though Jackie is a jerk, she is kind of a smart jerk. Though I would never let on that I thought she was smart.

"What does your teacher talk about anyway?" she asked me.

I didn't want to share Ms. Morgan with my family. She had said I was brilliant today, and Jackie wouldn't understand. She would just laugh at me. I shall keep her to myself.

"I don't really remember," I said.

"See," declared Jackie, pointing in my direction while trying to convince my parents with her exaggerated face of my apparent ignorance.

Jackie the Jerk.

30 PERCENT

"Hey, Mom."

"Yes, Jenny."

"What are we doing today?" I asked. Weekends seem to come and go, uneventfully. I wait all week for Friday night, then I blink my eyes and it's Monday morning, and I have nothing to show for it.

"I have to go grocery shopping, and do some cleaning around the house," she said.

"Yeah, but do we have plans today?"

"No, not really. I guess my plans are to get some things done around the house and make sure we have food for the week," she said. "I know it is not that exciting, and I might be adding to food waste in our country, but I must get it all done before the week starts."

"Does it take all day?" I asked.

Mom finally stopped moving things from one side to the next, appearing busy when she was just creating more chaos for herself. "What's wrong, honey? Did you have something in mind?"

I now had her full attention. "I was kind of thinking we could go to the beach?"

"The beach?" Mom stood there stunned. "Since when do you want to go to the beach?"

I looked away. My offbeat attempt at something new suddenly made me anxious. "Well, um, we never go, and today is a nice day."

"The beach is a 30-minute drive, and there is always traffic getting to the coast. It is more of an all-day event, not just a quick pop-in."

"Ok, never mind. No big deal."

I started to walk away to my room. I knew going to the beach wasn't something we could easily pursue. We would have to pack the car, get food, towels, and something to play with if we got bored. I *could* get it all packed quickly, but Mom showed little interest, and I didn't want to push the subject.

"Jenny?" Mom called out to me.

I turned around in the hallway, almost to my bedroom. Hopeful.

"Why do you want to go to the beach?" she asked.

Seeing only half of her in the hallway with her hand on her hip, staring sideways to steal a glance at me through the walls, I knew it was a lost cause. I gave it one more little push, anyway. "I don't know. We were just talking about it in class the other day, and I was thinking we never go, and it might be fun to see it first hand, since it is not *that* far away."

"Why don't you ask Jackie to take you?"

"NO!" was all we heard from the end of the hallway through Jackie's closed-bedroom door.

"Mom, no," I whispered. "I do not want to go with Jackie."

"Why not? You two don't spend enough time together," Mom said. "It would be great."

"There is a reason for that!" Jackie yelled again.

Mom came down to my level and whispered. "Just ask. You never know."

"*Really,* Mom?" I pointed to Jackie's bedroom door. "I think she is pretty certain she doesn't want to take me, or do anything with me in this lifetime."

"Just try," Mom said pushing her arms in my direction to shoo me down the hall. "Remember she will be graduating this year, and then she is moving off to college. This will be the last year you two are living together under the same roof."

"Except if she annoys everyone in her path and can't get a job and comes back to live with us," I said.

"Jenny, please," Mom said.

I had nothing further to say. If it was important to Mom *she* should try to make Jackie understand. I didn't want to spend the afternoon with Jackie anyway; she would just make me feel incompetent about something. I gave Mom the hard eyes, and walked back to my room.

Even if I did ask, Jackie was going to say *no*. It's not like she would actually feel bad enough to drive me to the beach.

Then I thought, *What if?* I guess I didn't really know, because I didn't ask her myself. Maybe there was a chance.

I really wanted to go to the beach. There was something

about the ocean waters calling to me. Something I needed to see for myself, not in pictures. I was desperate to feel the sand in my toes, and the cold water rushing up my ankles forcing me to make the decision to withstand the near freezing temperature or run back to my towel for warmth and comfort. I wanted to pick up shells and collect them. I wanted to gaze out into the 30 percent of our Earth's surface and wonder who lives in those deep waters, who makes a home. Do marine animals talk to one another, the way I talk to Jolene? Do they fight with their siblings like I do with Jackie? Do their parents leave for the day to their jobs and come home and make dinner? Do they know the difference between work and play, or is it all just play? I knew that looking at the ocean from the beach wasn't going to give me all the answers, but I wanted to be a part of it somehow.

I walked to Jackie's room quietly. With promise and fortitude, I raised my hand to knock on her door. It all felt so dramatic. Then, I paused and did some thinking. She might just say yes? She might just say no? There is absolutely no chance if I don't ask.

Knock knock.

"Don't even think about it," said Jackie, through the door. "I'm not taking you to the beach."

Now I know.

FEELING BLUE

Jackie's lack of affection didn't faze me, but it did make me wonder if I wasn't good enough. I never made it to the beach that day, and like every other uneventful weekend I was immediately back in class on Monday as if I never left.

Ms. Morgan's classroom was decorated with enthusiasm for the planet and all her students' art and projects. Our work was hung on the walls like when we were in Kindergarten. She had maps of the world, posters that made you wonder about wild places and animals. Ms. Morgan always said she preferred teaching outside but found herself inside more often because she wanted the most time with us instead of in transition. When I asked her if I could talk to her after class, she suggested, "Let's meet in the outdoor classroom at lunch."

I snuck away from the picnic tables without much

notice. I had the usual friends at school, but I wasn't really close with anyone. It didn't bother me, because at home I had Jolene and we did more things after school than I ever did with anyone at school for six hours.

I made my way to the outdoor classroom. It was a small space on the other side of the blacktop. Two years ago, a group of students built it after school as a present to the school community. It had open walls of lattice, rocks for the floor, and they constructed six benches that were placed around the inside of the space. At the entrance were two small boxes of sand with desert plants and large rocks for decoration. No one really hung out there. Most teachers didn't use it because they have said it's too difficult to keep students focused outside. I find that I am much more focused outside than inside the classroom. Inside the classroom I feel like I'm just going to get called on and have the wrong answer. Outside, I think about how great it is to be out of the room that my insecurities vanish and I no longer care anymore about being right or wrong.

Outside, everything is right.

"Hi, Ms. Morgan," I said.

She was eating a small sandwich, with her cloth napkin placed across her lap, and her reusable glass container to her left.

"Hello there," she said. "Come sit down."

I stepped upon the rocks, and enjoyed the noise they made under my feet. I noticed someone had scattered little blue stones. They shined bright reflecting the sun's rays.

"So, what's going on?" asked Ms. Morgan. "What did you want to talk about?"

I knew exactly what I wanted to say, but I had never talked to anyone about it before. I barely knew Ms.

Morgan. She made me feel comfortable, however. She made me feel like she wasn't going to judge me.

"Well," I started. *How would I start?* "The other day when you were talking about the web quest—"

"Yes," she said.

"I didn't know what it meant."

"No one did, Jenny. I was glad that Jaime asked."

She said his name correctly.

"Me too," I said. "It's just that, well, that was the first time that I actually noticed that others didn't know something. I wasn't the only one. Most of the time, I feel like I don't know what is going on in class. Everyone around me answers questions, or asks questions, while I sit there hoping I don't get called on."

"I hear you," said Ms. Morgan. "Though, the other day you had great things to say on the hydrosphere."

"That's another reason I wanted to talk to you. I am really interested in it. When you showed the picture of the spinning Earth all I was able to focus on was the Pacific Ocean."

"It's beautiful, isn't it?" she said. Her cheekbones lifted to meet her scrunched up eyes.

"Yeah. More than that, it is so big. It is way bigger than any of the continents."

"Great observation, Jenny."

I didn't want her to say that. I didn't want to be a scientist right now. I just wanted to have a normal conversation about how I felt in class. Why do teachers have to do that?

"Ms. Morgan, can I ask you something?"

"Of course. That's why we are here, right?"

"Yeah." I looked down at my hands. They were moving

around furiously. I leaned down and grabbed a blue stone from the ground and massaged it with my fingers. "It's just that, well." I didn't want to say what I was going to say, but for some reason I really wanted to tell Ms. Morgan. "I think I'm stupid, and I don't understand why?"

"First of all, you are not stupid," said Ms. Morgan. She put down her sandwich, wiped her hands, and moved her napkin to the side. She turned to me.

"That's what you are supposed to say," I told her.

"Why would you think that?" she asked me.

"It seems like everyone knows the answer to everything, or at least they are not afraid to raise their hand."

"I heard you are a good writer," she said.

"Writing is easy," I said. "You don't have to know anything, you just write."

"Writing is not easy for everyone, you know?"

"All you have to do is put your pencil down and that's it. In science and math, you have to know a million different things, and be able to talk about them with others. You have to experiment, and take tests."

"I understand what you are feeling. It would seem that way," said Ms. Morgan. "But I must tell you, they are the same."

"How can they be the same?" I asked.

"Well, writing is just a different way to answer a question."

"But, we don't write in science."

"Oh, yes we do. Look at what you wrote the other day. Look at your journal, what do you call that?" she said.

"Those are sketches and notes, not sentences," I said.

"It is writing, isn't it?" she asked me.

35

"Okay, okay. I guess you're right. It's just that it seems so hard to know everything. How do people do it all the time?"

Ms. Morgan carefully helped herself to the blue stone I had in my hand. She rubbed the sides of it, and then she held it up to the sun. She asked me, "What kind of stone do you think this is?"

"I'm not sure," I said. "It looks like the kind you buy in a bag at a craft store."

"That's what I was thinking," said Ms. Morgan. "What is it doing here, though?"

"I would think for decoration. It's different from all the other gray and white rocks." I picked up another blue stone. I held it up to the sun, like Ms. Morgan. It was beautiful the way it sparkled and became translucent. "Having the blue stones in here changes up the boring pattern and catches your eye," I added.

"Whoever put it here," she said. "I think was trying to bring about a smile."

"Maybe they knew people would like it?" I mentioned.

"Maybe," Ms. Morgan said. "Maybe they thought it would get people to ask questions."

"It is just a blue stone, from a craft store," I said.

"It is just a blue stone from a craft store," she repeated. "But, maybe it's something more?"

The bell rang. I dropped the stone back to the rock pile.

"Thank you for listening to me. Please don't tell anyone what I said," I pleaded.

"My lips are sealed," said Ms. Morgan.

OAT MILK

What Ms. Morgan said didn't really help, but somehow it made me feel better. Like I had an ally, or someone who wasn't going to laugh at me for things I couldn't figure out. I don't regularly get made fun of, but in class I generally have this feeling that I'm on the verge of something incoherent, which of course is an awful feeling, so I figure I might as well hide. Hiding is easier than being called upon with the wrong answer.

"Jenny?" Mom yelled for me from the dining room.

I was in my bedroom, staring at the wall thinking about the Pacific Ocean. I'm not sure why, but its blue expanse kept visiting my mind. The other day I started writing a poem:

Blue is the color of the sky and the sea,

Signs, and blankets, and words for me.

I got stuck here for hours, because it sounded lame.

Cap for the milk, blueberries and such.
Blue is the jelly bean I like so much.

To be honest, I don't really like jelly beans at all, and the cap for the milk is white, and it really isn't milk at all. Jackie has us buying almond milk. Then, after almost a year of our rough transition, she said we shouldn't be buying almond milk anymore, but make our own oat milk. Dad had been pouring almond milk into his coffee that morning, and I was enjoying a bowl of cereal. We stopped what we were doing and looked up at her.

"What?" she said.

"Well, honey," Dad said. "We started buying this because you told us it was better than cow's milk."

"I know, I know," said Jackie. "Things change. It's hard to keep up."

"What are you trying to keep up with?" Dad asked.

"I'm too tired to explain right now," she said.

Then she walked away to her room without so much as a glance in our direction.

Dad and I looked at each other for a moment, and then I went back to my cereal and he went back to his coffee.

"Jenny!" Mom yelled again.

"Yeah?"

"Come into the kitchen, please."

I threw my legs that I had propped up against the wall back down to the floor, and picked myself up.

I made it to the kitchen. "What's up, Mom?"

"Jackie has that thing we are supposed to go to tonight at the high school."

"*That thing*?" I asked.

"You know the thing, about something." Mom was busy setting the table. "Can you help me with this?" She handed me the forks and napkins.

"I don't think I know what you're talking about, sorry." I put the three place settings on the table. Jackie was apparently already at the high school. "Do I have to go? To whatever it is?"

"It's something for the newspaper. There are others from different school newspapers discussing topics." Mom was headed back into the kitchen to tend to what was cooking on the stove.

"Mom, this sounds awful," I whined. I could actually feel my face falling off my head, and melting down my body. I really didn't want to go. "I think I have been to one of these *things* before, and they are really boring. Plus, Jackie doesn't ever care if I'm there."

"I think this is very important to her, and I think we should all be there to support her," Mom said.

"All of us?" I asked.

"Yes, all of us." I stared at her furiously spinning food in a pan.

"Well, I have a lot of homework I need to finish."

"You will just have to finish it later tonight when we get back. Now, go tell your father it's time for dinner."

I stomped away. It is all so unfair that I need to be dragged to whatever event Jackie had. The problem is when I finally get to high school I won't be able to return the favor because she won't even be around.

I walked downstairs to Dad's studio. Across his screen

were little yellow birds flying out of eucalyptus trees. The next shot was a single Seagull perched on one leg staring out at the ocean, as if doing yoga.

"When did you get so interested in birds?" I asked him.

"I am not interested in birds," he said. He was staring intently at the screen with one hand on the mouse and the other on the keyboard. "OK...one...more...little...edit," he said slowly to himself.

"Dinner is ready," I said.

"I'm...almost...at...a...stopping...point." He was squinting so deeply I could barely tell if his eyes were open.

On the screen were pelicans jumping off a rock wall. It was a slow motion shot. Their wings were so wide and the lower part of their beak hung so heavy. I never realized they had yellow and red colored feathers on their heads.

It seemed Dad was always working on some fine detail. Something that no one would ever notice. Sometimes it was lining up the music to the right spot on the video that could take hours.

"Did you know we have to go to something tonight for Jackie? Because if you didn't and you're mad because Mom didn't remind you, I say we shouldn't go," I said.

Dad was still looking at the screen. "I know what your mother is talking about. It's a newspaper thing at her school."

Darn it!

"Do you even want to go?" I asked.

He still didn't take his eyes off the screen. "Of course I want to go. I am very proud of your sister."

I wanted to say, *but she's so annoying!* So I didn't say anything at all.

"Ok, there," he said. "All done." He finally lifted his

body from the computer and sat back cracking his knuckles, and then adjusting his back from side to side.

"What's with the birds?" I asked.

"Oh, I'm just editing something for a friend. It's a small job. Just want to knock something off my list before the end of the week," he said. Then he turned to me. "Why don't you want to go?"

"What?" I said.

"You don't sound very enthused about going tonight. Why not?"

"Really, Dad?"

"You know, Jenny, pretty soon Jackie will be out of the house." He walked toward me and placed his hand on my shoulders. "Believe it or not, you are going to miss her."

"Ugh, do you and Mom talk about this all the time?" I said. "She was saying something about this the other day. I think you two are going to miss Jackie waaaaay more than me."

"I'm not so sure," Dad said. "What's for dinner?"

"I really don't know, but I think it is going to be good. Jackie is not here to judge us, so Mom probably made something tasty and unhealthy."

We laughed as we made our way back up the stairs to the dining room table. Mom had dinner on the table and she was sitting there waiting for us.

"Steamed veggies over quinoa?" I moaned. "Jackie's not even here."

"I guess she is rubbing off on me," said Mom with a chuckle.

It wasn't funny.

CARBON EMISSIONS

The lights shined bright on the stage as we walked into the multipurpose room at the high school for Jackie's newspaper thing. There was a long rectangular table with microphones placed every three feet, and standing next to the table was a podium. There was a vase of clear water near the microphones and glasses for each speaker to clear their throats when the time came.

In the audience were rows of metal folding chairs. There were 10 rows and at least 10 chairs in each row. There were two sets of them, separated by a walkway down the middle. Were they expecting that many people to come listen to Jackie speak about the same thing she always talks about? She can be such a broken record.

I looked at Mom and asked, "Are they hoping for this many people?"

"I'm not sure, but I want a good seat regardless. Let's go to the front."

"Why? There are microphones. We will be able to hear her." I said.

"Knock it off!" Mom snapped. She had been in a rush all evening to get here, and she finally slowed down to yell at me. "You have been rude all night. Please, if you don't have anything nice to say about your sister, then keep quiet!"

"Jeez, Mom. Sorry."

"Well, I'm just tired of hearing you complain about your sister. I am very proud of her, and I think if you stopped to listen you may learn a thing or two from her."

"It's just that everything is always all about her," I said.

Mom found a few seats at the front and sat down. I followed her taking the middle seat between her and Dad.

"It's a big year for her. She is graduating high school," Mom said.

"Hey you two," said Dad. "I'm just going to use the bathroom before this gets started."

When he walked off, I turned toward Mom again, only this time I just kept quiet. There was nothing more to say.

Pretty soon the room was filling up, and the chatter among parents, other family members, and friends, lifted and encompassed the room, growing louder as everyone seemed to be speaking at the same time. A tall, thin woman finally came to the podium, and the noise slowly lowered to only a few whispers in the back of the room. "Thank you all for joining us tonight. We are thrilled to have the editors from four local high schools share with all of us their thoughts on some very important topics." She paused to smile, showing all her teeth. "I ask that you take your seats, and we will begin shortly."

Dad still wasn't back. I turned my head to look for him and I saw that every seat was taken!

"Is this seat taken?"

I looked up. It was another man, not Dad.

"Um, yes it is. My dad is sitting here," I said.

"Oh, ok. Thank you."

I turned to Mom. "He better hurry, or I might get lucky auctioning off his seat to the highest bidder."

Mom laughed.

"Sorry," I said. "You know, about being rude."

"I know." She patted my leg a couple times and then took her hand back.

Dad returned. "The place really filled up," he said.

The same woman returned to the podium. "Welcome to the Annual Young Editors Panel." She paused to allow time for the audience to clap. "We are here today to listen to some bright young minds discuss current topics they believe are important to their future, as well as yours." She took a moment to look at the audience with her wide smile. "These students are the editors of their school newspaper, and we are pleased to have them all with us."

Applause erupted around the room.

"We welcome, Josh Lyman from Cypress Cove High School, Jill Newman from Live Oak Prep, Jackeline Barajas from your very own Bayshore High School, and Kiran Shahani from Edgemont High School."

One by one the editors, including Jackie walked to their seat on the stage. The applause grew louder. Were they really clapping for these high school kids?

"Let's get started. Oh wait! Let me introduce myself. I'm Linda Robinson, and I assist the students at the Xpress

Newspaper and Magazine at San Francisco State University."

Believe it or not, I could see Jackie getting nervous. This doesn't happen often, but when she starts to take a clump of hair from the back of her head, and braids it really tight, then unbraids it, only to braid it again, I know she is nervous. Since this Linda-woman started talking Jackie has braided and unbraided that piece of hair three times.

Linda cleared her throat. "The first topic is about the influence of the newspaper on high school students, and how can more students needs and interests be reached?" Linda picked up her face from her paper. "Let's start with Kiran Shahani."

"Thank you, Ms. Robinson." He was dressed in black pants and a button-up white-collar shirt, with a red tie that was almost too short as it continued to sit on the top of the table. He tucked in under the table repeatedly.

"I would like to say that newspapers are still alive and well at Edgemont," he laughed. "There is a place for the written word, and for a physical copy of the news and entertainment." He moved his tie down again. "We are able to reach the students' needs through print as well as through digital media. We have set up multiple avenues for students to offer suggestions to our group and we are consistently reinventing our look to keep it fresh."

"Thank you, Kiran," said Linda. She looked down at her paper and then said, "I would like to ask this same question of Jackeline Barajas."

I looked at Jackie. I noticed the shirt she was wearing: *Education for Changes.* It was her brand, if you want to call it that. Something she uses to promote any one of her

45

causes. It was just a t-shirt, but when she wore a black blazer over it, she looked serious and professional.

She sat up straight in her chair and grinned at the audience. Her nerves seemed to ripple away. Oh no, here it comes. I already felt bad for this Kiran kid with his stupid red tie. She was going to eat him up.

"Thank you, Ms. Robinson." She cleared her throat, and glanced down at the papers in front of her. "While I want to sanguinely agree that there is still a place for print media, I must say it is on its way out." She glanced at Kiran before continuing on. "While many of us want to read from a physical copy and feel the ink bleed onto our fingers, it is without a doubt that the way in which we actually ingest our media and news is *online*. At Bayshore we have a full 'newspaper' online." She used air quotes when she said newspaper.

I always thought the air quotes were to patronize others. In fact, patronize is a word I looked up because I knew there was a word that describes the way Jackie spoke to me.

Jackie continued. "Since the staff at Bayshore Tides, our newspaper, has put most of our efforts into building a website—which regularly invites the student body to participate—we have seen our numbers grow immensely. Before our online presence we printed stacks of news-papers, and for a while had them folded into the local city newspaper, only to find we were left with bundles of fuel for bonfires. No one was reading the paper. Now, as we have shifted our efforts online we see a steady stream of visitors to the website, and participation in school events."

Jackie could go on forever. Someone would have shut off her mic in order to stop her. I looked up at Mom, who was smiling. She couldn't see out of her peripheral that I was looking up at her, so I turned to Dad. He held the same gaze, smiling intently at Jackie. I have to admit she was doing a great job already.

"Lastly, I would like to say that to-date we have saved approximately 33 trees in the past year. While that number may not seem significant, this simple fact means that we have saved nearly 23 pounds of carbon dioxide from entering our atmosphere."

"Well, thank you Jackeline," said Linda. "I'm happy to hear your paper, or well, your website is doing so well."

"Can I add something?" It was Jill Newman, another student editor on the panel.

"Yes, of course, Jill," said Linda.

Jill turned toward Jackie and said, "Jackeline, you say you saved 23 pounds of carbon dioxide?"

"Yes," said Jackie.

"Over one year?"

"Yes."

"Those numbers are similar to what one car produces in a single day. Hardly notable. I have read your editorials on what we can do to 'save the planet'." *Air quotes.* "How can you say that is even a feat worth touting?"

Holy Toledo! Someone just threw it back at Jackie, for like, the first time ever! What was she going to say? I turned toward Dad, whose smile faded. The same with Mom. Here it comes! Jackie didn't hold the appearance of someone who was told off, she simply smiled at Jill, and then turned her attention to the audience. She took the stack of papers in her hands and shuffled them, tapping them lightly on the table putting them in order. She placed them back down on the table.

"If I may, Ms. Robinson?" asked Jackie.

"Please," said Linda. Gesturing that the floor was hers.

"Thank you, Jill, for reading my editorials. I have also read yours, and I have to say you write well."

"Thank you," said Jill.

"Saving 23 pounds of carbon dioxide in the last 12 months is only a portion of what the students at Bayshore have been able to accomplish. With the advent of our online media, which is supported by many local businesses, we have encouraged less driving to school, and more use of personal bicycles. In fact, six months ago, with the help of our advertisers we were able to promote 'Tuesday Bike Day,' which has led nearly 50% of the student population to ride their bicycles at least one day a week. With 500 students riding to school we have saved close to 333,000 pounds of carbon dioxide, which is nearly 150 metric tons."

The audience and the editors were silent. Linda stood there waiting to see if something else would come of this. Jackie was content with her rebuttal. Jill looked annoyed.

"Well," said Linda. "This has really taken a turn from newspapers." She managed to get the audience to laugh along with her.

I turned toward Dad. "Did Jackie really get that going?"

"I'm not sure," he said, lifting his shoulders up and then back down without taking his gaze from the stage.

The discussion continued on for another 45 minutes. I felt awful for the other student editors on the panel. Jackie was relentless. She had an answer to each question asked by either Linda or the others. Those other students were not even in the same league as Jackie. *How did she do it?* I couldn't remember anything from class, or a book I read, or *re*read. I had to study, read it over, and still not do well on a test. How can Jackie, who is my *sister*, store so much information in her brain and be able to pull out what exactly she needed when she needed it?

SAVE THE BAY

The following week my class was headed out on a field trip. It was too early in the morning to be driving to school. Normally school started at 8:30 a.m. but today we needed to catch a boat at 8:00 a.m., so Ms. Morgan had us meet at school at 7:30 a.m. She had planned an all-day voyage with the Marine Science Institute. She had been talking about the details of the field trip for a couple weeks, as well as pestering us for permission slips from our parents. We had written thank you letters over the past week to those generous people who sponsored the majority of the trip. It really was a unique experience for us kids to get on a boat.

"This is a great experience for all of us!" Ms. Morgan said. "We are going to pull up nets, mud, and plankton to study the biodiversity of the San Francisco Bay, and how humans have a large impact on the success as well as the demise of our local waters."

She said we would learn some history about how the land and water has been operating over the last 200 years, and because of industry, overfishing, and changes to earth's surface the landscape and marine life has been so impacted.

"I get really sea sick," Lola announced to the class a couple weeks ago.

"Oh, you'll be fine," said Ms. Morgan. "The ride is gentle and the boat is big enough you won't feel much rocking."

"Just take dramamine in the morning," said Celia. "It will do the trick, and then you won't have to worry."

"Please talk to your parents first," Ms. Morgan interrupted.

No sooner had we arrived in the parking lot than we were being fitted for life vests and sent to the loading dock. Everything was happening so fast and we just seemed to follow the next person in front of us.

"This is so cool," said Brian.

"Is that the boat?" asked Lola. "It doesn't look that big. Do you think I'll get sick?"

"Didn't I tell you to take the dramamine?" said Celia.

"My parents didn't know what that was and they said I didn't need it," said Lola. "Now I think they may have been wrong."

"Everyone ready?" We heard a loud voice call out to us. We soon formed a circle around the docent. "Welcome to the Robert G. Brownlee. This 90-foot research vessel is equipped with great tools to give you all a better understanding of life here in the San Francisco Bay." I'm glad he was excited, because I think many of us were nervous watching the boat rock side to side by the dock. "Enough talk onshore, let's head on board. Are you ready!"

"90-foot, that's pretty big, right?" Lola whispered to me.

"You are going to be fine," I said to her. "If not, just hang over the side."

"That is not very convincing." She linked her arm with mine.

For as long as I have known Lola, she has been a worry-wart. She stresses over the smallest situations and asks so many anxious questions. When we were in the fourth grade she had a fear of butterflies. She was frightened with the way they flapped their wings. On a field trip to see where they migrated, she cried the whole time. Meanwhile, it was the most incredible experience I had the opportunity to witness. The butterflies clumped together in trees, holding on to leaves and branches and the company of each other. It was orange for as far as you could see through the trees. I told Lola to open her eyes so many times, but she refused.

We marched onto the boat and spent the next 15 minutes listening to safety guidelines, and Judy, the leader of this expedition, answered all of Lola's concerns. Then Judy asked that we stand up and look out the windows. We scurried to the circular windows to look out at the water.

"Whoa! How did we get out in the middle of the bay so fast?" asked Brian.

"We were moving while she was talking," said Jaime. "Didn't you feel it?"

"Not really," said Brian.

"That wasn't too bad," said Lola smiling for the first time. "I actually feel ok."

It was like she allowed a butterfly to land on her hand.

Judy then broke us up into groups where we would travel about the boat learning something new and interesting. We pulled up water to sample the small animals living below. We also tested the temperature of the water. As a whole group we pulled up a large net that took all of us working at the same time in a sort of circular heave-ho motion. Since we were unable to capture a marine animal in our net, we studied the animals they had ready in small tanks. It was like they knew we weren't going to catch anything.

When I had made it to the "history" portion of the tour, we studied maps of how the land had changed. The bay had been filled dramatically because of hydraulic mining during the 1840s and 1850s from the gold rush in the Sierras. The miners would blast out the land with intensely powered water hoses to pull away at the mountain in hopes to discover more gold. All those rocks filled up a third of the bay over a span of 40 years.

"Humans had made a strong and somewhat lasting impact on the bay in a short period of time," Judy said. "Just a few hundred years ago it was the Ramaytush Ohlone who lived here. From the oysters and clams they harvested there are still shell mounds here under some of these large buildings that sit on the perimeter of the bay." She pointed to the glass-walled buildings behind us.

We turned to look out at the many large Oracle buildings that stood shining and reflecting the water.

"Wouldn't the shells get crushed?" Lola asked.

"I'm sure there are many crushed shells below us, but when mixed with dirt and sand it creates a clay brick," Judy said.

"So, the bay has shrunk?" I asked.

"Yes it has," said Judy.

"Is that a bad thing?" I asked.

Celia rolled her eyes at me. Like Lola, I had known Celia since before kindergarten. We used to be best friends, but ever since my family moved homes when I was in second grade, she decided she didn't like me anymore. It was gentle at first, then with time it was like we didn't even know one another. All of our dads had become really good friends just living close to one another. As kids we played together almost every day. All the moms cooked the food, the dads talked outside, and the kids ran around the house stealing sweets and sugary drinks when no one was looking.

Judy's voice came back in, "Depends on what is important to you," she said. "If you like to see a natural setting and animals living in their own habitats, then filling in the bay would not be good. If you are interested in real estate, then you want to fill in the bay creating more *land* to build on."

Before we docked, we sat back down in the same place where we began our voyage. Judy asked us a series of questions, as well as let us ask a few questions of our own. I fell into a trance and stopped listening. I was thinking about how much the land changed over the last 200 years. If you never studied the land, you would probably have no idea how much the land had changed.

I raised my hand.

"Yes?" said Judy.

"If the bay has changed so much and has got more polluted over the years, what will it look like in 100 years?"

It got really quiet. This is what I hated. This is the very reason I don't raise my hand to ask or answer questions.

Celia turned to look at me then looked away rolling her eyes. Why does she always have to make such a repulsed face? I looked at Ms. Morgan who had the biggest smile on her face and was flashing thumbs-up at me.

"That is a great question," said Judy. "I'll turn it back to you. What do you think?"

This is not what I had in mind. "More pollution?" I offered.

"Why do you say that?"

What I really wanted to say was, *I asked you the question*, but what I finally said was, "Well, if there were less people 50 years ago and they were polluting then what is to stop even more people from throwing their trash or oil spills into the water?"

"People like all of you!" She pointed at all of us sitting there, grabbing our attention. "It's people like you that just learned about how beautiful the bay is and how if we continue to care for it then we can enjoy it for many more generations." She sounded like Dr. Seuss in the Lorax. "If you spread the word, and lead by example, others will follow. In fact, there were three women who started a movement in the early 1960s to help the San Francisco Bay keep a more natural state."

"Really?" said Ms. Morgan. We all turned to where she stood. "Tell us more."

"These three women wanted to protect the land from further development and preserve the natural beauty, and they were successful. Their organization is called Save the Bay. In fact, these women are credited with starting the environmental movement in the United States."

"How fascinating," said Ms. Morgan.

Judy checked her watch on her wrist, and then

instructed us with what to do with our life vests when we docked and reminded us to grab our jackets and lunch bags.

"I have another question," I spoke up again.

"Yes?"

"You had mentioned plastics in the bay and in the ocean earlier today. Are plastics in the ocean really that bad?"

"Of course it is," said Jaime. "What rock have you been living under?"

"Yeah, Jenny. Haven't you listened to anything we have been talking about?" said Celia.

"Ok, ok," said Judy. "To answer your question, the amount of plastic in the ocean is very bad. Have you heard of microplastics?"

"It's small pieces of plastic that have broken from larger pieces," said Arjun.

"Yes, thank you," Judy said. "I just read the other day that 1.9 million pieces of microplastics cover about 1 square meter of ocean floor. That is about a 3 foot by 3 foot area." She showed us an invisible box shape with her hands. "That number seems to grow daily."

It was hard to imagine that many pieces floating in a small area. It didn't make sense. It would seem we would be swimming in plastic and never even know it. Could that be right? It was like a huge problem that was invisible. I didn't want to ask. I was done with questions for the day.

While others were busy loading off, Judy casually walked over to me and leaned in. "Those three women I mentioned earlier?" she whispered. "Well, Save the Bay helped to support the plastic bag ban in San Francisco about ten years ago. That is proof there is a lot we can do to help."

We landed onshore and we were back in class for 30 minutes before the school day was over. Many of us planted our heads on our desks and rested. It was a long day at sea, and the sun had been blasting down on us from the start.

"Jenny?" Ms. Morgan asked. "Can you come here please?" I walked over to where she was sitting by the front door.

"I'm not sure if you are interested, but there is a documentary that came out a few years ago, called *A Plastic Ocean*. Have you heard of it?"

I shook my head.

"While so much has changed since it came out, it is a good place to start."

"It's ok," I said.

"What's ok?" she asked.

"I mean that I don't know why I was asking those questions earlier. I think I know the answers."

"Well, if you change your mind. Check it out."

Then she winked at me.

SCIENCE-Y

With so much new information, I decided it was time to be a kid with no worries once again. I hadn't seen Jolene in a while; she had been busy with family stuff, and it seemed like she could never squeeze out a minute. When she said yes to hanging out, I had to seize my opportunity.

"Mom, I'm headed out with Jolene!" I yelled from the front yard with my bike already peddling away from the house.

As soon as I got there, I ran into her home.

"Hi Eve!" I said. She is always the first person I say hi to when I come through their front door. Jolene's Mom, Eve, is probably the kindest person I know. She has a way of listening that I swear no one I know possesses. It's like she not only hears what I'm saying, but she wants to know more. Jolene says she is too much, but I say she gets me. I would love to be a student in her class. As long as I have known Jolene, there has always been some project Eve is working on at home for her class. She is one of those teachers that inspires kids to think outside the box.

"Oh, hello Jenny," said Eve. "I haven't seen you in a couple days. How are you?"

Eve was drying dishes off the rack. I don't think they have ever used their dishwasher. Jolene complains about having to clean the dishes all the time, and I always asked why she didn't just place them in the dishwasher. She said her mom thought it was a waste of water and electricity.

"I'm fine, how are you?" I said.

"Things are good here. How's school?" she asked. Now when Eve asks how school is going, she actually means it. There are so many adults that ask about school because it is a good go-to question, but they are not at all interested. I don't blame them. As kids, we say the same thing every time. Eve, on the other hand, is honestly interested, but I need to be careful, because before I know it we could be sitting there for hours talking about educational reform.

"We went on a boat yesterday for a field trip," I said. "And, that is something we never do at our school."

"Really? Where did you go?" she asked.

"We were on the bay looking at mud and plankton. It was actually really fun!"

"What a wonderful field trip. What did you learn?"

"Well, we talked about how shallow the waters are from so much sediment that was brought over from hydraulic mining in the 1800s. I was really surprised to hear most parts of the bay are only 15 feet deep."

"Isn't that interesting," said Eve. She was wearing an apron over her clothes that said *Spread the Love* across the top. "I took my class out there a couple years ago. We had a great time. I wonder if it is still the same?"

"Hey Jenny," said Jolene, entering the room. She was wearing overalls and her green Converse with the laces spilling out onto the floor.

"Hey Jo."

"Ready?" she asked.

"Yeah."

"We'll see you later Mom," said Jolene.

"Nice to see you, Eve," I said.

"Have fun girls," said Eve. She waved us away with the kitchen towel she still had in her hand.

Once out the door, Jolene said, "I'm glad I could save you."

"Save me?" I asked.

"From my mom. She was about to tell you everything she knows about the bay. She can go on forever."

"I wouldn't mind," I said.

"You might. It's boring stuff that you are not interested in," said Jolene.

We hopped onto our bikes and began peddling away from her house. Once we were neck and neck I said, "What makes you think I'm not interested?"

"You know, it's things that are *sciency*."

"I like science," I said.

"Since when do you like science?" laughed Jolene.

"I don't know," I said. "Lately I have been interested."

When my family moved to the neighborhood we live in now, Jolene and her family were the first people to knock on our door. Eve was holding a basket of fruits and vegetables she had grown from her yard, and a generous smile. Jolene's dad was quietly standing behind the women, as I learned was his general place in that family. Jolene was so excited she blurted out, "Let's get out here!" My parents seemed a bit reluctant when I looked up at them, but Eve reassured them they were in a safe neighborhood and the girls wouldn't go too far.

I remember that day so well. We had moved from a bigger neighborhood that had tons of kids, but we didn't get to run around past our own streets. Lola was just two blocks over, and Celia was across the street. When we went to Lola's we needed someone to walk us over. This new neighborhood was like a dream, and I had my own room in our new home. Sometimes I think Jackie hates me so much because she had to share a room with a crying baby sister for so many years.

Lola had since moved out of that neighborhood, and every now and again we got together. I had left behind friends and I was afraid I would have no one to play with after school. When I met Jolene that day, I was so relieved. Jolene was better than I could have imagined or wished for.

"What has you interested in anything about science?" asked Jolene.

"I'm not exactly sure," I said, even though I knew exactly what piqued my interest. "It's weird because I kind of feel like I'm connecting with something more."

"What have you been eating?" Jolene laughed.

I don't believe she was laughing at me, because she would never laugh at me. Though, today I wasn't so sure.

A PLASTIC OCEAN

Later that evening, as I was settling in to do nothing in my room, I wondered about what made me the type of person that was not *sciency*, like Jolene said. Could it be the very idea that Ms. Morgan suggested I watch that documentary and I had no interest? It could be that I don't retain information, or maybe because I am nothing like Jackie.

I really wasn't going to take Ms. Morgan's advice on the documentary, because I'm not a middle-aged person, nor someone in my twenties that is looking for an argument or a movement, or somewhere to donate money. Also, I just don't watch documentaries. Maybe because Jackie is always preaching about what I should and shouldn't watch. Or, maybe because I just don't like them. I have shows I enjoy watching that I never seem to have enough time for, why would I waste precious screen time with something that won't numb me out and then leave me feeling like I'm not good enough?

Having said that however, after watching 20 minutes of my latest show, and arriving at the familiar feeling of loneliness where I start to tackle all my depressions of having no friends, a big nose, frizzy hair, and feeling less than par in school after seeing all the characters with lustrous hair, who can sing!—I caved and decided to skim through *A Plastic Ocean* after all.

I could predict the storyline already: human consumption and dependency of plastics, and how those plastics eventually make their way to the ocean. The title gave it away.

While moving the big red dot from the ever-inching red line at the bottom of the screen further to the right, skipping through scenes, I landed on someone saying that there were, "plastics in every organism examined." I pulled the red dot back to the left just a bit and a horrifying picture of a dead fish stuffed with what I found out were plastic pellets, the same microplastics Judy had mentioned on our boat trip. Should kids be watching this? I could have nightmares! Despite the stomach churning sensation that made its way up to my throat, and my current uneasiness of mind, I pulled the red dot all the way to the left, and made the choice to start from the beginning. It couldn't hurt, I thought.

I hadn't realized I passed my screen time allotment until I heard Mom yelling for me from the kitchen. "Jenny, it's time to get off that thing!" I could hear her coughing from raising her voice and threatening her vocal cords. "Give yourself a break from those mindless shows, and do your homework!"

I shut down my laptop immediately, a sort of knee-jerk reaction in this particular situation.

"I'm actually watching something educational!" I yelled back through my bedroom door. I wasn't angry, I just needed to her to hear me without having to get up.

Then a wave of sarcasm crashed in. "If you have to say *actually* you should be embarrassed!" It was Jackie. Now she found herself yelling through her bedroom door.

"You should be embarrassed that you have nothing to do on a Friday night!" I called back.

"I am doing something! Just because I'm not out driving around, polluting the air, and engaging in useless small talk, doesn't mean I have nothing to do, dork!"

I only raised my voice louder: "That's because you don't have any friends!"

"Where are your friends, then!?"

"I cancelled my plans!"

"You don't have any plans! You're like five years old!"

"Whatever, Jackie! You're boring!"

"Good one, loser!"

"Whoa! What is going on up here!?" Now Dad showed up on the scene. "I can hear all this yelling through the walls down there! Is everything ok?!"

Without getting up to open my door, and put a halt to his insane level of decibels, I yelled again, "Jackie is being her usual rude self!"

"Jenny is pretending to watch something educational!" Jackie yelled.

"You know! I'm going to miss this arguing! How about you Sofia!?" Dad yelled to Mom, though I'm pretty sure they were standing right next to one other.

"I'm not sure! I might need to head to the store for cough drops if we keep this up!" Mom shouted back.

I could hear them laughing with one another. I actually found myself laughing as well. Though I wouldn't let them know. It was kind of funny that all four of us were yelling through closed doors in our home.

Would I miss this? It is hard to tell at this moment. I mean, what would it be like not having Jackie around to make fun of me or put me down? What if Mom and Dad took a genuine interest in what I was doing? Must have been nice for Jackie to have Mom and Dad all to herself before I was born.

"Hey Mom!" I started it back up.

"Yeah!?"

"Can I please watch some more?! It really isn't mindless, I swear!"

"Yeah right!" yelled Jackie.

"Shut up, Jackie! I'm not talking to you!"

It sounded like my parents were whispering. I couldn't quite hear what they were discussing, maybe considering giving their throat a bit of a break. Most likely, though, they were deciding whether they were going to parent or just give in and let me watch more.

Then my door flew open. My eyes left the blank wall to the open door.

"What are you watching anyway?" Jackie stood before me. She was tall, as I was sitting on the floor. Her hair was wrapped up into a messy bun, with her glasses sharing space on her head. Her toes woven through the carpet, and her toe nails half painted and chipped, as usual.

"Why do you care?" I asked hugging the laptop to my chest.

"Just want to see if you're telling the truth," she said. "What you think is educational could just be a jean jacket."

"It's called *A Plastic Ocean*, as a matter of fact," I said with pride. "My teacher recommended it just to me."

"Why? Because she sees your plastic straws from Starbucks you and Mom continually buy?"

"I'll have you know that they have a different type of lid that doesn't need a straw," I stated. "And to answer your question, no, because Ms. Morgan—" I paused. I still didn't want Jackie to know I was taking an interest in something she might also share.

"Well?" said Jackie. She threw her arms up with impatience.

I said nothing.

Instead of walking away, she started back up again. "Just so you know. It is a good documentary and if you have any sense, you'll finish it."

Before Jackie could leave I asked, "Have you seen it?"

"I watched it when it first came out. It taught me a lot about how plastic is in almost everything we use and how we don't actually have a proper way of recycling most of it." She paused. "It was really the documentary that changed my life," Jackie added.

"You were only 13 years old," I said. "How can your life be changed that much?"

"I know what you're thinking. But, before I cared only about myself and what was cool. I was interested in buying new clothes and getting frappuccinos."

"What! You? I don't remember you ever caring about anything other than saving the planet," I said.

"Four years ago you were still so young. Why would you remember that?" said Jackie. "Mom and Dad were involved in everything at your school and taking you all over the place."

"What are you talking about?" I asked.

"What do you mean?"

"What I mean is that Mom and Dad are always doing things for you, and never for me."

"That's just not true," said Jackie rolling her eyes.

Then, out of nowhere, Jackie bent her knees, cracking them as she came down and took a seat next to me on the carpet. Both our backs were up against the wall, her legs stretching out past mine, her shoulders just above my own. She politely grabbed the laptop from my hands and placed it on her thighs. She opened it and clicked the play button.

"I have been feeling like I need a refresher on plastics," said Jackie. "It's like rereading a good book."

I looked up at her, startled. Was this a joke? Was she going to laugh in my face and say, *Sucker*!

She didn't. She simply turned toward the screen, and the two of us jumped back into *A Plastic Ocean*.

WATER DISTRIBUTION

The following Monday, Ms. Morgan continued the discussion from the boat. "If you could all bring your eyes to me," said Ms. Morgan standing at the front of the class before the whiteboard. "Open up your Evidence Journals, we are going to talk more about the ocean." Ms. Morgan's eyes opened wide and her smile matched their size.

We did what we were told while she started up the projector. Soon a blue light appeared on the whiteboard, and there was a large image that simply stated, *How does the ocean play a role in our Earth's four systems*, with today's date neatly typed at the bottom of the screen.

It really wasn't a simple question. It was far more complex, as I had learned from the documentary. I not only watched the documentary, but Jackie filled in where I needed more understanding, adding more detail, and her opinion of course. To say the night was weird was an understatement. I had a mixture of apprehension, just waiting for Jackie to say something mean, and total rapture listening to what she had to say. It actually went well, which I wish wasn't such a surprise.

"Let's talk about water distribution here on Earth," Ms. Morgan started up. She held up a two-liter plastic bottle. "Here, we have 2000 milliliters of water." Then she pulled a small bottle of blue food coloring from her pocket with her other hand. She squeezed out a few drops into the bottle.

"Whoa!" said Jaime.

"That's so cool," said Brian. "The way it mixes together is neat."

We were all mesmerized. In fact, we all became very silent as we watched the blue food coloring blend in with the clear, colorless water.

"This represents all the water on Earth," said Ms. Morgan, shaking the bottle to mix the two together more. "For purposes of measurement, we will say that all the Earth's water is represented as 2000 milliliters."

She put down the big bottle on the small table next to where she was standing, and pulled out three graduated cylinders. These are the kinds of tools that make us all feel like scientists. We generally want to fill them up and then look at them by bending our knees to really study them at a horizontal focal point. Then do it all over again. We say we are pretending to be scientists. Ms. Morgan says we *are* scientists.

"Now, I'm pouring out 50 milliliters, from the 2000 milliliters." As she did this she asked us, "Any predictions as to what this represents?"

"Drinking water?"

"I don't know?"

"Maybe just 50 milliliters?"

"You are all mildly correct. This represents all the freshwater on Earth." She placed the cylinder next to the two-liter bottle. It was an incredibly small amount when you compared the two side-by-side.

"What do you think this big bottle represents?" she asked us, tapping the two-liter bottle.

"Salt water," said Jaime.

"Yes!" yelled Ms. Morgan. She jumped as she said it and nearly spilled all the water out onto the floor.

"Now, watch this." She then pulled water out from the 50 milliliter cylinder. "Make silent observations," she told us.

The next graduated cylinder held about 15 milliliters.

She pulled out a dropper from her pocket, and put what seemed like one tiny drop into the last cylinder. We had no idea what she was up to, but we waited patiently for Ms. Morgan to explain. I had a faint memory from when I had to research the hydrosphere, but like most things, I couldn't hold onto much information. Most information is stored for about 24 hours, maybe 48.

"This here is 34 milliliters, and this represents all the freshwater on Earth that is frozen." She moved to the side a bit. "This one that is 15 milliliters is all the fresh water that can be found in the ground. This last one, here," she pointed to the tiny, lonesome drop. "This one is point five milliliters. It represents all the surface fresh water. What we think of as lakes and rivers."

She paused, looking at us. "What do you think?"

"That's it?" asked Celia.

"What does it take to pull it from the ground?" asked Arjun.

"This means that most of the Earth is covered in salt water," I said.

"Duh," said Celia.

"Well," I spoke up again despite Celia's eye rolling. "That means that what happens to the ocean can have a huge impact on our world."

"I think Ms. Morgan wants us to realize that there is not that much drinking water available," said Celia. There she was again, always trying to make me feel inadequate.

"Actually, Jenny, that is a great observation. In fact, everyone here has great observations. There is a lot that can be taken from this model," said Ms. Morgan. "Okay everyone, take a seat."

We hadn't realized we had all taken leave from our seats to get a closer look at the water distribution model.

"Jenny," said Ms. Morgan. "You bring up a really good point. If the ocean covers 97 percent of all Earth's water, then the health of the ocean is very important." She took her eyes off me and directed them to the class. "How does the ocean play a role in all of Earth's systems?"

"If the ocean makes up that much of the Earth, then it probably plays a big role in the hydrosphere, specifically the water cycle," said Arjun.

"Great observation," said Ms. Morgan. "Anyone else?"

No one seemed to raise their hands after Arjun's comment. It kind of summed it up for most of us. The ocean was endless and far reaching. The spinning Earth from a few weeks ago played again in my mind like a movie. When the image reached the Pacific Ocean, I could see how much space it took up. If everything I saw on the documentary last night was accurate, then humans were basically filling our world with plastic. It wasn't just the idea that it was in the ocean, it was our world. I raised my hand.

"Yes, Jenny," said Ms. Morgan.

I cleared my throat. "Well, last night, my sister and I watched a documentary called *A Plastic Ocean.*"

Ms. Morgan winked at me. No one else seemed to care or notice, thankfully. Well, except Lola who smiled at me. She knows that doing anything with Jackie can be tough.

"I know that this is not exactly what you are asking, but," I paused to look around. No one was gawking at me. I wondered if they were even listening. "There is a lot of plastic, and other garbage that is thrown into the ocean every single day."

Celia turned towards me with her *duh?* face.

I continued. "If the ocean is as big as you say, then all the plastic thrown into the ocean is actually filling our world as a whole."

"Save the turtles!" yelled Joshua. He managed to get the whole class laughing at me.

"Dude, plastic is poisonous," I said to Joshua. "It's not a joke."

"Ok," said Ms. Morgan. "What are you trying to say, Jenny?"

Why was it when I opened my mouth, it came out wrong. Anyone else could say something and the others would agree, or at least left them alone. I am tired of this role I have to play. I finally decided that I had something to say.

"What I'm trying to say is that we humans tend to think that our plastic consumption and eventual disposal doesn't affect us because we can't see it. The reality is that there is an island of trash floating in the Pacific Ocean that is three times the size of France! And, what's really crazy, is that there are even more patches of trash in the Pacific Ocean."

"You are correct, Jenny," said Ms. Morgan. "Does anyone know what that island of trash is called?"

"The Great Pacific Garbage Patch," said Joshua. "And, it's not actually an island or really a patch."

"Thank you for that, you are very accurate Joshua," said Ms. Morgan. "This so-called area has been growing in size for more than 70 years!" She threw her arms up into a wide-open embrace. "In fact, it is stated that in just thirty years there will be more plastic than fish in the ocean."

"Most of the garbage is plastic, and specifically fishing nets," Joshua added.

"I heard that it is impossible to clean up," said Arjun. "It just keeps spinning around and around, and there is no good system to actually pick up all the pieces."

"Those are called gyres," I spoke up.

"What is?" asked Arjun.

"When you say that it keeps spinning and spinning around, that movement is because of an ocean gyre. Basically big ocean currents," I said. "The gyres move around and collect what is in its current, and as it moves that plastic sort of stays in one general place. Over time it has become a huge expanse of trash, made up of mostly small plastic pieces."

"Yes, Jenny," said Ms. Morgan. "To add to this, one of the reasons is the patch—or, sorry, area," she looked at Joshua. "As it continues to grow, that plastic, as we learned on the boat the other day, does not biodegrade, but only breaks down into smaller and smaller pieces called microplastics."

"In other words, plastic doesn't go away?" asked Lola.

"Correct," said Ms. Morgan.

"If we know this, then why isn't more being done?" Lola asked.

"Actually there are many people around the world working towards a cleaner ocean, and there have been invented systems to clean up the trash," Ms. Morgan said.

"It seems to me that there wouldn't be a need to clean it, so much as to stop using that much plastic, right?" I added.

"What was the documentary you watched?" asked Celia.

"*A Plastic Ocean*," I said.

I thought Celia was going to laugh at me, but instead I saw her write it down. Then I saw Arjun write it down. Then Ms. Morgan took an expo marker and wrote it across the whiteboard. It seemed everyone in class wrote down the title.

"It's on Netflix," said Ms. Morgan.

"That's cool," said Jaime. "But, not everyone has Netflix."

"My mistake," said Ms. Morgan. I could tell she was trying to find a solution in her head.

"It came out a few years ago, but it has a lot of great information," I said. "I didn't want to watch it at first, but I gave it a chance."

"Ms. Morgan, you should assign us all to watch it," said Lola.

"I don't want to make it an assignment," she said. She smiled at Lola. "But, I do recommend it. Maybe you can get together at someone's house?"

"Is it long?" I heard someone ask.

"Not really," I said. "There were definitely parts where I had to ask my sister to explain what was going on, or who a certain person was. I did pause it a few times to better understand."

I looked around and noticed people were listening to me, for like the first time. What was even more startling, was that for a moment I wasn't embarrassed. What was happening?

After school that day when Dad picked me up and asked how my day went, I said, "Fantastic!"

"*Fantastic*?!" he repeated. "Really? Sounds exciting, share with me."

"People in my class actually listened to me, and for once they didn't think I was the class airhead," I told him.

"Jenny, you are not an airhead."

"I know that." He stopped at the red light, and we exchanged glances. Dad looked sad for me. Today was not a day to be sad, however. "Listen, Dad. When everyone seems to dub you the airhead in class, it is really difficult to rebuild a reputation. I'm not worried, though. Because today, I was no longer the airhead."

"What happened to change everything?" he asked.

"It's not that important, really. What is more important is that I have some work to do."

"What kind of work?" He was showing a genuine interest.

"I need to tell everyone about how bad plastic is and how if we continue to use plastic we are going to be swimming in garbage."

75

"Now you're sounding like Jackie," he said. The light changed to green and he drove forward crossing the intersection.

"Really?" I said.

"A little." He braced himself.

"That's cool," I said.

VEGAN MARSHMALLOWS

After dinner I asked if I could go to Jolene's house, which is normally not an issue. In fact, Mom and Dad barely notice when I ask to leave. However, tonight they were overly excited. Dad was all smiles, and Mom kept rubbing my back. I didn't realize my happiness meant so much to them.

I grabbed my bike from the garage and filled up my water bottle before I left.

I walked into their home the way I always have. They were finishing up dinner and were on to hand washing all their dishes. Eve did the washing, and Jolene did the drying.

"Hey Jolene," I said. "Hi Eve."

"Hey Jenny," Jolene shouted. "My mom actually bought stuff for us to make s'mores outside on the fire pit!"

"Thanks, Eve," I said. "I wasn't expecting anything."

"You're welcome," said Eve. "I was trying to find vegan marshmallows for a hot chocolate fundraiser at my school, so I thought why not have s'mores."

"Vegan marshmallows?" I asked.

"Yeah," said Jolene. "There are pig's hooves in there."

"Pig's hooves!" I yelled.

"Well, the gelatin that makes marshmallows have that sticky consistency comes from pig's skin," said Eve.

"That's weird," I said. "So how are the vegan marshmallows sticky?"

"Different plant parts," Eve told me.

"Why wouldn't we use plants in the first place?" I asked.

Eve shrugged her shoulders. I knew she had a good answer, but she appeared tired. Maybe it was a long day at school. She didn't seem to have anything left to give to the conversation. I recognized that familiar expression from when my Mom gets home from work.

"All the ingredients are in the pantry," said Eve. "Your dad started the fire outside. It's probably ready."

"Thanks, Mom," said Jolene. "Can I go?"

Eve looked at the dishes she wanted Jolene to dry. "Oh, fine. I'll stack them on the rack this time."

"Thanks," we said in unison.

We grabbed the graham crackers, vegan marshmallow, and chocolate and headed outside with the skewers. The fire was roaring. We found our usual tree stump seats around the fire pit to sit. Without wasting any time we stuck two white globs on top and extended our skewers. It wasn't long before Jolene had her marshmallow in flames.

"Yours is on fire," I said to Jolene.

"I know. I want to burn it." She twisted it around to ensure the entire marshmallow would soon be charred. "It looks cool."

"It does."

Jolene pulled back and blew out the flames, then stuck it back in. We sat mesmerized by the orange and yellow that was glowing and radiating heat. It was so beautiful the way the flames swirled around one another, like they were dancing.

"Jenny?"

"Yeah?"

"What are you thinking about?" asked Jolene.

"Nothing, why?" I said.

"You have been staring so long into the fire. I figured you were thinking about something important."

I was still lost in thought about what happened in class earlier that day, still enjoying the moment. If the rest of the class could listen to a brief summary of the documentary, then maybe we could work together for something bigger. How could I do more?

"Actually, I was just thinking about how cool the fire looks," I said. "But, also I did have a great day at school."

"What happened?"

"I finally felt smart."

"What happened?" she asked again.

"Well, we were talking about Earth's water distribution, and I had watched a documentary on plastics in the ocean, so I shared some information that I could actually remember," I said. "And, people listened."

"We're doing work on plastics right now, too," said Jolene.

"You are?" I asked, turning toward her. "Like what?"

"Well, it's actually a project Jackie put together."

"Jackie?" I paused, confused. I took my gaze from the fire to Jolene. "Like my *sister*, Jackie?"

"Yeah. She comes in and talks to our class. Her and my mom are working together for the time being. I guess it's something for her senior project."

"Wait, what?" I was taken aback. I shuffled on the wooden stump to look at her. The fire was still raging. Jackie was helping at Jolene's school and I didn't know anything about it? Jackie didn't mention anything. In fact, Jolene hadn't said anything.

"When did this start?" I asked.

"Like, two weeks ago." Jolene looked back into the fire. She sort of brushed her feet over the dirt below and scratched her head.

"I don't understand?" I said.

"What do you mean?" asked Jolene.

"How is it that you, *and* your mom, *and* Jackie are working on a project and I have no idea?"

"I guess it didn't come up," said Jolene. She looked away.

"I sort of think that would come up at some point in the last couple of weeks," I said.

"Why are you mad?" Jolene asked. "It's not a big deal."

"I'm not mad, I just figured I would know about it, that's all."

"Well, to be honest, Jenny, you spend a lot of time hating Jackie and telling me about how annoying she is and that you can't stand her. I just figured you wouldn't care," Jolene said.

I wasn't sure what to think. How could Jackie not even

mention it? We had actually sat down and watched that documentary together the other day. She did say she needed a refresher, but I assumed that was for personal reasons. Then there was Jolene. I mean, I guess she was telling me now, but it only came out because I brought it up. Eve didn't even say anything. It felt weird. Almost like they were all trying *not* to let me know.

"What's wrong, Jenny?"

I looked at her. My face said nothing. Or, maybe I was giving off the impression that I was really bothered and upset. Why was I upset, though? Shouldn't I be happy they were all doing something positive together?

"How did this start?" I asked.

"Well, every year my mom teaches a unit on the ocean. The last two years she has kind of branched off to talking about the health of the ocean, and that has basically become plastics and other garbage in the ocean." She placed two more marshmallows on her skewer and proceeded to burn them to a black crisp. "Your mom told my mom that Jackie was needing to fulfill a requirement for her Senior Exit project and was looking to do something about the ocean." She pulled out her skewer from the fire and blew out the flames. "My mom said she could lead an advocacy campaign at her school, and that was how it started."

"So Jackie goes to your school, and does what?" I asked.

"She always has some sort of presentation we watch, then leads us into an activity of some sort. It's actually really fun," said Jolene. "She is very different from the way you describe her at home."

I had built my s'more, but lost my appetite. It sat in my

hand, sticking to my skin, and leaving chocolate ooze across my palm.

"Jenny, what's wrong?" asked Jolene. "Why do you seem so mad about all of this? I mean, I do this work with my mom every year. Even when I was too little to understand, I was always helping her with projects, and learning about the ocean."

"But, you have never talked about it before with me. We are best friends, and I had no idea," I said. "It makes me feel like you thought I was too dumb to talk to."

"No way," said Jolene. "You just never showed interest. Plus, we have fun in different ways, like buying candy and riding bikes."

We didn't say anything for a little while. I stared into the fire. There was so much I wanted to say, but there was no kind way to explain how I was feeling.

"These marshmallows don't taste any different," Jolene finally said, breaking the silence.

"Well, I am interested in more than candy and bicycles!" I yelled.

I threw my s'more across the yard, and turned to leave.

"Jenny, where are you going?"

I didn't want to talk anymore. I just wanted to get out of there. My supposed best friend thinks I'm too dumb to understand the ocean. I went from having the best day in class, back to my normal self, except I fell even harder. And, it hurt.

I rushed home in the dark, left my bicycle outside the front door, and went straight into my room and shut the door. I threw my head into my pillow.

I do have more to me than people see. I have big ideas, and I really do care about the world around me. Why was it that only the superficial side shows up? What was I doing that made it hard for everyone to see that I was more than junk food?

I needed to write it all down. I pulled out a journal that I received as a birthday present a few years ago. It had a lock, that I knew with any logic or perseverance could be opened without the key. You could shake it and the flap would fall open to reveal all my inner thoughts. Except this journal was nothing but a bunch of empty pages. I had not written one single world. In fact, when I unwrapped the box I was thoroughly disappointed because I knew I would never take the time to write inside.

Until today.

I grabbed the silly little key that was dangling next to the lock. No security there. I opened it up and found a small little pencil inside. It was much too tiny to grip, so I tossed aside and grabbed a pencil that was sitting on top of my desk.

November 17

I will not address this to anyone, because the only reason I'm writing is because I might just start screaming, and I don't want my parents to come running. I just want to be left alone. I'm writing today because I have discovered what I already knew. That everyone thinks I'm dumb. Even Jolene, my best friend, thinks I'm too dumb to talk about anything with depth. Apparently, Jackie has been working with Eve's class, which is also Jolene's class, for like two weeks, and no one bothered to tell me. Jolene said it was because she didn't think I would be interested anyway, and all I talk about is how much I hate Jackie so why would I even care.

I stopped writing and let the pencil fall onto the journal, and slowly roll off onto the carpet. I sat for a while like this, stunned and saddened. I stared at the wall, thinking about everything and nothing. And, then I started to cry, and I cried really hard. The tears just kept coming. I couldn't possibly wipe them away. It was like a flood erupted in my eyes, and like a mudslide, wiped out my face. My special, incredible, epiphany of a day was crumbling before me like the ashes falling to the bottom of the fire pit.

I guess there is still always choice. Isn't that something Dad always says? *We live by the choices we make.* I grabbed my pencil from the floor and brought it back to the paper.

Part VI:
The Think Tank

LA NIÑA

"This might not work," said Lola. "But there's something I have been thinking about."

"You never know," said Ms. Morgan. Her shoulders went up to her ears, and she let them drop down as she took a sip of her coffee.

I sat back in my chair. Lola had a way of telling a story that seemed to last forever and never get to the point. I reached into my jacket pocket and pulled out a crumbled page from my diary. When I finally stopped crying last night, and took a moment to just breathe, I actually had a moment of clarity. I had ripped out the page to keep it with me for when I wanted to get down on myself, for when my mind tried to convince me I am not good enough.

My mom had long ago given me a pocket angel. She told me to keep it with me always and reach for it when I needed strength. I have no idea where the little angel is, but I knew what she meant. This entry is my little angel:

November 17, 2020

I don't hate Jackie. In fact, I think she is the smartest and most passionate person I know. Jolene doesn't think I'm dumb, she just wants to have fun with me. My classmates can be mean, but I am the one that lets it bother me. Ms. Morgan is inspiring, and she wouldn't have suggested that I watch that documentary if she didn't think I cared. I'm actually not dumb. I just didn't know how to say what I was feeling or thinking. I guess I have always had something to say, I just didn't know how to start. So, okay, here I go. I think I may have just found my voice.

"You know when there are events at our school, not like an all-school event, but smaller ones where the parents have bagels in the morning, or when clubs get together," said Lola.

Upon hearing Lola's voice come back in my conscious mind, I folded up the paper quickly and shoved it back into my pocket, looking around to make sure no one noticed me.

Everyone was nodding their head in response to Lola. We often tried to sneak a treat that was meant for a parent, when no one was looking, or plead with whoever was standing over the table that we were getting a pastry for our teacher. Oh, we know what Lola was referring to.

"Well, I was thinking, what if there was a set of reusables plates and forks that the school owned that could be used for these meetings, so we are not always using paper and plastic."

Everyone sort of made comments to one another around the room. From the various whispers people seemed to think it was a great idea.

"Who would wash the plates?" Brian asked.

"The people that use them," said Celia. "I mean, do you all wash your own dishes at home? Can't be that hard to do it here in the school kitchen."

"I think it is a great idea," said Ms. Morgan. Then asked us, "How would you convince the school to buy reusable plates and utensils?"

"Couldn't we just ask?" Lola said.

"Well of course you can," said Ms. Morgan. "What I mean to say is how are you going to convince them to spend the money?"

"We can tell them what we have been studying in class, and tell them how important it is to us that we do more to eliminate single-use plastics in our own school," said Lola.

"Okay then, let's pitch the idea to our administration," said Ms. Morgan. "Everyone, for your homework please write up something that can be presented to the administration. For now, pull out your evidence journals and let's talk about how the ocean affects our coastlines."

I could tell Ms. Morgan was eager to keep our scientific investigations moving, while keeping our activism on the back burner for now. Still warm, but just simmering for when we moved it to the front.

The administration is tough to convince when it comes to spending money. We needed to be prepared for why they would say no. While Ms. Morgan was showing us a keynote about coastal erosion, my mind was jumping to many options for how we could get the money.

"Now, with your group, we are going to build a model simulation of a cliff and ocean waves," said Ms. Morgan.

She passed out a clear, plastic container to each group, an empty cup, a hand shovel, and a square piece of cardboard. "We are going to head outside for this," she said. "Can two of you grab that bucket of sand on the table for me?"

Jaime went for it, and while he tried to pull up the bucket, he couldn't lift it. "Dude, this is really heavy."

"Yes, I know. I put it on a cart this morning from my car and brought it to the classroom," said Ms. Morgan. "It requires two people."

Brian jumped in to help. The two of them grabbed the handle together, and from there it was manageable.

"Where do you get the sand?" asked Celia.

"The beach of course," said Ms. Morgan, laughing a little. As if thinking where else would someone get sand. "I picked it up this morning before I came to work."

We knew Ms. Morgan lived on the coast, and drove over the hill every morning. She talked about the ocean a lot because it was so close to her, and she wanted to keep it beautiful.

We walked out of the class and headed toward the open field. I caught up with Lola. "Hey, if the administration doesn't want to spend the money, maybe we can ask the PTO? I bet they have money in the budget for this kind of thing."

We found a spot in the open field to set down our materials.

"That's a good idea," said Lola. "Thanks."

Ms. Morgan's voice came back in, "Now, using your

hand shovel, dig out some dirt. Then take that dirt and pack it into one side of the container, only filling it up about halfway."

The dirt was hard to dig up. It was dry and crumbled. She instructed us to add only a little water to make the dirt pastier, but not too much that the dirt should turn into mud.

"Now, I'm coming around with sand," said Ms. Morgan. "One of you will reach into the bucket and pull out enough sand to fill the empty side of the container. I would say about an inch high." Jaime and Brian were the first to shovel out sand. "Use the cardboard piece to separate the dirt and the sand," Ms. Morgan added. "Make sure the two don't mix."

Lola turned toward me while we were trying to separate some of the sand that got under the dirt. "Thanks for starting all this, Jenny."

"It's not me," I said. "It's Ms. Morgan. I don't think I would even care, or know about plastic being such a big problem, if she didn't recommend the documentary."

"Yeah, she is cool," said Lola. "But, you seem to actually care."

"I don't know what I'm thinking," I said. "It's just that after seeing that documentary, I can't unsee what is happening to our oceans. You really should watch it."

"I will," Lola said.

"Now, using the hose, fill the cup with water," said Ms. Morgan. "You are going to slowly pour it over the sand so that the water level is half way up the cliff, or the dirt."

The water was cold out of the hose, but it was nice to clean off the dirt and sand from our hands.

"Remove the cardboard, still trying to keep the sand

and the dirt separate," said Ms. Morgan. "Now use the cardboard to make small waves in the water. Go slow, and observe what happens."

Lola pulled out the cardboard and started carefully making waves. Even with a gentle push, the water was moving quickly. The sand was swimming all around below the water's surface.

"What are you noticing?" Ms. Morgan asked us.

Lola handed me the cardboard, and I switched to now making the waves.

"I have some ideas about what we could do, and it goes along with your idea about buying reusable plates," I whispered to Lola.

"What do you have in mind?"

"Well, there has to be a way that we can do more, you know?"

A small piece of the dirt fell from the cliff and started floating further into the water. "Oops," I said. I tried to pull out.

"Just let it happen," said Ms. Morgan who was walking around and observing our model.

"I thought you said you didn't want it to mix," I said.

"To build the model, yes. But let's observe what happens when the waves come to play."

Pretty soon more and more dirt was mixing. The mound we packed in was slowly losing shape and was falling into the water.

"I would like for you all to walk around and observe other models," said Ms. Morgan. "Don't disturb their work, just use your eyes to see the differences and similarities."

We walked around with our evidence journals drawing

sketches or writing down our observations. I really loved how my journal was coming together. As the year went on it was filled with drawings and small speech bubbles, lots of arrows connecting one idea to another. Ms. Morgan had advised us not to scratch out anything or erase, just make space for new ideas or outcomes. My evidence journal felt like a journey. I still had the puppy stickers on the front, but last night I ripped out a picture of the ocean from a magazine and glued it on the back cover.

As I walking around I noticed that all our models looked similar. There were some models with more of a mixture of dirt and water, and others where the water still looked clear. We settled back to our own models and took a seat in the grass.

Once we were all seated, Ms. Morgan asked us, "What is the sand made up of?"

"Very small pieces of rocks," said Joshua.

"Yes, and what is special about those very small pieces of rocks that makes it move with the waves?"

We had to think about that question for a moment. No one answered. After 30 seconds of confusion and silence, Ms. Morgan suggested, "Talk to others around you and come up with some ideas."

We turned to talk to one another, but none of us had an answer. Instead we just started talking about how hungry we were and how we were so close to lunch we could actually taste our food.

"The sand is light in weight," Ms. Morgan finally said. "Therefore it moves around easier, depositing itself on the shore making beaches."

"We knew that," said Arjun.

"Well, why didn't you say anything," said Ms. Morgan.

"I guess we figured that was too easy to be the answer."

"That is what often happens," she said. "We think if it is too easy it cannot be right. Not everything is out of our reach. Use what you know, what you have heard, and try it out."

I never had a teacher like Ms. Morgan before. Maybe all teachers thought it was ok to make mistakes, but no one actually supported that theory. She made it seem like it was actually better to make a mistake than to have the correct answer.

"Now, how do waves affect the land?" Ms. Morgan continued.

"It causes erosion, which eats away at the cliffside," said Joshua

"Depending on the size of the waves, it could take down a lot of the cliff," said Jaime.

"What causes the waves to get bigger?" Ms. Morgan asked.

"Wind," said Brian.

"Yes, wind from storms!" Ms. Morgan said. She paused. We could see her mind was thinking a thousand different things, and she had to chose just one for now. "Has anyone heard of the ocean conveyor belt?"

We had because she had mentioned it before in class. We tend to remember most of what Ms. Morgan says because she makes it easy for us to make connections. None of us responded however, because although the name sounded familiar, we couldn't seem to come up with any content.

She walked us out of the grass, to a large patch of dirt. "Come follow me. I need a whiteboard, but since we don't have one I will have to improvise." We stood around her in a lopsided and loose circle. She had dragged the bucket of sand over and dumped out what was still inside onto the ground below.

Ms. Morgan then drew a rectangle with rounded edges into the sand. "Try to see this as a side view of the ocean," she said. "On this side is the Arctic, and on the other side is the South Pacific." She wrote in the names, but it was hard to really decipher the letters. I could make out the "A" and the "S."

"Now, we know that it is cold in the Arctic, and the water in the South Pacific is warm, right?"

We nodded our heads in agreement.

"What do we know about water when it is very cold?" she asked.

"It turns to a solid," said Joshua.

"Yes, it turns to ice and then it gets very heavy," said Ms. Morgan. "Cold water sinks. But, the salt does not freeze, it sort of stays toward the top."

She drew little arrows going down the rectangle on the Arctic side. "What happens with the warm water from the South Pacific is that it wants to swim up north to sort of recreate the ocean water that had sunk." She then drew more arrows, this time on the top of the rectangle moving from the South Pacific to the Arctic.

"What do you do when you are cold?" she asked us.

"I grab a beanie," said Brian.

"Sometimes my mom turns on the stove in our house and we stand around it in the morning," said Lola.

"You want to get warm, right?" said Ms. Morgan. "That's what the cold water that sunk wants to do. So it travels down south looking for a beanie, or to turn on the stove." Then she drew arrows on the bottom half of the rectangle from the Arctic to the South Pacific.

Before Ms. Morgan could finish drawing the arrows, Celia burst out, "Then that water gets warmer and rises because it is less heavy!"

"Exactly!" Ms. Morgan then drew the last of the arrows, going from the lower South Pacific to the surface water.

Many of us were now drawing this model in our evidence journals. I tried to follow all parts, but basically it was like a moving wheel, going around and around.

"This is what we call the ocean conveyor belt. The currents in the ocean, that are moved by the wind, are keeping this machine going. And, when it is going, it is transferring energy and water, and even little animals," said Ms. Morgan. "It also keeps our climate happy, keeping places from getting too hot or too cold. Pretty neat, huh?"

"And, that happens all the time?" Celia asked.

"All day long," said Ms. Morgan.

I wrote it all down, not wanting to miss a single bit of information. I loved drawing arrows around the page. Arrows connected everything.

"Now, what do you think happens when the ocean temperature warms up?" Ms. Morgan asked.

"Like, what is happening because of climate change?" I asked.

"Yes and no," she said. "The temperature of the water has always had fluctuation in degrees. When the surface temperature in the Pacific Ocean gets warmer near the middle, like say, southern Mexico, it can have a large impact on weather."

"Like what?" Lola asked.

"Well, what happens is that there is a low pressure system around us that causes us to have a more wet winter, as in more rainfall and storms. Does anyone know what this phase is called?"

"El Niño," Joshua said.

"Yes!"

"How did you know that?" Jaime asked Joshua.

"I heard it on the news before when they were talking about the weather," said Joshua. He really seemed to know everything, which is generally annoying, but also really amazing.

"That's cool." Jaime nodded his head to Joshua, and Joshua nodded back in an agreement that made his news and weather watching something cool.

"The opposite of this is a phase called La Niña, where we have colder waters, higher pressure systems, and a dry winter where we live," said Ms. Morgan.

"In other words, when the temperature of the water changes, there are big changes to our weather," I said. "Which means that when the ocean is holding in a lot of carbon dioxide and it gets warmer, we might start getting a lot more storms."

"Our weather is definitely affected by climate change," said Ms. Morgan.

DON'T REINVENT THE WHEEL

While I was trying to figure out why there weren't more people like Ms. Morgan who made learning interesting, I also thought about Jackie. Did she make it fun in Jolene's class? I hadn't spoken to either of them for a couple days now. This avoidance is somewhat difficult to pull off when you live in the same house, and this person I'm desperately trying to ignore just so happens to be my sister. My anger couldn't go on forever, and it wasn't serving me, so said Dad.

"Jenny, I understand and acknowledge your feelings toward this situation," he had said to me. "However, letting yourself sit in your anger and absorb your thoughts is unhealthy. At a certain point you need to decide if you want to be joyful or mad."

"Jackie is not absorbing my thoughts, trust me," I said

when he interpreted my journal entry. I slapped my diary shut, and put the cap back on my pen. "I have other things on my mind."

"All I'm saying is that when you make peace, you will be happier, and it will open more doors to opportunities for a stronger relationship," Dad said. "Maybe even a friendship?"

"Easy for you to say," I mumbled.

"Why is it easy for me?"

"You make friends easily, and people seem to like you immediately."

"That's not entirely true," Dad said. "There are always the haters out there."

"*Haters?* Dad, Really?"

"Sorry I borrowed a word from your dictionary." He laughed because he knew it sounded lame. "Jenny, there are people that despise my work, and think I do it all wrong. There are plenty of people that think I need to focus on different issues with my film projects."

"That seems hard to believe."

"You are never going to make everyone happy."

"And that doesn't bother you?"

"Sure. Sometimes I let it get to me." He grabbed his mug of coffee and looked deep inside, swirling it around. "But, if I let what everyone thought of me dictate my life, I wouldn't do the work that I do. There will always be someone who disagrees with you, but you can't let them take you down." He took a big sip of the coffee now, tilting it back toward his face. "Now in the case of you and Jackie, I suggest talking to her about what is bothering you, and see how you two can move forward. You don't have to agree with what she is doing with Jolene's class, but you can at least talk about it."

"Dad, you're confusing me," I said. "First you say that I shouldn't let the 'haters' get me down, then you say that I need to work it out with Jackie. I don't get your logic."

"Ok, let me say it differently, and I'll be very direct." He set down his coffee and grabbed both my shoulders and looked me straight in the eyes. "Jackie is passionate."

I pulled my head away from Dad's gaze and looked into the distance just so I didn't have to make eye contact. "I know, I know. I have heard it before."

"Listen," Dad said, bringing my head back into the conversation with the palm of his hand. "She works hard, and there are people that do not agree with her stance, or they think she is too uppity. She doesn't let them stand in her way, because she believes in the movement. Her work with Jolene's class is a wonderful project that is inspiring the youth. You are just upset because you were not included."

I opened my mouth to shout out everything I was holding in. Dad put up a firm hand in my face. "Understandable," he said. "Now, is it worth it to be upset when we both know Jackie is doing a good thing, and you have decided years ago that you didn't want anything to do with Jackie?"

"Jeez, Dad. That's not fair."

"What's not fair?" he asked.

"You are putting all the blame on me," I said.

"There is no blame here," Dad said.

"What are you talking about, then?"

He pulled back his hands. He picked his mug back up, and took another sip.

"Jenny, all I'm saying is that if you spent less time

being annoyed with Jackie, you might find room for a relationship that might just surprise you."

I was going to have to talk to Jackie eventually, but I knew she was going to be condescending and rude. At this point she didn't even know I was ignoring her. She was going on about her life not talking to me, and it didn't matter to her in the least. She was completely oblivious to my silent protest. In other words, it didn't matter. I mean I did want to know what she was doing in Jolene's class that I could do in mine. Such a predicament. I would need to take my pride, crumple it up into a ball, and throw it out the window if I was going to move forward. Wait, no! I couldn't throw it out the window. I could at least put in the recycling bin.

Looking back on that conversation now, I understand what he was trying to tell me. I knew what he was going on about, I just didn't have the strength to make it right. Plus my thoughts were consumed with plastics in the ocean, and I had no idea what to do with those thoughts, or where to start. I couldn't waste any more time on being upset or trying to mend my relationship with Jackie.

I grabbed my silly diary-slash-journal-thingy and went for a walk outside. I figured if I could write it all down, without distractions, until there was nothing left to write, I could come to some sort of conclusion. The only way to see past myself was to think about it for a really long time until all my thoughts were thought and I could finally see the thing, whatever it was, with a clear mind.

I walked into the woods that were at the back of our neighborhood. It was a safe place and close to home. I could scream and someone would definitely come running. A little further in was a beautiful grove of eucalyptus trees that were set back, surrounded in a barrier of poison oak that separated them from the path. Today, I decided to carefully hop over the poison oak and sit among those trees. I knew they were blue gum eucalyptus trees, and I knew that everyone said they were invasive. They were everywhere I looked, and they were tall. Those trees must have been there for decades. At what point do we say they are no longer invasive, but part of the local ecosystem? That was too much for me to decide at this moment.

I laid on the ground, face up, and pulled my legs up onto the tree to rest, the way I did so in my room against the wall. I placed my journal across my chest, and I looked up in the sky to the tops of the trees. I stared into the pure nature of it all and just let myself be still. If there was anyone around I had no idea, and I was perfectly happy in my perceived isolation.

There is something incredibly relaxing about being in nature. It's like everything slows down, and time almost stops. It really makes whatever is bothering me seem nonexistent. The only thing that mattered was being right there, under those trees.

Then it hit me! I knew exactly what I wanted and needed to do. Looking up at the extensive forest was like looking at the map of the Pacific Ocean, and it suddenly became clear. What I wanted to do was too big to wrap my head around, but I needed to start somewhere. I mean I couldn't tackle the entire problem, even if I wanted to.

If a documentary could inspire me, maybe I could inspire those at my school with a documentary?

Holy Toledo! I could see the entire project run into my head racing like horses on a track. Around and around it went and I could see every turn and mistake, and all the people on the sidelines cheering. Not for me, but for the cause. I could see everyone that was important to me involved, and I could see how to bring us all together. It was all there. I had the greatest idea ever!

I ran all the way home and immediately to Dad's studio downstairs.

"Hey Jenny," he said. "Everything ok?"

"Everything is great," I said, still gasping for air. "I need some help."

"Sure, what can I do for you?"

"Dad, how do you make a documentary?"

"Well, that's a big question. There are many components." He stood up from his seat in front of his computer screen and stretched to one side. He scratched his head and looked at me. "You need the footage, you need to edit the footage. There is music involved, interviews of course," he said. "It takes a lot of time and collaboration."

"I have a vision!" I announced.

"Do you want to make a documentary?" he asked me.

"I do, but I don't know what I am doing."

He sat back down, and said, "One thing I always say is you can never be prepared enough, and when the time comes to film, you will always feel underprepared."

I grabbed my notebook and started writing it down. Knowing the way my mind works, I was not going to remember anything. "Go on," I said.

"You look very serious about this," Dad said. "What are you writing?"

"Don't pay attention to me, just keep talking," I told him.

"Ok, ok. I'm not going to stand in your way. Where was

I?"

"You were saying I need to be prepared because I will always feel underprepared," I said.

"Yes. When filming a documentary you have to capture the moment. In order to document, you must be ready to film life happening before you. You cannot be sidetracked, and you must focus on your subject."

"Okay." I was furiously trying to get everything down on paper.

Dad leaned into the conversation. I think he had been waiting for me, or anyone really, to ask him about his life's work. "You need to tell the story, Jenny."

I nodded my head.

"Once you feel that you have gathered the material, you head back into the studio, and fulfill your final product. You mix it up and produce your vision."

"So, my vision is what leads the project?" I asked.

"Not necessarily, but I will say stay with your vision."

"Thanks, Dad. Even though that was really confusing." I started heading out, back upstairs to start on my project.

"Wait, are you leaving so soon?" he asked. "What is this all about?"

"It's complicated, but actually, well, not at all. I know what I want to do."

"Okay, tell me more about your vision."

I turned back around. I really didn't want to talk about it anymore; I just wanted to get started, but I guess I owed Dad an explanation.

"Dad, I know people care about the environment, but not enough people know that people care. Do you know what I mean?" I said.

"I think so. Do you mean that people agree but they

don't talk about it? Is that it?"

"Kind of. It's like we all need more Jackies out there so more people know that others are interested, and then together we can do more." I set aside my notebook and pen, and slapped my hands on my knees. I took a deep breath. "It's like, we all need more people to say it out loud. There needs to be more people showing and saying what they are doing to normalize the care our planet needs."

Dad was listening. "Isn't that what Greta Thunberg is already doing?"

"Totally! She is great because she is so big and important people listen to her," I said. "What I'm talking about are the people that can't talk to government officials, and, you know, speak at conferences. What about the people that are not taken seriously? Or think they can't do anything about anything?"

"From what I hear, Greta was not taken seriously at first," Dad said.

"I know, but do you hear what I'm saying," I pleaded.

"Of course. It kind of reminds me of when I was younger and was first getting into documentary filming. Someone told me point blank, 'You are not going to reinvent the wheel.' It was hard to hear, and it could have deterred me completely. What I remember that day was deciding that I had a story to tell, and I wanted to tell it with all my heart."

I looked intently at Dad. It is always weird for me to think of him as younger, with dreams and failures. He always seemed enthusiastic about life, so it's odd to hear that maybe life wasn't perfect or laid out in front of him.

"I can see you have a story to tell," he said. "If you feel you are the person to tell it, then you need to do it. Don't let anyone stop you. There are a lot of naysayers out there, but you are also going to find supporters as well, probably more."

"Thanks, Dad." I grabbed my notebook again.

"One thing I will say, if you want to do this well, learn about cameras, audio, and editing." He laughed, but he was also rubbing his eyes as if he were to rub them off his face.

"Dad, how am I supposed to learn about all that when I want to get the story out fast?"

"I can help you, if you would like."

"Would you?" I asked.

"Of course, Jenny. I would want nothing more than to help you with anything you need. And, since it has to do with filming, there is no way I could turn it down."

"Do you want to hear about the vision I have?"

"I'm ready."

SMALL, MANAGEABLE STEPS

If you ask yourself, *Where do I get started*, when a large project looms over you, and you have never tackled something of that size or depth, and you are worried that you are under qualified...well you just need to start with a list. At least this is where I started in order to compart-menttalize my thoughts:

1. Stop using plastic products
2. Make flyers or posters to put around campus
3. Make up some sort of narrative to share the idea with other classes
4. Get others interested in...
5. Okay, now...How?

How, is definitely the question. Or, is it, *Why*? Yes,

why! Once you know why you care, then you can figure how to get your project going. So, why should people care? Why do I care? I care because when we wipe out marine life because of habitat loss and lack of food, then we wipe out the majority of our life on this planet. Plus, if we don't do something about the plastic problem, there will be micro plastics in everything that we eat and drink, and in our air. No one really wants to eat plastic.

Why does this matter? Because there is a domino effect that will hit life on land, and then humans will be impacted.

Aren't we already impacted? Why does no one see this?

Now I'm back to the *how*.

How can I show others *why* they need to care?

It was all too much. I was having an argument with my own mind. Where does anyone get started? I needed to talk to Eve, she'd know what to do.

I entered Jolene's house the way I always have, speaking with Eve first. Only this time I intended to have a purposeful conversation with just Eve, and only Eve.

"Hi Jenny," she said. "I haven't seen you in a couple days. How is everything?"

"Things are great!" I said with a huge grin across my face, without a worry in the world.

"Well that's good to hear," she said. "I don't mean to pry, but I heard about your argument with Jolene. Have you two been able to work it out?"

"Oh, yeah, that. I haven't spoken to Jolene about it, but that's ok. I actually came here to speak with you."

"Me?" she asked.

"I actually want to talk to you about the project going on in your class that Jackie is a part of."

"Everything ok?" She was puzzled.

"Yes, completely," I said with utmost honesty. "This is a good thing!"

"I think it would be best to talk to Jolene first. She was pretty upset after you left."

I didn't think it was fair the way Eve said that to me, as if I had no right to be agitated. "I was upset too," I added. I wanted to say that while I was able to move forward, and I may have overreacted, I was hurt. Instead I said, "I will talk to her soon."

It didn't seem to satisfy Eve much. She wanted me to make it right, and I just wasn't ready to do that at this moment. She stared at me waiting for me to physically respond by walking up the stairs and into Jolene's room. I wasn't ready, and it wasn't going to happen today.

"Ok," said Eve, finally giving up. "Now what did you want to talk to me about?"

"The work you have been doing in your classes with Jackie about the ocean. I would like to do something like that in my class."

"Have you spoken with your teacher?" Eve asked.

"Sort of. She knows that I am interested, and she knows that I want to start getting others in my class interested. I'm pretty sure she would help me with anything if I asked."

"She sounds like a supportive teacher."

"She is! She is a great teacher. I think she is the reason that I'm so interested in the ocean." I finally took a seat on one of the counter stools, and took my jacket off to hang on the back. I never stayed long enough talking to Eve to actually sit down, but today I needed to get comfortable.

"So she knows that I want to do something, I just haven't told her what I want to do," I said. "That's because I didn't know what I wanted to do before. I now have a great idea."

"You have my attention," Eve said, joining me on another stool. "What is it that you need from me?"

"The only other person that I know that cares about the environment is Jackie, and she has always been so intense, a sort of all-or-nothing attitude," I said. Eve pushed a bowl of strawberries toward me. I grabbed on and took a bite. "She is not afraid to get in front of a group of people. The idea of being the face of anything scares me. But, as I have been noticing, there are more people that have similar ideas and interests, but they are just not as vocal. Like we all keep it to ourselves. For example, I never knew that you and Jolene did a lot of work with oceans in class. And, the other day, I started actually asking questions and bringing up ideas in my class, and people listened. It's almost as if all that interest had been there the whole time."

"Well, insight is a beautiful thing, Jenny," said Eve. "What is it exactly that has your interest?"

"I think it's hard to care about the ocean when you don't live near it, or see it regularly. It's like it's not there, just something on a map that doesn't actually exist in the real world. I've come to realize how bad the plastic problem really is. For some reason something clicked and I could finally see how impacted the oceans are from plastic waste. I knew it was happening, like all of us do, but most people, including myself, are not doing anything about it."

"That's not entirely true," said Eve. "There are many organizations that are putting all their efforts into cleaning up, people who bring awareness, and still many others who are finding alternatives to plastic use. All you have to do is a quick internet search and you'll find them. Trust me, they are out there."

"Then why is the problem getting worse?" I asked. "Shouldn't we see less plastic in the ocean, instead of the numbers growing?"

"That's a great question. Though, in many ways I would say it is not getting worse. It may feel like a standstill, or a time of transition, but again you don't have to look far to see that many others are aware of the plastic problem and solutions are popping up all the time."

"If what you say is true then why wouldn't more people put in the effort to avoid plastics, and just overall trash?"

"It's hard," Eve said. She placed both her hands on the counter top. She looked them over. "Our lives became more convenient with plastic. In the beginning no one really knew that it was going to stick around and not biodegrade. In order to stop plastic use businesses would have to drastically change their ways. They would have to spend more money to make those changes, and the consumers, us, would have to make conscious choices for the planet regularly, not just in the times when it is convenient."

She was right. Though it was the same thing I kept hearing. Businesses are too big to reach. It was too expensive. They weren't going to buy in if they lost money. Consumers aren't going to change their ways. There is no use in trying.

"Do you think that with more time people will understand?" I asked.

"Time," Eve said, nodding her head. "That's interesting. Some would say time is running out."

"This brings me to why I came here," I said. I took a deep breath and then smiled.

I proceed to tell Eve that we needed to bring this action of plastics and trash to the youth, in a way that created accountability, not just awareness. She told me she couldn't believe how mature I sounded. I continued to tell her that we could bring it to our schools and collaborate on a project that could eventually bring more schools together. I jumped into the details of the project and the work involved, and was firing off at a rate my voice couldn't keep up with. I just talked and talked, and smiled, and waved my arms around, and said, *You know what I mean?* more times than I care to admit.

"Ok, Jenny," said Eve. "This is a great idea, now let's bring that big picture into reality."

"Ok, what do you mean?"

"I hear what you are saying, *and* you need to see the manageable steps to take, otherwise this wonderful idea of yours doesn't lift off."

"Ok."

"What you are proposing is going to take a lot of energy from a lot of people. It is not something that is going to happen overnight, or over the course of a week."

"I understand, but I really want to do this," I said. "And, I really think it is possible."

"Have you spoken to Jackie? I bet she would have great feedback, and she is probably willing to help, or doing something along the same lines."

"I haven't yet. I came to you first because I was hoping my class and your class could be the first collaboration. You being the private school and me from a public school."

"How about this," Eve started. "You talk to Jackie about what she is doing in my class, then ask your teacher if that would work in your class, then we will see how the collaboration could blossom. What do you think?"

I was feeling dismissed. "I guess that is a start?" I said.

"You need to start somewhere. All ideas need a feasible plan in order to grow. Do you know what that means?"

"Yeah. It means that I need something that will actually work, not some crazy dream."

"You need roots before you can bloom," Eve said.

I heard what she was saying. Did she understand what it was that I was trying to do, though? I went to Eve for guidance, and all I got was how to slow down and go talk to Jackie. Since I am polite, I said, "Thank you. I'll do that."

"Come on back, and let me know how it goes," she said.

I got up from my seat and put my jacket back on. I grabbed one more strawberry from the bowl, smiled at Eve and waved goodbye. When I turned the door handle, I looked back around to say one more thing.

"Eve?"

"Yes, Jenny?"

"I'll be back."

"I know you will."

TRASH GYRE

Eve was right. I needed to start small, and talk to others, which was slightly different from what Ms. Morgan said the next day at school, "We need to walk-the-walk." She led us out to the blacktop and armed us with buckets and said we needed to clean up our own school yard before we could begin cleaning up the ocean.

It was a good idea, and any time spent outside of the classroom was always a plus. While out picking up bits and pieces of hard-to-grab garbage, we came across an area just outside the blacktop where all the trash seemed to pile up. We found the red stick from the cheese and crackers snack pack. We saw the corners of plastic chip bags where they had been ripped off. We picked up the flimsy plastic lid to a chocolate and pretzel-stick container. There were a few larger items, but mostly it was the small discarded pieces that didn't seem worth picking up in the moment, that got swept up in the wind and found themselves in a swirling eddy on the ground mixed with leaves, making it much more difficult to sift through and scoop up.

It was the perfect ocean gyre simulation I had learned about in the documentary. Somehow with the weather patterns, the wind, and the trees, all the small pieces that got left behind from snacks and lunches swirled around and around until they ended up here.

Here was an opportunity to start small, but still go forward with the project.

The following week I had sent Ms. Morgan an email outlining what I had in mind. I had worked on it all weekend. I filled countless pages with my thoughts and ideas. I asked Dad nearly a million questions about filming. I could tell Jackie was starting to notice, but she was too busy with school to butt in.

Ms. Morgan took care of the authorization forms for the class, allowing me to film for the school project. In my eyes it wasn't a school project, it was going to be much bigger, but for now, we kept it simple. Like Eve said, slow down, start small, and take manageable steps.

Dad loaned me a camera I could take with me to school. It wasn't his best camera, but it did the trick, since we couldn't use cell phones at school. I started by documenting the class picking up the trash, and really focused in on this new trash pile.

I made it a point to go out there every morning to see what would turn up from the day before. With the documentation I could prove a point, because I would have eventual statistics. That seems to be what people wanted: data.

Every morning we were met with trash. It wasn't as big as when we first came upon the scene because we started picking it up now, but it gathered nonetheless.

After a week of picking up the trash, Ms. Morgan opened up a discussion.

"If the trash keeps coming back, then the problem is not with having students or a janitor pick up it," Joshua stated. "It's that the trash needs to go in the can. People are being lazy."

"Actually, dude," said Jaime. "The wind can pull trash out of the cans. And I have seen squirrels and crows pull out trash when they think no one is around."

"I once saw a squirrel take an entire sandwich in a plastic bag from a lunch table!" said Lola. "They are sneaky."

"Then what happens to that plastic bag that the squirrel doesn't eat?" I said. "It ends up in the gyre out there." I pointed out our new favorite spot to look for trash.

"So, what do you think we should do?" asked Ms. Morgan. "Turn and talk to those at your table, and come up with five solutions." She flashed up her hand, emphasizing the number five. "Don't worry about the possible contingencies, just list ideas and we can discuss them as a class."

We immediately pulled our seats to face the center of the table and dove right into the conversation.

"Obviously the animals are starved," laughed Brian. "And, they need to go out searching for food that is not in their usual diet."

"Actually, you have a point," I said. "But, for a problem we can try to tackle today, I think we need to—"

"Lids!" interrupted Lola.

"Lids?" I said.

"Yeah, if there were lids on the garbage cans then the animals couldn't get in."

"I think there are lids," said Brian, feeling embarrassed for Lola's ignorance.

"What I was going to say," I started again. "Is that we need to convince people not to have so much trash and waste in their lunches."

"Now, that's a good point," said Brian. "If people didn't have all that packaged food, then there would be less floating around."

"Okay, that's one idea. Ms. Morgan said we need five ideas," said Lola. "If we can't think of any, I will write down lids and we can forget that Brian totally shamed me."

We laughed.

"What if we stick to this overarching solution, and then think of five ways to implement it?" I said.

"Okay, so what would that be?" asked Lola. "I'm confused."

"It's ok, just listen. We could hold an assembly showing people the footage I have collected, and then show some options of how to pack their lunch."

"I'm pretty sure we have had ten thousand assemblies about bringing reusable containers," said Brian. "It's the same thing every year, and then a few in between. I think Ms. Morgan has actually led a bunch of them."

"Well," I said. "No one is listening. How do we get them to listen?"

We sat there and thought silently. Our heads tilted up, our eyes squinting at the ceiling, as if ideas would fall from above.

"I like the footage idea," said Brian. "Maybe we could still do an assembly, but instead of the usual, it could be something different."

"Like a challenge!" shouted Lola.

"Yeah, like challenging everyone not to put trash in their lunch for a month and see what happens," I said.

Just as we were getting started Ms. Morgan's voice cut through the chatter of the class and she redirected our attention. "I'm hearing great ideas," she said. "Would anyone like to start?"

Lola threw up her hand quickly.

"Go ahead, Lola."

"We talked about a bunch of stuff, but what we came up with is having an assembly urging students not to put trash and plastic waste in their lunch."

"Another assembly," grumbled Celia.

"Not just another assembly," I said. "It could be based around showing the footage of the trash outside, like proof. Then we thought instead of showing people the reusable containers like how it is done every year, we could create a challenge of some sort."

"Oh, so your little video is going to lead the way," said Celia. "You are going to just take the lead on everything?"

"That's not what I'm saying, Celia. I was thinking that it would be more interactive, and I think that the footage shows what is happening in a way others can see, not just hear."

"I think it's a great idea," said Ms. Morgan.

Celia raised her hand.

"Yes, Celia?"

"Can I go?"

"Of course," said Ms. Morgan.

"We came up with a plan to create reusable bags for everyone at the school. That way we could promote less plastic waste" she said. "We could make them ourselves and hand them out."

"Why don't you charge for them so you can have money for the supplies," I suggested.

"I was thinking of a donation jar, so everyone could have access to at least one, regardless of money," said Celia. "You know, not everyone can afford them."

"Another great idea," said Ms. Morgan. "What would you make the bags out of?"

"We were thinking either beeswax or we could sew together a piece of cloth with either a button or Velcro."

"There is a concern of capital for the materials," said Ms. Morgan. "Nonetheless, we could combine both ideas," said Ms. Morgan. "We could make the bags, then have an assembly with the footage to show why the baggies are so important to use. And *reuse*."

Everyone seemed to agree with Ms. Morgan that combining the ideas was the best solution. Celia looked annoyed. Why was she always so angry with me?

After class I was determined to find out. When we had packed up and filed out of the classroom, I caught up with Celia.

"Hey, Celia, can I talk to you?"

"Why?" she said, though she couldn't be bothered to look at me.

"To be honest, I want to know why you hate me so much."

"I don't hate you," she said, and walked away.

So I ran after her because I wanted answers. I tried to

catch up with her again. "Then why are you always so rude to me?"

She didn't respond; she just kept walking.

"Hey!" I yelled. "Why won't you talk to me?"

Celia turned around, and said, "Why do you care?"

"Because I don't understand."

"Do you need me to spell it out for you?" she said.

"I guess so."

"You really want to know why?" she shouted.

"Yeah," I said.

"Because you think you're better than everyone, that's why."

I stopped walking. "What are you talking about?" I said. "I don't think that at all. Where would you get that idea?"

She was on a mission to get rid of me, but I wasn't finished. I started walking again to meet up with her.

"Celia, we have known each other since we were babies. We used to be best friends. Now you treat me like your enemy."

She finally stopped marching down the hallway. I saw her shoulders drop, and her head hang with agitation.

It wasn't that long ago that we used to hang out all the time. Our dads would buy these little cookies that are made of peanut and marzipan. They were individually wrapped with a little rose on the top. We could eat ten in a row, which would necessitate lots of hot chocolate, and of course water.

"The thing is, Jenny, when you decided to move out of the neighborhood, you also decided that Lola and I were no longer good enough for you."

"That's not true!"

"What about your little friend, Jolene?"

"What about Jolene?"

"When you met her, we were done," said Celia.

"You think that because I met Jolene that *we* were no longer friends," I said.

"That's when we stopped hanging out, isn't it?" she said.

"I moved. We couldn't hang out unless one of our parents drove us."

"You never wanted to come back. We always had to go to your new house and hang out with your new best friend."

"Why didn't you say something?" I asked.

I was trying to remember if that was accurate. We moved out of the neighborhood three years ago, and at first Celia and Lola came over fairly often. I did introduce them to Jolene, but Jolene was so cool, I never thought Celia didn't like her. I never really went back to my old neighborhood, and we did slowly stop seeing each other altogether. It wasn't my fault. I didn't mean for it to unravel. Nothing was intentional. It just sort of happened.

"I thought you liked Jolene?" I said.

"I mean, she's nice, but she's not like us," said Celia.

"Like us?" I asked.

"Yeah. She is like that perfect little house type family."

"What are you even talking about?"

"You changed, you know that. You changed to be like her."

"I really have no idea what you are talking about. I have not changed," I said.

"Do you remember what your old house was like?"

I remembered Jackie and I sharing a bedroom. I

remember being outside all the time playing with Celia and Lola. There was a lot more noise. We got together with our neighbors more often than we do now. It was different, sure, but I hadn't changed.

"Celia," I said. "Why are you really mad at me?"

"I already told you," she said.

"Because I moved? Because I made a new friend?"

"Yeah, and you think because of your new house and your new friend that you are better than me."

"I don't think that," I said. "I never once thought that."

Celia didn't say much after that.

"Celia, you know that's not true," I said again.

It seemed she was through with me, and discussing the matter.

It seemed I was finding enemies at every corner. First Jolene, now Celia.

DO YOUR RESEARCH

When something weighs heavily on your mind, it's hard to push it away. I was trying to move forward with the footage, but Celia kept popping up. I had sat at my computer for a really long time, and probably could have finished already if I wasn't so distracted. The good news was that when each clip uploaded and appeared on the screen, I was more than satisfied with the outcome. I actually captured what it was that I set out to do. The blacktop gyre was loaded with trash the first day, and it was easy to see that specific location accumulated trash every day. I had footage of the pile every morning for five days. While I do not want to get ahead of myself, I could see the power of documentation.

I heard a knock at my bedroom door.

"Yeah?"

"Can I come in?" It was Dad.

"Sure. I'm just looking at my footage."

"Music to my ears," he said.

Dad opened the door and stepped inside. He was in his usual blue jeans and cotton collared shirt. He was never dressed up nor dressed down, just casual, and always with a smile.

"Can I check it out?" he asked.

"Of course," I said. "I am looking at trash piled up at my school."

Dad knelt down beside me and made room for himself on the carpet next to me.

"How come you never sit in a chair?" he asked. "It's not as easy for me to get down here."

"I like this spot because it's closest to an outlet, which I need," I said picking up the cord that was plugged into my laptop and the wall. "Plus, it's more comfortable on the floor with my back against the wall, than slumped over in a chair."

"Probably better for your posture, too," he added. "So, what are we looking at specifically?"

I told Dad about the gyre, and my need to document it to prove that the trash kept coming back. He nodded, but didn't say anything.

"What?" I asked.

"Oh, nothing."

"Obviously, there is something," I said.

"I don't see much here. A few pieces of trash in each shot, sure," he started.

"Our class is going to hold an assembly at school, and I am going to show how the trash accumulates every day. Our hope is that people will understand that their trash ends up somewhere, and then eventually to the ocean."

"Ok, I see," he said. "That's very cool. When is the assembly?"

"We haven't set a date."

Dad leaned in closer to the laptop. Slowly he took control of the mouse and was zooming in on an empty bag of chips. He asked, "What do you see here?"

"Is this a trick question?"

"Not at all," Dad said. "If you take away the noise what do you see?"

"That's not the point, though. The students need to see that their trash is ending up in the corner of the blacktop."

"Yes, I understand. Seems to me you have two stories here. One of irresponsible behavior getting trash in the trash can, and another of making unhealthy choices."

"Dad, you sound like Jackie."

"She generally makes a good point," he said. "What if students were made more aware of their eating habits?"

"Well, actually, that kind of came up in class. Not exactly eating healthy, but we discussed alternative options for food packaging. That's when the assembly idea came up. Of course Celia had to embarrass me in front of the class, like she always does."

"Celia?" I could tell Dad was about to describe the Celia he knew. The one who wore ruffled dresses and two pigtails, pulled back so tight her eyes seemed to stretch to her ears.

"Yes, the same Celia."

"Embarrass you?" Dad asked. "How, or should I say why?"

"She has to make me feel stupid. She rolls her eyes at me any time she can, and she actually told me yesterday that she thinks *I think* I'm better than her. Can you believe that?"

"What did she say to you in class?" Dad asked.

"She said something like I wanted to lead every project with my film idea," I said.

"And?"

"It wasn't that big of a deal, considering she always puts me down. I tried to talk to her after class, but she didn't really want to talk to me and kept saying that since we moved I became a jerk," I said. "Well, she didn't say jerk, but you know what I mean?"

"You know, Jenny, her family has been through some hard times lately," said Dad.

"Really? Like what?"

"Well, Luis, her dad?" Dad waited for me to make the connection.

"Yeah, I remember Luis," I said.

"Well, he is pretty sick."

"What? What kind of sick?"

"Well his kidneys aren't doing so well, and he can't work."

"But, he's going to get better, right?"

"It has been almost a year now." Dad looked away from me towards the door.

Luis and my Dad had been friends before Jackie or I was born. Luis worked as a mechanic. He could fix anything, was what everyone said. After working all day in the shop you could still find him under a car or truck of one of our neighbors. Celia liked fetching him the tool he needed in the moment, or holding the lamp for him when he worked into the night.

Mom and Dad moved into that neighborhood the day

after they were married. Luis was the first one who came over with Celia's Mom, Conchita, with a flan to welcome them. Conchita made the best flan. Seriously, when you slid the side of your fork down inside to carve out a bite sized piece there were never any air bubbles, just pure cream and caramel sauce dripping from the top. Celia said she was tired of flan at every gathering. I always asked her to grab a slice for me. I couldn't get enough.

"How come I didn't know about Luis?" I asked.

"I'm pretty sure we have discussed it around you," Dad said, looking back at me. "Your mother and I try to visit once a week, after work usually, just to pop in, bring food, just try to stay positive for them."

"I had no idea."

"Well, you have been caught up in what is going on in here," said Dad, placing his index finger on my head. "Sometimes we can sit at the same table and not hear what anyone is saying when we are lost in thought."

"That only happens when I'm trying to tune out Jackie," I laughed.

"Anyway, keep up the work on this project of yours, and let me know how I can help," he said.

He brought one knee to the carpet and then leaned on my shoulder with his left hand to help him up. "Don't be an editor. It's a lot of sitting, and back pain."

"But, you love it, Dad."

"Ok, then, at least get a stand-up desk."

When Dad left my room, I went back to my footage. Dad had a point, there wasn't much there. It wasn't compelling, which means it wasn't going to be the call to action that we were hoping to garner.

It was time. I knew it. I stood up, with more ease than

Dad, and decided to make the walk to Jackie's room. It wasn't going to be easy. She would most likely turn me away, but I would use soft eyes with her and talk about the stuff she likes.

Knock, knock.

"Come in," she said.

I crept in very slowly, holding the door as a shield in case a shoe came flying in my direction.

"Hey, Jackie," I said.

"Oh, it's you," she said, though she gave me the courtesy of looking up. "What do you want?"

"Well, I am working on this project with my class about plastics in the ocean, and I heard that you have been doing things with Jolene's class, and I was wondering if you had any good ideas about how we can get more people at my school interested."

Jackie closed up her laptop, scratched her messy bun, and turned toward me. "I heard about your little project," she said.

"You did? From who?"

"Who do you think?" she said. "Mom told me. She also told me you needed help."

"I never said I needed help."

"She also said, you said you didn't want my help, but that you would probably come ask me sooner than later."

How embarrassing. *Thanks a lot, Mom.*

"First of all, you don't even know what you are doing," she started. "You got all excited when Dad loaned you a camera and now you think you are going to make the next best documentary, and everyone is going to watch. What you need to do is understand your cause."

I knew she would be dismissive and rude. This time

though, I took the beating instead of walking away, and waited for her to speak again.

"So many people want to fight for something. I think we, as humans, want to find that kind of passion that fuels us to do greater things. We want to be heard, and we want to make change. We see things that we don't agree with, and we find a bit of motivation, but when things get tough, we back out."

I was listening.

"The other day we watched that documentary together, then you got jazzed up and wanted to save the world from plastics. Let me guess, you want to make your own documentary, but you don't know what to do now that your inspirational fairy dust has worn off."

"Not exactly," I said. "I still want to do the filming and sharing so others can see. I just don't think my footage is that great, and I came to you to see what I could do to really get people's attention."

"Attention for what?" she asked.

"For plastic consumption, that eventually makes its way to the ocean," I said.

"Do you even know anything about the ocean?" Jackie said.

"Yes."

"Like what?"

"I know that most of Earth's water is salt water, and that the Pacific Ocean is the biggest ocean," I said. "I know other stuff, too."

"Why don't you do some research about the ocean and come back to me. Then we can talk about getting people's attention."

"Where do I start?" I asked.

"A Google search for starters," she said. "Now go, because I have a paper I'm working on that is due tomorrow, and I really need the head space and time to finish."

I turned and walked out, like a deflated balloon. She couldn't have been more dismissive. First Eve, now Jackie. Not that I was completely surprised, but she could have at least given me a bit of guidance besides a Google search.

"Oh, Jenny?" Jackie said.

I knew she had it in her, she wasn't going to leave me hanging. I quickly turned around eagerly anticipating what she would impart. "Yeah?"

"Close the door when you leave."

So much for that.

OCEAN LITERACY

I sat down with my laptop, ready to type *ocean* into my old friend Google. I looked around my room, at all the paraphernalia I had pinned up that had nothing to do with rising sea levels or fossil fuels, and more to do with what was popular and staying up-to-date on the latest fashion trends. I had the current stickers of wanderlust stuck onto my full-length mirror, the tapestry of the tarot card, The Sun, covering half my wall, clothes taking up space on my floor, and the chotskies I had my mom purchase every time we stepped into a store. I was definitely not the poster child for climate change mitigation.

Jackie was right, I needed to beef up my knowledge.

I wasn't going to learn it all from Ms. Morgan, or from school in general. I had to hold myself accountable for gathering information, or else I was stuck in the waiting game of life, where I stand by and stick around for something or someone to tell me what to do or where to go. I was quickly discovering that no one was really going to lead the way, or hold my hand. The door wasn't going to open on its own; I was going to have to turn the handle.

But, first I needed a key.

O-c-e-a-n.

Images of blue scenes filled the screen almost immediately upon pressing enter. Large, barreling waves, underwater ecosystems, colorful sunsets, and aerial views of white water shores. Scrolling down I found the familiar Wikipedia site, ready to give me any and all information, if I was willing to drudge through the encyclopedic-style writing.

National Geographic and the National Oceanic and Atmospheric Association, or simply NOAA, came up a few times with educational articles. Then there were the small activist websites about pollution that revealed themselves as I made my way further down the first page of possibilities.

What struck my attention was the word literacy. *Ocean literacy.* As if there was a sort of proficiency of knowledge to the ocean, like being able to read a book, or learning a new language. As if the ocean had a form of communication with which to learn and understand.

I found a short document that detailed the principles of ocean literacy, and how each student should attain this knowledge by the time they graduate high school. There were various organizations that contributed to this guide, and it all started from some workshop a bunch of educators attended where their combined passion for the ocean rolled into something that could be shared with schools and other organizations with the intent to educate. It was called the Ocean Literacy Framework. Their main goal is to educate the population, mostly students, about the ocean.

The phrase that captured my consideration, and made me feel as if Jackie wrote it, stated that an "ocean literate person can communicate about the ocean in a meaningful way."

I was not ocean literate.

The document was not of great length, but it held enough information to give me a starting off point from which to round up more information.

I could not help but wonder, did every teacher know about this? If these are principles that should be learned by the 12th grade, was it actually being taught in schools? No wonder the ocean is a disaster, no one was taking the time to teach it. No one was learning enough to comprehend its importance, and its place in the world.

I read that most oxygen on our planet comes from organisms in the ocean. Our oceans soak up harmful chemicals, like methane, and it takes in a lot of the carbon dioxide in our world. Almost all bodies of water make their way to their way to the ocean, no doubt collecting chemicals and debris along the way.

That was a lot, in just one paragraph.

After skimming through the framework, I clicked on a National Geographic article that was simply titled: *Ocean*. The article was written for my exact age group. After reading through the basic information I had already gained in Ms. Morgan's class, it went on to discuss the world under the surface. The mountains, the trenches, the millions of marine lives that make up the ocean.

Oceanographers. Those who study the ocean.

Only five percent of the ocean has been explored. If the ocean makes up three fourths of our planet, that means that less than thirty percent of Earth has been explored. What did that even mean?

I wasn't quite sure, but I suddenly had an idea, and I needed help. Again. Mom was right. Everyone was right. Everyone around me was always right in hindsight. Why does it take so long to figure it out? With every step I needed someone's help.

I picked up the phone and dialed.

"Hello?"

"Hello, Celia?" I said.

There was no response on the other end. I kept my breathing silent so it wasn't too annoyingly needy and heavy on the other side.

I waited.

She knew it was me, and I knew she didn't want to talk to me.

"Celia?" I asked again.

Nothing. She hadn't hung up, which made me believe she was at least curious as to why I was calling.

"I'm sorry to hear about your dad," I said.

Nothing.

"I'm sorry I haven't been a good friend."

Nothing.

I sort of felt like I was leaving a voice message. I didn't expect a response anymore, so I continued. "I spoke with my dad the other day, and he told me that your dad has been sick for a while now and that it has been hard for your family."

"When did you start to care?" She finally spoke up. It

was meant to hurt, but I was thankful she reciprocated in some way.

"I guess I was oblivious. I wasn't being a good friend," I said. "I moved and I met Jolene, and I never thought about taking care of our friendship. I just assumed it would always be there, no matter what."

Celia went back to the silent treatment.

"I'm sorry," I said.

She let out a big sigh. "What do you want?" she asked.

"I want to say I'm sorry, and I want to see if you will forgive me. I know it doesn't mean anything, and I might be worse off for saying this, but I really had no idea how you felt. I realize now I was being selfish. I'm really sorry."

"Why now?" she asked.

"Well, to be honest, you have really good ideas in class, and I thought we could talk about them and see how we can work together."

"So, this is all for your little film?"

"No!" I just got myself in a corner. "Well, not exactly." I sounded superficial and phony. How was I going to get out of this one? "What I want to say is that I want to be your friend again. I also think we can work together on this ocean project."

She made me wait again.

I looked around my room again, at all the lame posters on my wall, and the stuff I idolized: face masks, and fluffy anythings. Who was I kidding? Celia could see right through me.

"Well—" she started.

"Yeah?" I jumped at the prospect of her conversation.

"Just so you know, people that don't live in good neighborhoods care about the environment too," she said.

"You don't have to have a big house and a fancy education or job to know that you want to make this world a better place."

"I know," I said, though it sounded so stupid coming out of my mouth. I was confused with what she meant, and so far everything I have done or said has gone wrong. I needed to just stay quiet.

"We see it first hand, and we don't have the option to buy metal straws or organic cotton," Celia went on. "All the stuff you are talking about with the ocean, it's important to me too. Even though I can't buy better alternatives, or convince my parents to even recycle, doesn't mean that I don't care."

"Celia, I never thought that at all," I said. "Honestly."

"Maybe, maybe not," she said. "I just want you to know that there are others out there that really care and we are working twice as hard in our own homes to make it right. I'm not the only one. There are many others. People you know."

I had no words. She was hurt, and I didn't know if I could make it better. In fact, I could be the reason she was hurt in the first place. I was able to piece together what she was referring to. It was now obvious. The difference between Jolene's family and Celia's family was huge. Celia's parents had to work long and late hours. Celia's house was old, and the neighborhood was loud.

I was right in the middle, never feeling good enough for one side, while at the same time considered a snob on the other. I wouldn't share this with Celia because my perception of problems wouldn't give her circumstance value or meaning, but leave it feeling small. It was like we were living in two different worlds, and I didn't know how to build the bridge to connect us together again.

"Celia?" I said. "Are you still there?"

"Yeah, I'm still here," she said.

"Maybe that's exactly why we need to work together, to bring out more voices and to let people know it is okay to speak up."

Celia said, "I feel ok speaking up. I don't want others to feel they can't."

I was not the one to make all the wrongs right. I couldn't fix all the pain she felt, but I could start today with something.

Or, maybe I just needed to listen.

"Okay," said Celia. "Why did you call?"

I let out a huge silent sigh on my end. In just a matter of seconds I imagined Celia and I, and even Jolene and Jackie, spreading the message of plastics, and single-use plastics especially, to others. I saw us creating options for all families. I saw us starting a non-profit where we could help others find their voice and be heard, and for times to change.

"Well, I was just doing this research and I realized if people don't know enough about the ocean, how can they build the desire to take care of it, right?" I said.

"I totally agree," said Celia.

ENVIRONMENTAL JUSTICE

Celia and I spoke on the phone a few times in order to build our idea to spark more interest and understanding of the ocean. Then she came over to work on the keynote presentation together using my laptop. We had plans for bright graphics and a couple borrowed videos that could explain what we had to stay more succinctly. Ms. Morgan agreed to let us build a large model of the Pacific Ocean in her classroom. She also warned us about time.

"Don't try to do too much in one hour," she said. "You are going to find the discussion, which is the best part, will take up a lot of the time you planned for the model."

Celia and I looked at each other, and mentally flipped through all that we had planned. Then without rehearsal we simultaneously asked, "Can we have two hours?"

Ms. Morgan reluctantly agreed. I'm only assuming it

was a win-win, seeing as she wouldn't have to plan anything, and we were doing something she was into.

"Oh, and one more thing," I said to Ms. Morgan. "This might get a bit messy."

"Sounds perfect," she said.

Back at my house, we kept ourselves busy trying to find how to best display the ocean floor, as well as why it was important to teach, and why was it important to even build a model in the first place.

It was great having Celia over at the house again. She really was like family to me. She was so comfortable with my parents, and even Jackie, that it put everything at ease. Celia said our house felt cozy.

I did miss Jolene, and I really wanted to mend our little feud sooner than later. With too much time in-between she might forget about me, and then before we know it we will become strangers with distant memories of friendship now forgotten. It had been almost three weeks without speaking with Jolene and confronting the situation, and when I say situation, I am referring to me throwing my s'more across the yard and running away like a big baby. I still wasn't ready to reach out to her, and she was not reciprocating in the least.

I was keeping myself so busy I wasn't paying attention. Our disagreement did cross my mind, but I had so much to occupy my time, and time was flying.

"Where are we going to get something that will hold the model?" Celia said.

"I have no idea," I said. "I mean how big do we want it to be?"

"Really big!" She spread out her arms to reach as far

as she could. "Something that catches the attention of others walking by. Maybe we could even display it in the multipurpose room, or use it for when we have the assembly."

"There are so many things. I just want to do it all!" I said. "There isn't enough time, and I get all crazy in my head."

"Don't worry, let's just focus on this for now, and we will get to the assembly later," she said.

It was weird how we were instantly friends again. She needed acknowledgement and I needed awareness. A perfect exchange.

Without invitation in walked Jackie.

"Hey Celia," Jackie said. "Nice to see you."

"You too," said Celia.

"What are you two working on?" Jackie asked.

"Who are you, *Mom*?" I said.

"What? I can't ask questions."

"You can, but your tone was too nice," I said.

"Whatever," said Jackie. "Is this part of your little ocean project?"

"Yeah," Celia chimed in. "We are going to talk about the ocean floor, and then build a massive model of it in class."

Jackie just nodded her head.

"We just need to find something to hold the model," said Celia.

"What materials are you using to make the model?" asked Jackie.

"Salt dough," I said.

Jackie nodded her head. Then she said, "What about plywood?"

"Where would we find plywood?" Celia said.

"I bet there is a piece laying around somewhere. You definitely shouldn't spend money on it," said Jackie. "Maybe we could go to a construction store and see if there are any scraps. I bet they would be cool with it if we said it was for a school project."

"Ok, who are you, and what you did with my sister?" I said.

"Whatever," said Jackie. "Do you want my help or not?"

"We'll take it," said Celia.

When we dropped off Celia, her mom Conchita, came running out with a fresh batch of móle to give us. She had unintentionally disguised it in a large plastic butter container.

"I just made this," she said. "Warm it up tonight with some chicken legs. Mmmm." She pursed her lips together, as if she was drinking in a mouthful of her own móle. "It will be so good."

"Thanks, Conchita," Mom said. Then Mom gave her a sideways glance, with a tinge of embarrassment. "Jackie is a vegetarian."

"Then warm up some tortillas, and slip in some jack cheese. You will love it!"

"Ok, that sounds good," said Mom. "We can't wait."

Mom went to the store and bought both drumsticks and jack cheese. Since we always had tortillas at home it was easy to get the dinner going.

When Mom put the dinner on the table, we were like wolves digging in. "This is delicious," said Jackie. "Have you ever made móle before, Mom?"

"Of course, but it has been a long time. I'm so glad she gave this to us; I had no plans for dinner tonight."

Jackie was devouring saturated tortillas with slices of semi-melted cheese stuffed inside. "So Jenny," she said. "What's up with you and Celia. You two friends again?"

"We were always friends," I said.

"Right," she said. "So, not talking or hanging out for a couple years defines friendship."

"We are working on the project together in class, and it is kind of bringing us back together," I said.

I swirled my rolled-up tortilla in the móle and sunk it down lower so the sauce reached higher up, making my next bite even more delicious. It made me think of our old house, in the neighborhood Celia still lived in. There was always a reason to gather with friends, like a birthday party for someone on the block, or a baptism, or wedding festivities still going into the night.

"Dad?" I asked. "Why *did* we move?"

"Um, well," he started. He scratched his head. "There were a few reasons."

"Like?"

"We wanted to upgrade our home for one." He looked up from his plate at Jackie and I, and proclaimed, "Isn't it nice having your own bedroom?"

"Yes," said Jackie, nodding her head with definite agreement.

"What are the other reasons?" I asked.

"Probably the fact that it is hazardous to your health living over there," said Jackie.

"Well, that is not it exactly," said Dad. "At least not anymore."

"What do you mean, Jackie?" I asked.

I saw Dad and Mom exchange glances at one another.

As parents they understood an unspoken language, where a glance could explain a thousand words of hurt, punishment, joy, and disappointment. They looked at one another as if they knew what the conversation up ahead entailed and they were either going to put on their gloves or sit back to observe.

"There used to be this crazy hazardous recycling plant, that basically put a bunch of VOCs in the water." She took another bite, then wiped her mouth with the cloth napkin she begged Mom to buy. We started with just four napkins a year ago, and now we can barely close the drawer.

"That closed down over ten years ago," Mom interjected.

"Yeah, because the people found out why they were getting sick," said Jackie.

"What are VOCs?" I asked.

"Volatile Organic Compounds." Jackie said those hefty words with a flair of arrogance, as if I should already know the meaning of the acronym.

"Ok, but what are those?"

"Basically, a bunch of gross chemicals that if they get into the ground, like they did in our old neighborhood, they seep into the soil and groundwater, which is the water we use to cook and clean with, and we ingest them, and get sick." Jackie's head leaned to the left and to the right with every breath she took.

"Sick? Like how sick?"

"It could be a headache, or more severe like kidney or liver damage." Jackie said it all so matter of factly, like it was common knowledge.

Mom sighed. I looked in her direction, but she dropped her head down to her plate and stayed silent. I turned back toward Jackie. "I don't understand," I said.

"What is not to understand?" said Jackie. "Basically—"

"Stop saying basically," I said. "None of this sounds basic."

"Ok, ok. Let me rephrase. Celia's neighborhood is part of an unincorporated part of the city, which means that there are no elected officials, like city council, to oversee what happens, and they don't get to have, or not have, what the bigger city gets. This means that they get taken advantage of because there are less regulations. In other words, big companies like that recycling plant are able to do whatever they want regardless of consequences to the health of the community, so long as their business flourishes." She took another bite, and wiped her mouth.

"That doesn't seem fair at all," I said. "How does that even happen? How can they get away with that?"

"Well, to be clear, because of grassroots efforts from the community, they were able to shut it down ten years ago like Mom said, and they got the EPA to clean it up," said Jackie. "Now, as far as why they got away with it for as long as they did, well that's called environmental *in*-justice."

Ms. Morgan has brought up the phrase "environmental justice" before. She had said that it was the rights of everyone, no matter who you are, to have access to a clean environment to live in, as well as information and the ability to decide what develops around them. What was happening in our old neighborhood was the complete opposite.

"I know I don't know much, but my teacher had told us about environmental justice earlier this year, and this all seems to break the law. How do they get away with it?"

"Because, people of color get taken advantage of all the time," said Jackie.

"Ok, well there is more to the story," said Dad.

"Not really," said Jackie. "People that are not considered a threat are going to be controlled, and unless they do something drastic, nothing is going to change."

"What I mean to say, is that there are other factors involved," Dad said.

"Yeah, like what?" said Jackie.

She waited for Dad to respond, but he didn't seem to come up with a reply. Were there other factors? There had to be. You can't just come in and wreak havoc upon people and get away with it. Right?

"Can I ask another question?" I said. Dad and Jackie both turned to look at me. "If you are saying people of color get taken advantage of, how would that same situation be different in a neighborhood like ours now?"

"We would have access to information and time to ask questions, and time to refuse or set our own regulations," said Jackie.

"So, no one was given information?" I asked.

"Not full information, sort of like small print, you know?"

"But, why do companies get away with it?"

"They seek out places and people they know will not raise a fuss, and then slowly seep into their community."

"This sounds like a horror movie," I said.

"It is," said Jackie. "And, it's happening all the time."

"All the time?"

"Look it up," she said.

Mom and Dad had slipped out without our noticing, leaving just Jackie and I to discuss the issue. The table was mostly cleared except for the plates and forks in front of us. Jackie was soaking up the remaining móle on her plate with the last tortilla that had stayed warm in a folded kitchen towel still on the table.

I was having a hard time understanding how this could have happened, and that it was happening in other parts of the world. I must have held a confused look on my face, because Jackie reached over and put her hand over mine, and said, "I know, it's a lot to grasp."

I looked down at her hand on top of mine. I couldn't remember the last time we held hands, or even close enough to touch one another. It was a *lot*.

There were so many reasons to be upset with people and big companies. It wasn't just plastics, it was oil companies not wanting to move towards cleaner options, and it was corporations taking advantage of people in poverty and people of color. It was all too much. How could I possibly want to build a model of the ocean floor out of salt dough when there were bigger problems, in my own city!

I threw my head on the table, and let my arms catch my fall, cradling my deflation like an empty bird's nest.

"I get overwhelmed all the time," whispered Jackie. She had come close to my ear, as if she didn't want Mom or Dad to hear those words if they were listening from the other room.

I turned my head just a bit to see her with one eye. She was staring right at me, her hand extended toward my shoulder.

"There is so much going on in the world that I want to help with and make right. It piles up and I feel overpowered and helpless," Jackie confided.

"You do so much," I offered. "How can you feel helpless?"

"There are many people that are working towards a better planet, raising awareness, marching and protesting for the future of our world, and yet the carbon emissions keep rising, and the climate is changing, and those who are most affected are those who have little say in the matter."

"So what do we do?" I asked. "The small things that I'm trying to do with my class seem so trivial compared to the bigger issues. I'm not even the one living it. Celia is the one. In fact Dad said something about Luis had kidney damage. It's probably from the VOCs you are talking about."

"We are all affected in some way," Jackie said. "Even though I had the ability to appear as if I am on the fighting side without being directly affected, I carry so much pain all the time."

"What do you mean?"

"I worry that we can't do enough to avoid a catastrophe. I try my best, but sometimes I get really down."

Mom and Dad must have been listening from the kitchen, because at that moment they both emerged and sat back down at the table. Like Jackie had laid her hand on mine, Dad reached out and put his hand on Jackie's hand. Then Mom reached out to my hand.

"I don't know what to say that will make this better," Dad started. "But, I want you to know that you can talk to me about any of your fears."

"I would be lying if I said I didn't also worry about our changing world. These conversations are hard and uncomfortable," Mom said. "I am so proud of you for all the work that you do to let people know what is going on, and for being a strong example. As it is, you have inspired all of us at this table."

The corners of our mouths all turned upward toward our eyes. I knew there was resiliency here. Then Jackie filled up with tears. Mom came in for the rescue, scooping up Jackie in her arms. Jackie had never needed anyone, and I knew Mom kept her distance so as to give Jackie the space she desired. I suppose at this very moment, they both threw out their self-made rules and jumped into what was necessary.

"It's just so hard," she cried.

"I know, I know," said Mom.

"Nothing great is easy," Dad said.

Jackie pulled back and started to wipe away the tears. "Sometimes I just want to do so much."

"You are doing great things," Mom said. "Don't be so hard on yourself."

"I'm super proud you are my sister," I said.

That just about did it for Mom. She completely lost it and didn't care what she looked like or what we would have to say. Mom could barely breathe. "That makes me so happy," Mom said.

Both Jackie and I looked at her like she was some sort of gremlin that washed up onshore.

"Okay, okay," said Jackie. "Let's not get ahead of ourselves here." She quickly dried her tears.

Mom's display of emotion actually allowed us a breather from feeling so much, which seemed like the precise adverse reaction we craved.

With some time to gather ourselves, I finally broke the

silence and said, "I know I already asked this earlier, but what do we do?"

PLASTICS ON THE MAP

All that Jackie had told me about Celia's neighborhood made my heart ache, and I felt guilty. My family was able to move to a cleaner neighborhood, but Celia didn't have that option. Jackie said that it was not the time to feel guilty, and that no one wanted to hear I was feeling that way. She said, "You need to take action, and you need to listen."

Listening was proving to be the one of the biggest lessons. I had to listen to so many people around me, and do my research. I needed to open up to what others had to say. Dad's naysayers had a point, I wasn't going to reinvent the wheel, but I knew that something had to be done.

I went forward with the ocean floor model, because that is what I could do in the moment. It was important, and I knew that it mattered.

Celia brought the project together before the class, and I sat in the back filming her go off! For all the eye rolling she gave me, she really did have something to say, and she came alive. Others in the class easily listened to her, and she led them to be intrigued with the bottom of the ocean.

In true Ms. Morgan fashion we included the important people that made it their life's work to bring the ocean to others, like Sylvia Earle and Susan Humphries. Sylvia Earle had said that when she saw the depths of the ocean and all the beauty is when she fell in love. Because of her love of the ocean, we were all able to learn more.

We showed the videos and we explained why we wanted to share them. Then we split the class into two groups. One building the model, and the others were sent on a web quest about single-use plastics that Ms. Morgan put together.

"Please read the articles," said Ms. Morgan. "There is great information in there, so much more than I could ever teach."

I had looked at the list, and it seems Ms. Morgan found every relevant and factual online article she could about plastics, microplastics, why we use them, and solutions to our ever-growing plastic problems.

Jackie somehow found us a 4 x 4-foot piece of plywood. She had said, "Don't ask where I found this, just be thankful." So we didn't ask any questions. Mom said she would buy the ingredients for the map. In class, we discovered we needed to make way more dough than we originally planned. We also found out that we were going to need more than just two hours.

Every one of us had a part in molding the dough. We

filled the entire board and we built up mountains, and carved out trenches. We labeled points on the map, where Japan was and our home, the San Francisco Bay. We also put in the Midway Islands. It was at that point that we got really creative.

"We have to put plastic on the map!" said Brian.

"How?" asked Jaime.

"Pull it out of the trash and glue it on," said Brian.

Just like that we had our floating "patches" in our Pacific Ocean.

As we were researching plastics from the web quest, more ideas came up that we could make happen, which was incredibly empowering. A couple students decided they needed a camera as well. They borrowed a simple point-and-shoot from Mr. Porter in the office and went around campus photographing where there was garbage. They came back with pictures of discarded plastic cones, used paper towels caught in the bushes, cardboard boxes, plastic wrap, a broken garden hose. Those same students that captured the images grabbed a few more students and they started picking up the trash and bringing it back to the classroom. All the while I wish I had Dad here to film where I couldn't be. I did my best filming what I could.

"Can we print these photos?" they asked Ms. Morgan.

"Of course," she said. Which was the word she kept repeating. Everything was ok, and welcomed.

Off they went to find a way to print the photos.

"What if we pulled out the trash from the cans outside and showed people what they are throwing away?" said Lola.

"That's gross," said Jaime. "But, I kind of like it."

Those two then went off, digging through the trash

like raccoons, pulling up dirty bottle caps and yogurt containers and plastic spoons. Lots of plastic spoons!

When they returned, Lola shouted, "What if we had an art show!"

It was getting wild in the classroom. Ideas were bouncing off the walls, and Ms. Morgan kept saying of course. Over the next week she basically gave the class free rein to create and spread the message of plastics. It was crazy how it evolved. Each time we walked into her classroom, it was like walking into a workshop where our ideas mattered and we could explore what we wanted. We could work with anyone, and because of this we worked with people we hadn't before. We worked with people who shared the same ideas and different ideas. While there was a big picture, there was no plan. We just kept coming in the next day fueled with ideas and ways to clean up, and Ms. Morgan sat back and supported us.

Lola had found a discarded bulletin board in the school dumpster that was thrashed, but she saw it as a foundation for the trash she and Jaime pulled out from the cans. With an Xacto knife she carved out the shape of a heart and the two of them started gluing on all the pieces they gathered.

The model of the ocean floor was coming along. It was no longer the center of the project, but another important piece. Filming was hugely important to the entire cause. I zoomed my camera in and captured the slow blue strokes of the paint brush along the salt dough making the ocean, filling in the cracks of added texture.

I leaned into Celia and whispered, "I had no idea this was going to be so big."

"I know, it's crazy how everyone is finding something

they can do," said Celia.

"Can I tell you a secret?" I said to her.

"What's up?"

"I have no idea how to edit this footage."

"Just ask your dad," she said.

"I know. It just seems like a lot. Like I'm going to miss parts."

"It *is* a lot."

"Not helpful," I said.

Ms. Morgan walked over to the two of us. "This is going so well! I can't believe the enthusiasm around the room. I couldn't be more proud."

"Yeah, we were just saying how crazy it is," said Celia.

"Are you still going to make the baggies?" Ms. Morgan asked Celia.

"Totally. We are thinking we can pass them out at the art show," I said.

"The art show?" Ms. Morgan asked.

"The one Lola was shouting about on Monday."

"I heard her mention it, but I didn't know it was happening," said Ms. Morgan.

"Oh, right," I said. "I guess she only just shouted it out like a maniac without a cause." I looked at Ms. Morgan with pleading eyes. "I think it's a good idea."

"Yes, of course," she said. "But, what do we have in mind here? When is it happening?"

"We haven't figured out the details yet," said Celia. "We are on it."

Ms. Morgan then left to tend to Jaime's hot glue gun burn, leading him to the sink and holding his hand under cold water.

"What are we going to do?" I asked Celia. "We don't

know anything about an art show."

"Dude, we don't have to do anything. It is already happening. Look around," she said.

Lola was finishing up her heart art that was a least three feet wide and two feet tall. It was massive and filled with rubber gloves, chip bags, bottle caps, plastic utensils, glue sticks, empty tape rolls, and plastic baggies. She and Jaime titled it: "Plastic Heart, Bleeding to the Ocean." They planned to place bottle caps from the bottom of the stand that would hold up the heart, every couple of inches along the floor all the way to the large ocean floor model we built as a class.

The photography group managed to get photo paper and printed out nine different photos from around the school, which they placed in a 2 x 2-foot array on a large wooden board with a simple tack to hold up each image. Across the top they titled it, "We are Living in Trash."

Brian, Arjun, and Joshua took it upon themselves to collect empty plastic water bottles over the last week and put them together to make one tall and wide water bottle. Arjun brought in a trash can from home, turned it upside down, placed their whale of a water bottle on top, then taped the words to the bottom of the barrel: "REFUSE."

Everyone was contributing facts about plastics in the ocean from the web quest and printing them out on small sheets of paper that they stapled to a long wooden pole that was anchored down with a couple bags of sand. It was a tree that held up limbs of plastic parts. It was simply titled, "Plastic Tree."

The classroom was erupting in projects and awareness, and I was getting it all on film.

YOU NEED A COMPASS

It was time to take all that footage and start editing it to tell a story. While that sounds very exciting, I was at a loss.

"Dad, I really need some help," I said. Holding my laptop in my hand, and carrying around a mop of hair on my head that looked like it ran through a cattle ranch.

"I'm telling you, it's tedious, and it takes time," he told me.

"How do you do this? There is so much footage that I want to condense into ten minutes."

"Why ten minutes?" he asked.

"I figure we can get our point across and not lose our audience in that amount of time."

"Ten minutes is a long time for your age group," he said. "Where are you planning on showing this? Social media?"

"I'm not sure exactly," I said. "We had thoughts about the assembly."

"I remember you mentioned that," he said.

"Then, it morphed into an art show."

"Really? An art show, that's very cool. Sounds like quite the endeavor."

"You should see some of the art we created. Come here, look at this." I flipped through a few clips of the art we made in class on my screen. Dad nodded his head.

"This is great work, and your camera work is not too bad."

"Yeah, I'm kind of surprised myself," I told him. "Guess I'm learning from the best."

Dad smiled. "So what's the plan?"

"I really don't know, and I'm getting scared." I slumped down into myself. "I know that I'm not the only one that is a part of this project, but I feel very responsible for making it all come together to showcase, and I'm scared I'm going to mess it up."

"Sounds like you need some help," he said. "And, some direction."

"I have direction, I just don't know where to go," I said.

He laughed. "Can I buy you a compass?"

"Dad," I said. "That's not funny. I'm really worried that everyone's work won't get noticed, and all the filming will sit on my computer filed away for no audience."

"Well, get it out there," he said.

"It's so much work," I said. "Sometimes it feels silly."

"Silly?" Dad repeated.

"Yeah, like here are a bunch of kids looking through trash and making art. It has been done a thousand times, what makes us unique or worth watching? How are we different?"

"That is not where your head needs to go," he said. "Do you believe in the project?"

"Yeah."

"Then who cares what others think. If you think you have something to say, then shout it out."

"Ok!" I said. Dad was like my personal cheerleader. I felt like a football player ready to burst through an opening banner fully charged for the big game and all that was riding on its success.

Dad patted my back and then sent me off to work on the editing.

There was only one way of getting it done. I went back to my room, sat upright against the wall, faced my computer, and committed to making at least a first draft of this video story.

Hours must have gone by without moving from my seat, because when I finally got up to use the bathroom, my body felt like it was going to crack like a breadstick and fall to pieces. I limped down the hallway, dragging my body with me.

"Hey, how's the video going?" Jackie asked when I passed her bedroom.

I jumped with her unexpected words. "Oh, you scared me," I said, catching my breath. "It's going."

"Need any help?" she asked.

"Um," I started. I still wasn't used to her kindness. It was unnerving. I still braced myself for her to take it all back and laugh in my face. She never really laughed in my face, though. Jackie just had a way of talking that I didn't like. However, nowadays her tone was softer and more approachable. Was it her, or me?

"Actually, it would be great if you could look it over and give me feedback. I just finished getting it all in there, but I haven't added any fine details," I said.

"You really put together the footage?" she asked.

"Yeah. Like I said, it's not great, just a start."

"I'm happy to look it over," she said. "Right now?"

"Sure. I'm just going to use the bathroom, but you are welcome to my computer."

When I came back into the room, Jackie was deep into the video. I waited for her to finish before I opened my mouth to apologize for all that was terrible.

"Ok, where did you come from?" Jackie said.

"The bathroom?" I said confused.

"No, I mean, where did this come from?" She pointed to the screen.

"From the stuff we are doing at school."

"This is part of your ocean floor model project with Celia?" she asked.

"That's how it started," I said. "Well actually, it started when you and I watched the documentary together." Then I remembered the boat trip and how that may have been the spark, though maybe it was before that? "No, actually it started when Ms. Morgan showed us an image of a spinning earth." Then I wondered if it was actually the image, or if it was Ms. Morgan herself. "I'm not really sure anymore how it started, but this is where it is now."

"And, you got your classmates to buy into it?"

"Yeah, they were cool with the whole thing," I said. "Why, is it terrible?"

Jackie didn't say anything. She just played back the video. I sat down next to her and watched alongside. I

159

wasn't sure what she was thinking. Was it awful? Or, was it kind of good? I was nervous to ask.

"What are you going to do with the video?" Jackie asked.

"I'm not quite sure what to do with the video. I have an idea, but I don't know if it is *feasible*," I said. "Like you said a couple weeks ago, I really don't know what I'm doing. Dad just told me I need a compass because I lack direction. It all looks pretty dumb. Is that what you're thinking?"

"I didn't say that," she said.

"Is that what you are thinking?" I asked again.

"Listen. I'm really impressed."

"What!?" I yelled.

"Yes," Jackie said. She looked up from the screen, and saw me smiling. "Calm down. Don't let that go to your head."

"Wait, y*ou* are impressed with *me*?"

"I think the work you are doing is good," she said. "I have some suggestions, but I'll be honest, I'm kind of blown away."

"Stop! Now you're making fun of me."

"Not at all," she said. She brushed me off. "Do you want to hear my suggestions?"

"I guess?"

We sat there for three more hours while she told me to cut this, keep that, let the live audio play there. Jackie pretty much hacked up the entire piece, and left little resemblance to what I had initially created. It was beautiful! It was actually enjoyable to watch, and it had somewhat of a storyline.

"Where did you learn to do all of this?" I asked.

"You think you are the only one Dad imparted knowledge onto?" she said.

"This doesn't even look like my work anymore," I said.

"This is all your work, I just made it look like something someone who is not your family might want to watch," she said.

I understood what she meant.

"Thank you," I said.

"You know, you have done a lot of work here," Jackie said. "You should think about collaborating with more people."

"That's what I want to do, I think," I said. "We want to put together an art show and invite our whole school."

"I could see that happening," she said. "You could have this video play in the background, or you could introduce the show with the video. Either way, or both. Where are you thinking about holding the event?"

"I really have no idea. Our multipurpose room?"

"I hate to say this, but you are not going to get a lot of people to show up, except everyone's parents," said Jackie.

"What should we do, then?"

"It doesn't mean you shouldn't try. I'm just saying don't expect a lot of people."

"I want it to be big. I want people to come and see the art, and hear us talk," I said.

"Sometimes you have to start small, or just start somewhere," she said. "It's ok if it's the multipurpose room. It's probably where you need to start."

I felt so discouraged. It mattered so much to me that a lot of people showed interest. It mattered that those in my class felt acknowledged. "How did you get all those people to show up for the editor's panel?"

"That was a combined effort by many people, not just me. All of us editors told our friends and family. Linda from San Francisco State obviously told people. We put it in our newspapers, and put up flyers. The school had its own promotions. Plus it is an event that has been going on for a few years now, so people knew it about it already."

"I could do that," I said. "I could advertise, and get others to do the same."

"Ok, so you get hundreds of people to come see your art, then what?" she asked.

I didn't have an answer that I thought was good enough. It was the same story I continued to repeat: let people know, raise awareness, stop using single-use plastics. I didn't have any really good solutions, except that if more people knew about our polluted ocean, then more people would care, or at least take it seriously enough that some parts of it could become a reality. Nothing was going to change if it didn't happen at a higher level. Our individual efforts are important, but they are not enough.

"I just want people to care," I said. "When I went on that boat trip with my class I was told how much the bay had changed because of humans. I also learned about a few women that decided they would come together to try to save the bay, and they actually made a difference and inspired many others. I want to be like that."

"It's not about you," Jackie said. "It's about the cause."

"I didn't mean that. What I meant is that I want to make a difference so that our planet isn't ruined before I even get a chance to see it, or anyone else. It's not me, but I feel the need to do something. I want to let everyone know that we can make change and that we don't have to accept that our ocean is going to one day in the near future be so polluted that marine life ceases to exist. That there are no more coral reefs, or that the islands in the South Pacific are forever loaded with trash in the shore break."

"I get it, I get it. I'm here to help," said Jackie. "I know how we are going to start. But, you have to know we can't do it alone, we are going to need help."

FRIENDSHIP MATTERS

Jackie came up with a few ideas and said her friends may be willing to help. That's when I realized that I needed to call my friend.

My next stop was Jolene.

It had been a month since we saw each other, or even spoke to one another. I saw her a couple times riding around the block through our front window. I wanted to run outside and just start talking to her like nothing had happened, but I knew that was the wrong move. Plus I was scared she would ride away and ignore me.

There was no reason she should be kind to me. I was the one who acted like a baby. I was the one who walked out on her.

Today was the day to be brave.

Normally I would just walk into their home, but this

time I felt I needed to knock. Eve was there to answer the door.

"You're back," she said. "Good news, I assume?"

"Yes," I said. "Well, actually, is Jolene here?"

"She sure is. Just up in her bedroom. I think she is doing homework, but you might find her watching some show instead."

"Thanks."

Eve stepped aside and let me in. I went right by her and raced up the stairs. For some reason walking up the stairs was always too difficult, I needed to run, and skip a step in between like I was training for the high jump.

Jolene's door was slightly open. I tapped lightly with my finger nail, and then let myself in. She turned around. "Whoa, Jenny," she said. "I wasn't expecting to see you."

"Hey." I wasn't sure what to do next. I mean, I knew what I wanted to say, I just didn't know if I could start talking about it, or if I needed to wait.

"What's up?" she asked.

"Um, well, I wanted to come over and see how you are doing," I said.

"I'm fine. How are you?"

She was acting so polite, and as if nothing had happened. Well, nothing had happened in the last few weeks. Maybe she was ok with not being my friend. Maybe we were better off not seeing each other every day. She did have other friends at school to hang out with. She probably kept herself busy the entire time, and didn't even realize we hadn't hung out.

"I'm good. I mean, I'm well," I said. She threw me off. I was expecting her to tell me I was the worst. "What have you been up to lately?"

"Just school and basketball. You know, same old thing. What about you?"

"School."

"That's cool," she said.

"Jolene, I'm sorry I acted like a baby. I know I didn't handle that well."

"It's ok," she said. "I just figured you were busy and had other things on your mind."

This was weird. She didn't even seem bothered. I didn't know what to do. I felt stupid for even thinking our friendship mattered. "Ok, well, I guess that's it," I said.

"Ok, cool," Jolene said. "I guess I'll see you later."

"Ok, bye." I turned around and walked out, closing the door behind me.

"Dude, get back here!" she shouted.

"Oh, my gawd." I swung the door open, and I threw my hand over my heart like it stopped beating. "I totally thought you hated me."

"No way. I'm so glad you came over." Jolene reached over and threw her arms around my shoulders, squeezing me tight like a boa constrictor. "I have missed you so much!"

"I missed you too. I was so nervous to talk to you because so much time has passed."

"Me too. I kind of figured you really hated me and that was basically the end of our friendship. Then I saw that Celia was coming over to your house a lot and I thought for sure we were done."

"No way!" I said. I sat down on her floor, crossed my legs and felt a huge wave of relief sweep over me. "You have no idea how happy I am that you don't hate me."

"Sometimes we just need space," she said.

"I guess?"

"I don't know, that's what my mom said. She said that you were busy with some project and that it was good for you, and that you would probably come around when you were ready," Jolene said.

"That's not exactly how I thought it out, but it is kind of true. How did she know that?" I said.

"She's a teacher. That's what she does. She knows what kids are feeling. It's so annoying to be her daughter," Jolene said. "She always seems to know what is wrong with me, and she's so nice about it all the time. It drives me crazy!"

We laughed because it was true, and we laughed because it wasn't as bad as she was making it out to be.

"So what's up with this project you're working on?" she asked.

THE BEACH

Without wasting any time, Jolene and I were back, and to make up for time we lost, we managed to get Eve to take us to the beach that weekend. When she said yes, I immediately asked if I could bring another friend. She was happy to accommodate, and soon we were at Celia's house to pick her up.

The three of us sat in the back seat together, already eating the chips we begged Eve to buy. "Please, Mom," said Jolene. "Can we just go to the beach like regular people and eat junk food?" Eve easily gave in. I don't think what Jolene said really had any effect on her decision. I kind of think she was happy to make the day fun for all of us, and if that meant buying chips then she was going to cave.

The ride to the coast was about 30 minutes, if there was no traffic. However, anywhere in the Bay Area there is traffic. Apparently it took an extra 20 minutes, but we had no idea. We were laughing and joking and trying to save some chips for later, which proved to be an impossible task. When we parked and grabbed our stuff, I made my way to a garbage can to throw out the bag.

"You didn't save me any?" Eve said.

"Sorry," I said, feeling sheepish.

"It's ok, I'm kidding. I'm glad you enjoyed them."

We settled on a spot that gave us some freedom from other groups on the sand, where we could be as loud as we wanted, and yet not too far that carrying our bags would become tortuous.

It wasn't a particularly warm day at home, which meant the temperature at the beach was even cooler. It didn't really matter, we jumped in the freezing water anyway in just our bathing suits. It felt like a thousand needles poking into my feet and ankles. There was actually pain from the cold temperature of the water.

"Ah!" Celia screamed. "I can't take it!"

She started running out onto the sand. I grabbed her hand and pulled her back. "Just wait in the water a little longer, it will get warm. I promise."

"It's not going to get warmer, we are going to go numb," she said.

"Either way, it is going to get more comfortable," I said.

Celia ran out anyway and buried her feet into the sand. After looking out at us, still in the water, she finally decided she could muster the strength to withstand the cold for however long it took to go numb.

"Let's go in deeper," said Jolene.

I was quick to follow. Celia was again hesitant. Jolene

and I ran in anyway, figuring Celia would follow us eventually when she got over the cold.

We let the waves crash onto our bodies. We ducked underneath them, and jumped above them. After just a few minutes, I finally let my feet lift off the sandy floor and I started to move my arms in the shallow water and began swimming. My body went horizontal and I relaxed into the movement of the waves. It was so freeing being out there. I couldn't take the smile off my face, or feel less than wonderful.

I could forget about everything out there. I didn't have to worry about saving the planet for a moment. I didn't have to worry about being confident, or using my voice, or trying to learn and absorb everything. I could just be.

After a little while, Jolene and I decided to go back to our warm towels. We found Celia there wrapped up in her own towel, not sharing in our same joy.

"If you just wait in the water long enough, you forget the cold," I said. "I swear."

She just looked at me.

"It's not that bad," I said.

"It's not the cold," she said.

"Are you ok?" Jolene asked.

Celia grabbed her towel tighter around her body, and looked down. I decided she didn't want to talk about whatever was bothering her, so I let it go. I didn't want to bring up anything that might embarrass her in front of Jolene.

"Eve?" I called out. She was sitting at a distance, lost in a book. "Can we eat our sandwiches now?"

Without looking up from her book, she said, "Go right ahead."

I grabbed all three and passed them out. Soon enough, Celia was talking again and whatever had been bothering her seemed to slip away.

After reaching a point where we were full enough, Celia asked, "Do you want to go for a walk and collect shells?"

We wrapped up the other half of our sandwiches to save for later, and stuffed them back into the backpack. Jolene skipped over to her mom to let her know we were going to walk down the beach, then caught up to us as we walked in the shallow water.

There weren't many shells, and those that we saw were mostly broken. Celia kept leaning down and picking them up, then tossing them to the side when she was dissatisfied. Then she picked up a small blue piece.

"Is that sea glass?" I asked her.

She spun it around in her hand, and squeezed it with her thumb and index finger.

"Looks like plastic," said Jolene. "Definitely not sea glass."

Celia sort of shrugged her shoulders. She held onto it anyway, and we kept walking.

There was something so special about walking in the sand and the salt water. From the moment the Pacific Ocean caught my eye all those months ago, to physically being a part of it at that very moment was bringing it all together in a way that filled me with incredible optimism for the future, and just plain happiness right here and now. I let my eyes wander, and I let myself get caught up in conversation with Jolene, who was talking about wanting to travel the world on a unicorn.

When we came back to our spot, we sat back down on

the blanket we had originally set up, and laid down. Celia continued to sit upright and sift through all she had collected on our short walk.

"Look at all these small pieces of plastic," Celia said.

I sat upright, and let my eyes adjust to the bright sun. Laid out in front of Celia was a wave of colorful plastic shards. In a way it was really pretty. Like art.

"You found all of that?" asked Jolene.

"It was all there," she said.

"This beach looks so clean, though," said Jolene.

"Right?" I said.

"I kept thinking I was going to find a shell or sea glass, and every time it was this," said Celia holding a red triangular piece of plastic.

We looked at the pile. I was instantly ashamed that I had bypassed it all. I was so caught up in the moment of fun, that I didn't think to look down at my feet long enough to see what was below.

"Hey girls," Eve said. "Let's get ready to pack up."

"Ok," said Jolene. "Let's jump in one more time!"

"I'm going to have to get numb all over again," I said. "Are you going to come this time?" I asked Celia.

"No, thanks," she said. "I'm just going to clean this up."

Without any more thought, Jolene and I quickly ran into the water.

When Eve dropped Celia off at her house, I got out of the car to walk her to the door.

"I'm so glad you were able to come today," I said. I leaned in to give her a hug. She returned the gesture.

"Thanks for inviting me," she said.

I pulled away and said, "Can I ask you a question?"

"Sure, what's up?"

"Were you mad at me and Jolene?"

"No, not at all," Celia said.

"You seemed upset when we were in the water. If I did anything wrong, please let me know."

"You did nothing wrong," said Celia. "I just can't swim. When you two wanted to go further, I knew I wouldn't be able to."

"You can't swim?" I asked.

She shook her head. "I guess I never learned how."

"I'm sorry. I didn't know. I would have stayed on the shore with you."

"It's ok, really. I mean I was a little embarrassed, but after a while I just figured I could do other things instead of swimming. It's not a big deal. I'm not worried about it. Honest."

"Ok," I said. "Well, I'll see you on Monday at school."

We waved at one another, and then I ran back to the car, and off to my home.

ECO-ANXIETY

When I walked inside, Mom and Dad were already seated at the table eating dinner.

"Are you hungry?" Mom asked.

"Totally!"

"Perfect timing, we just sat down," she said.

Mom had made another stir fry, and since I hadn't eaten in hours, it actually looked like the best meal ever made.

"Jenny, I hear you are doing great things with this art show," Mom said.

"Well, thanks to Dad for inspiring me with the camera work."

Dad smiled at me with what seemed filled with a decade of hope that one of his daughters would one day want to follow in his footsteps.

"There is still so much to film," I said.

"What is the next step?" Mom asked.

"I want to document what we do in our everyday lives to be part of a solution. Then I want to see how Eve's class can be a part of it."

"This sounds like a big project. Are you getting any help?" Mom asked.

"Ms. Morgan is super supportive, and the class is totally on board," I said.

"I'm glad you are reaching out for help," said Mom. "It will be what gets you through the tough times, or when you feel like quitting."

"I'm not going to quit," I said. "Mom, this is so much bigger than me. This is about getting everyone involved. This is about people believing in themselves and talking about what is important."

They both laughed at one another.

"Why are you laughing? Are you making fun of me?"

"No," Mom said, still continuing to laugh. "Not at all."

"Then what is so funny?!"

"It's just that you have made it your life's purpose to hate your older sister and all that she wants to accomplish, and now you sound just like her," said Dad.

"And, that's funny to you?"

"Relax, Jenny," said Mom. "It's that you two have so much in common, and now you are finally seeing it."

"It's not funny," I said.

They continued to laugh, even louder now.

"What now?" I asked.

"You sound just like Jackie," they both said.

At that moment, Jackie came home. She was holding a stack of books in her hand, with her hoodie draped over her head.

"We were just talking about you," Mom said to Jackie, wiping her eyes.

Jackie set down her books and took a seat at the table. "It's easy to do," she smiled.

"We were talking about how you and Jenny sound so much alike these days," Mom said.

Jackie didn't say anything.

"Is everything okay?" Dad asked.

"Yeah, totally," said Jackie. "I just have a lot on my mind."

"About what?" Mom asked.

"College," Jackie said.

"How is the application process going?" Dad asked.

"I'm done with all of them." Jackie started serving herself the rice and vegetables that were on the table, skipping over the chicken Mom had prepared. "It's just tough to know where I want to go. I know it's not forever, but how will I know exactly what I want to study? There are so many options."

"I can tell," Dad chuckled as he stared through the books Jackie has brought in. "You have an interest in so many subjects."

"Right?" Jackie said.

"Don't worry about that now," said Dad. "Your major will come to you in time. You might even change your mind after your graduate."

"There is so much I want to learn and be a part of," she said.

"That's how I feel right now," I said.

They all looked my way, then Mom and Dad immediately went back to Jackie. I guess my problems were small.

"Jackie, honey," Mom said resting her hand on Jackie's hand as she does. "You will know."

Jackie started eating, and Mom pulled her hand back. It must be a lot to think about. Where to go, what to study, moving away from home. To me it all sounded exciting.

Jackie interrupted the brief silence, "I mean, I know all this stuff, but where do I go from here?"

"You mean, like now that you know more, you have to do something about it?" I asked.

Jackie turned to me and pointed. "Yeah, just like that."

"That's how I feel right now," I repeated. "Like awareness is a lot to hold on to."

"It brings up stress and uncomfortable feelings," Jackie said. "Then you look at the world around you and see what's going on, and you're supposed to choose one thing to put forth your efforts when there are so many things that need help."

"Like this art show and the video project," I said.

"You are doing great stuff," Dad said to me.

"It's the best thing I have ever been a part of," I smiled. "But, when I reach the goal of raising awareness, what comes next. What do you do with it?"

"You take action," said Jackie. Her eyes lit up.

"Of course you do," said Mom. "Just like you are doing with your college applications. You are choosing to further your education. Not everyone has this opportunity, you know."

"I know," said Jackie. "Thank you Mom, and Dad."

"Of course," said Dad.

"Jenny," said Jackie.

"Yeah?"

"You take action."

Part VIII:
You Take Action

BREAK FREE FROM PLASTIC POLLUTION

When I stepped into my class I was armed with a really big idea. I can say now that no one saw it coming.

I knew what I wanted to say. I stayed up all night filling up the pages of that insignificant, yet powerful little diary, sharpening my pencil too many times to count. That same adrenaline that kept me up was still pumping throughout my body.

Last night when I was listening to Jackie, I realized that taking action was the answer, but taking action wasn't easy.

"Good morning everyone," announced Ms. Morgan. "Isn't it a beautiful day?"

We mumbled our musings, and like robots pulled out our evidence journals to begin our discussion.

I didn't want to waste any time. "Ms. Morgan, can I

share something?" I asked.

"Yes, of course," she said. Ms. Morgan sat back in her chair and gave me her full attention.

"I know we have all been thinking a lot about the plastics we use, and no matter how we seem to take the effort to dispose of them correctly the garbage in the middle of the Pacific Ocean seems to grow." My hands were shaking. "Ok, so there are so many people advocating for less plastic consumption, and still the garbage grows. There are people that have spent decades of research and energy trying to convince others to stop using plastics, engineering designs to clean up the garbage, and still it grows. It's like this never ending, nonstop one step forward, five steps back routine."

I was going to need a huge canister of courage funneling into my body at a rapid rate, like oxygen tank divers use to study the ocean. This time though, I was no longer waiting to see Celia's eyes roll, or hear Joshua tell me that everyone already knew this. No one interrupted me, and no one was doodling in their journals either.

"I was thinking, we need to stop plastic consumption at the governmental level. And, we need to convince our Congress that if they don't take charge of this problem, then they are willingly subjecting everyone to a sub-par existence." I practiced last night, looking up the right words to sound not only smart but hopefully motivating.

Ms. Morgan clapped her hands together. I think the class thought she was applauding me, so they joined her, and soon the room was erupting in cheers. There I was on my soapbox. A place I never dared to stand upon. A place I never dreamed would mildly feel comfortable. It was all so dramatic.

"Well, well, Jenny," said Ms. Morgan. "Spoken like a true Earth steward."

"What are you talking about?" Jaime said.

I looked up, eyes wide.

"Huh?"

"What are you saying we should do?" Jaime asked, this time with a bit of impatience.

"Oh, right, ok. So there is a bill that has been sent to Congress, and we need to convince our representative to vote yes on it when it gets to the time of voting it through," I told them.

"What's the bill?" asked Brian.

"It basically forces the people who make the plastic responsible for recycling it. I can read it to you, it's not long." I turned to Ms. Morgan. "Can I share it?"

"Of course, please do," Ms. Morgan said, opening her arms to the audience before me.

I got out of my seat and walked to the front of the room. "Can I use a marker?" I asked Ms. Morgan.

"Of course," she said.

"To sum it up there are five parts to the bill."

I grabbed the first expo marker I could see and began scribbling on the whiteboard. I understood now when teachers write erratically across the board and their words are oftentimes indecipherable. It is the excitement of knowledge, and the speed at which those thoughts are brimming from their heads that cannot meet the will of the hand.

"Last night I was thinking a lot about what to do, and I saw this bill, and I think it pretty much sums up what we want to do. We just need to convince others that it is important," I said. Then I turned to the whiteboard to start writing. "You can find this information online, but first this bill will require that people that make the plastic come up with a way to recycle the plastic."

I looked back at the class, and I saw Lola getting it down.

"The second part of the bill would have a deposit system for drinks. Like, you could get money back for recycling the plastic bottle." This time I didn't turn to face the class, I just kept going. "One of the main goals would be to ultimately eliminate single-use plastics, which is huge! There would also be requirements for the type of plastic manufactured, as in the only plastics allowed would have to be a form that is easily recycled. And, the last important part of the bill wants to make sure that we, the United States, are not shipping our waste to places that cannot actually recycle it."

I wrote down the last word on the whiteboard, and finally turned back around and faced the class. Lola was still getting down all the information. I saw a couple others writing down some notes.

"Ok, so you know I'm your girl," Celia started. "But, I need to ask, what do we do about it?"

"We write letters!" I said. "We tell our Congresswoman that we think it is important and she should vote yes on it."

"Thank you, Jenny," Ms. Morgan chimed in. "My heart couldn't be happier! I think this is a fantastic idea."

"Would they actually read our letters?" Lola asked.

"Why not?" said Ms. Morgan. "There are people in their office that most likely will sift through them. The basic idea is that if you get enough people that want something badly, then the representative will have to do the will of the people. This is after all a democracy."

"Yes, but does letter writing actually work?" Lola asked again. "Do people still write letters?"

"Of course it works. Your voice is the strongest thing you have right now," Ms. Morgan told us. "Unfortunately you cannot vote, but you do have the power to make change in other ways. In fact, your voice is so important because what happens with this bill ultimately affects your generation the most."

"But, we are just 25 kids in a class, how will 25 letters make a difference?" asked Brian.

"Your enthusiasm can be infectious," Ms. Morgan said. "What if you wrote a letter *and* told someone else about the bill? What if you spread the word around?"

"How?" he asked.

"We could make posters!" Lola interrupted. "We could put them around the school. We could talk to other classes about it, and maybe we could get others to write letters. We could make calls. We could make flyers and put them in places around town."

"Yes, you can do all of that!" said Ms. Morgan. "Let's first start with some research. Everyone grab your laptop, and look up the bill."

"I can write it on the board," I suggested.

"Go ahead," said Ms. Morgan.

This time I put more effort into the shape of my letters: Break Free From Plastic Pollution 2020.

I'm not sure why Ms. Morgan continued to give me chances in class. I felt like this wasn't even science class anymore, it was more like a class in activism. When I told Ms. Morgan, she said that it is science. "Part of science is collecting data and knowing when to share your findings."

"This bill isn't our data," I said to her.

"No, it's not, but the other parts are," she said. "You have collected data on trash at your school, you have documented students in action. You are taking something that is personal and urgent that affects our world, and now you are rolling up your sleeves and doing some real problem-solving."

I nodded my head.

"Are you telling me that is not science?" Ms. Morgan said.

I couldn't argue with that.

THE WEBSITE

I was ready to take this idea further, but I needed to first figure out what we were going to do about this art show. It was already gaining some strength so I couldn't just let it fall between the cracks. Jackie said that we would need a venue for the art show that was big enough to hold a lot of people and one that wouldn't charge us a fee for holding our event.

"I thought you said I wouldn't get a lot of people to show up," I asked her.

"Well, that was when you didn't have me helping," she said.

Jackie was officially over the multipurpose room and was ready to move on to a place off campus. She said we needed some buy in from our larger community. She said I needed to be bold and confident. "If you want to make

187

this happen and change some minds and get this off the ground, you need to be ready to talk to people that are not your classmates or their parents. Are you ready?"

Jackie said we were going to need the video done to secure some funding, which frightened me. *Funding?* I immediately asked Dad for some help getting the video polished, and he said "Sure." In fact, he dropped everything he had going on. "I'll ask one of my friends to write some music for it."

"Actually, one of the kids in my class wrote a song about caring about the planet and how we can help. Maybe your friend can work with my friend to put it together?" I said.

"Sounds great. Get me the lyrics."

Jackie then invited me to the newspaper meeting at her school. I had never actually walked into one of her classrooms—it was really cool. I was happy she would let me listen in on what went on with a high school newspaper. I had a pen and notebook to write down ideas I could share with my class.

"Ok everyone," Jackie started. "This is my little sister who I was telling you about. She has a really good idea, and she needs our help."

"What are you doing?" I mouthed to Jackie. She put up two gentle hands and told me to relax.

I was suddenly so nervous sitting around all those high schoolers. They all sounded so smart, and just older. What was I even doing there? All I could do now was smile, mostly because everyone was looking at me.

"Here is a video she put together about what she has been doing with her classmates."

"Um, Jackie, the video isn't done," I whispered. "Please

stop. I'm so embarrassed."

"It's ok, Jenny," she said. She turned around and clicked a few buttons. Soon my unpolished video of trash on the blacktop, and my classmates running around making art out of garbage was displayed on the screen. I thought I was going to faint. My breathing was so shallow and fast that I thought I wasn't actually breathing. Was I having a panic attack? This is not what I thought was going to happen at this meeting. I had no choice but to sit back. I would only make it worse if I started mumbling how much it sucked, and how I desperately needed a paper bag to breathe into.

When it was through, the ten people in the room clapped. I just looked down at my feet. What was happening? Jackie hadn't told me what this meeting was all about. She made it seem like it was going to be a learning experience, where I could see what she was doing at her school and how I could apply that to my project.

"Ok, so this is where we come in," said Jackie. "She needs a website."

"On it, Jackie," someone said from the back.

"She also needs some graphic art for flyers for the event she will be hosting," said Jackie.

"It's ok, really," I said. "I can do it myself."

Jackie came over to me and whispered, "Remember when I said you are going to have to be confident. Believe in your work. It's ok. People want to help."

"We can work on it," said another girl.

"Great, thank you," said Jackie. "Jenny is going to stick around, so please ask her any questions as to how she wants it to look."

"I bet you all have better ideas than me," I said to

everyone. My voice was shaky, and it creaked like an old door.

"Stop being embarrassed! You have great ideas," Jackie said. "Oh, one last thing," she turned to the group again. "I want to run an article on how this young group of students is trying to raise awareness of plastics in the ocean through their art show, and how they are pushing for the Break Free From Plastic Pollution bill."

"I can do that," someone shouted out.

Everyone got right to work.

When Jenny finally slowed down and sat down next to me, I asked, "What the heck was that?"

"Jenny, I know it's hard to accept help, but this is how it works. You can't *do* everything, and you can't *be* everyone. It can't be a one-woman show. It won't work. There are others with skills you don't have. Learn to be assertive."

"I'm not good at this," I said. "I've never done this."

"I know, you're like five. Just be polite and say thank you."

"Thank you?" I mumbled. "Seriously, Jackie."

"Seriously, what? For once in your life I think you have something good here. Let me help you."

"Why are you being so nice to me?" I asked.

"I like what you're doing," she said.

"Thank you."

THERE IS NO PLANET B

It was quite a rush being around all the high schoolers. They were kind, they asked me a lot of questions, and they seemed interested. When I left I knew that I needed to hold up my end of the bargain by giving them content for the website.

Next move was to document our class writing letters to our Congresswoman. I brought Dad in this time.

Before we entered the classroom, Dad said, "Jenny, don't lose focus of your subject. I know that I am doing the filming, but you are the director. Don't get distracted. Sometimes you only get one opportunity to get the shot."

I took my regular seat, and Dad sat at the back of the class.

"After much research and discussions on plastics, we are ready to draft our letters," said Ms. Morgan. "As many of you already know by now, Jenny is looking to document the project. She has brought her dad in to help. He will be filming, and Jenny may pull you aside to ask you some questions."

"We are going to be famous!" yelled Brian.

"I hope so," I said.

Everyone started writing. It was a typical Ms. Morgan environment: the class was loud and working at the same time. We were out of our seats and still getting the words written on the computer. Dad was walking around with his camera acting as if he wasn't there at all. I was following him around to see if he was getting what I wanted. I could hear the conversations among my fellow classmates. I didn't have to tell them what to say, they were saying it all on their own. This must be what Ms. Morgan feels when we are on task and actually discussing the current topic.

"Hey Jaime, can I ask you a few questions," I said. "In front of the camera?"

"Sure, why not?"

"Cool, thanks."

He stood up from his seat and met me at the front door. I clipped the microphone onto the collar of his shirt.

"Whoa, Jenny," he said. "When did you get so professional?"

"This is all my dad's stuff that he's letting me borrow."

"That's cool."

"Ok, there you go." I stepped back behind Dad so as not to be in the shot.

Jaime adjusted his shirt and ran his fingers through his hair. "How do I look?" he asked lifting his eyebrow for effect.

"Great!" I said. "Let's get started, can you tell us what you are doing here today?"

"Well, so, um," he started. He paused, then said, "Jenny, you know what we are doing."

I looked at Dad nervously. He shook his head as if to say don't worry, and smiled.

"What am I supposed to say?" asked Jaime.

"Of course I know what we are going to do, I just want you to summarize what we are working on at this very moment for the camera."

I looked at Dad again. Without losing sight of his shot, he whispered, "Relax, just give it some time."

"Well, um, see there is this bill called 'Break Free From Plastic Pollution 2020' that basically makes companies like Coca-Cola responsible for all the plastic waste they create."

I smiled at him and told him with my eyes to keep going.

"So um, as a class, we have been studying the ocean, and we found that so much plastic waste gets thrown into our ocean and stays there disrupting marine life and filling up the waters. It's hard to clean it up, so it just sits there, getting bigger and bigger, and the pieces are getting smaller and smaller but never really going away." He scratched the side of his face, then looked around. I waited.

Dad said that it is best to just wait for the interviewee. "Have patience," he had said, "and when they are ready they will elaborate without you having to ask more questions."

"So we figure if people can't make better choices, then we need to set up a law to help," Jaime said. "What we are doing is writing to our Congresswoman to vote yes on the bill so it can make its way to the Senate. It's not quite there yet, there are all those committees and things that need to happen, but when it gets there we hope she will vote yes!"

"Thanks, Jaime. That was great!" I said. "Can I ask another question?"

"Sure." He was beginning to feel more comfortable in front of the camera.

"Why do you care if this bill gets passed or not?'

"Why do I care?" he asked. A look of puzzlement crossed his face. It was as if I asked him to divide 367 by 8976.

I nodded.

"Well, that's kind of a big question." He took his hand and rubbed his opposite shoulder, like the answer might be right there in his muscle. "I care because, I care about the place I live in. I don't want to live in a bunch of trash. Is that good?"

"Thanks, Jamie," I said. "You were great."

I went on to ask others in my class about why they care:

"I want to be able to visit all those islands one day and not see trash everywhere."

"I care because someone doesn't, and so I need to care more."

"I care because it's the right thing to do."

"Like Ms. Morgan's shirt says, *There is no planet B.*"

"I care because, well, why not?"

I knew Ms. Morgan was listening, and I hoped she felt proud. I was proud. I think Dad was proud. It was pretty much the best day of my life.

"Make sure to print out your work and hand it to me," said Ms. Morgan. "I have addressed this manila envelope and we are ready to send it out when I have all the letters together." She held up the large yellowish envelope and shook it in front of us like a bowl full of raffle tickets.

"Dude, this is really awesome," said Brian. "I don't think I have even done something that actually mattered."

"Thank you to Jenny for getting this started. And, thank you to her father, Pedro, for coming in."

"You can call me Peter," Dad said.

"Thank you, Peter," Ms. Morgan said again.

I HEAR YOU, I SEE YOU

The letters were sent off.

Check.

I had the footage.

Check.

Jolene said that I needed to meet this girl in her class, Melanie, who lived on the coast, and made going to the beach her life, except when she ventured over the hill to go to school five days a week. Jolene said Melanie lived in a house on the water that had a lot of open space. She said it would be perfect for the art show.

When I told Jackie, she gave me a face of disgust.

"What?" I said. "What's wrong?"

"I don't know," she said. "It sounds, um, I just don't know."

"I'm not sure what that means, but the way Jolene

described the place, it seems worth visiting, don't you think?"

"I was thinking of asking the San Mateo County of Education," said Jackie, her frown now all smiles. "They have a bunch of conference rooms, and they are familiar with this type of event for students."

"We can look at both, right?"

"Sure, I guess."

"I'll check with Jolene and see if this girl's house is even an option, and together we can ask the other place," I said.

I called up Celia and told her all the latest updates, then we sent an email to Ms. Morgan to see what she thought. Of course, we were met with a bunch of emojis and yeses.

In class the next day we presented all our ideas and new information to the rest of the community. They were very excited to hear about the website, and the possibility of having their art showcased.

"This is actually going to happen?" Jaime asked.

"Well," I said. "I hope it does. I haven't found a place for the art show. But, it's just a matter of time."

There were so many more people who were now involved, and waiting on my word. I had never been in charge of anything. I didn't really know exactly what I was doing, I just knew something needed to be done. Yet, I had this horrible feeling that soon enough Jackie's friends at the newspaper would discover I'm a phony. Some silly little kid with no direction who watched a documentary one day and was going to save the turtles. The other day when I went to the beach with Jolene and Celia it was so much fun *not* thinking and worrying, and releasing all that responsibility. I just wanted to have fun. We ate those chips from a plastic bag without thinking twice.

The problem is that it is hard to unsee all that we have learned. That day at the beach, while we were having fun being carefree, Celia had found a heap of plastic on the beach, and I then found out that Celia can't swim. Our world seemed like an exhausting place to live in. I found myself asking if it is better to remain ignorant, or to be mission driven.

Jackie was constantly fighting, she barely took a moment to settle in and just be, like how I felt at the beach for that small moment. I cannot recall a time when I saw Jackie sitting on the couch watching TV, or just sitting without preaching about something she found important. If she rested, I never saw.

It had been four months since I set my eyes on the spinning Pacific Ocean, and since then so much had happened. I could see how putting in an effort could shake things around, and while I had moments of being proud, I wondered if this was the kind of effort that needed to be upheld day in and day out. That thought was frightening. At what point do you get to sit back and watch the beauty of hard work and determination unfold? Would it ever happen?

So, when Jackie asked how the plans were going I didn't have an answer because there was too much going on in my head.

"Hello? Is there anyone in there?"

"Um, yeah. Here," I said.

"Here?" Jackie asked.

"I'm here."

"Whatever, anyway. Did you ask about that place?"

"What place?" I asked.

"That friend of Jolene that has a big place on the water?"

"Oh, yeah, sorry," I said. I felt like I needed to shake my head to come back into consciousness. "I haven't. But, I remember driving by it with Eve a few weeks ago."

"And?" Jackie's neck elongated and was reaching toward me.

"The place is really cool. It is all gray stone, and the bottom floor where the art show would be if we chose that place, is surrounded by glass walls. You can see right inside from the street. Of course it was empty when we drove by."

We were sitting outside on the lawn in the backyard. It was spongy and soft, and was the exact spot to sit on a warm, sunny day. I had been sitting out there by myself feeling useless and unmotivated, when Jackie came outside to join me and check in on my progress.

"Are you going to talk to that girl, or her parents?"

"Yeah, of course. I thought you didn't even like the idea?"

"Whatever."

"Though, I kind of feel weird now," I said.

"Why?" Jackie asked. "What's weird?"

"Hey, this is off-topic," I started. "But, did you know that Celia can't swim?"

Jackie shook her head.

"Don't you think that's odd. Like, don't all kids know how to swim?"

"No. You aren't born knowing. It's not some inherent trait we are gifted," said Jackie. "You have to be taught."

"Who taught us?" I asked.

"Dad mostly taught me how to swim, but you were

given swimming lessons. Don't you remember?"

"Kind of." Though I could barely form a memory.

"So, getting back on topic, why are you feeling weird about talking to this girl?" Jackie said.

"I just don't know her, that's all."

"There are so many people you don't know, that you have never met or crossed paths with. You need to lean on others and reach out, even when you are scared," Jackie said. "Otherwise you'll never know what could happen. Or worse, you'll never do anything with your life."

"Don't be so dramatic," I said.

I heard what she was saying, and I had been stretching myself lately. Asking this girl wasn't what was scaring me, though. I actually wasn't afraid of her. I was afraid that if it all worked out that I would mess it up.

"How is your documentation going?" Jackie asked.

"Jackie, how do you find time to do it all?"

"I guess when you want something bad enough, you find the time," said Jackie. "To be honest, sometimes I'm not quite sure. I sort of keep going."

"The documentation is going great, really," I said. "It's easy to point a camera and shoot. The editing is where I feel a bit stuck. It takes forever!"

"The website is almost complete," said Jackie.

"Really? Wow, that's fast."

"Well, it's simple when you know what you are doing. Remember it's not going to be the best of the best, but as long as you sit and listen when they tell you how to publish and understand all the settings, you'll do just fine."

All of this was happening too fast for me. I stood up from the grass, and took a few paces in the opposite direction. My heart beat revved up, and my breathing was suddenly difficult. "Ok, I need to say something." I wasn't sure how to say what I was feeling. I turned around with my back to Jackie. I was nervous and uncomfortable, and I needed to finally let it out. "I have no idea what I'm doing."

"Duh," said Jackie.

I didn't want to turn around, but I was too curious to see her reaction.

"It's obvious," she said. "But, listen, that is how everything starts." Then she waved me in, like she had a secret. She waited for me to kneel back down, then she whispered, "I still don't know what I'm doing. I have to fact check myself all the time."

I just stared at her, because I didn't know what she meant.

"Sometimes I say things because I think I heard it somewhere, but not because I am one hundred percent certain."

"So?"

"*So*, I go back and look it up and I find that sometimes I'm wrong," she said. "Like I made something up because it sounded good, or it was only slightly true. That usually happens at home though. When I'm at the paper I have to be really careful."

"I still don't get it," I said.

"Whatever," Jackie said, now waving me away. "My point is that nobody knows what they are doing. A lot of people sound like they do, but they are faking it."

"What does that mean?" I asked.

"It means that it is very normal to feel the way you are feeling." Jackie said, exhausted with my lack of comprehension.

"Ok, but I seriously don't know what I'm doing, and I feel like people are going to find out. Or I am going to mess everything up, and I'm scared because I feel like there are so many people counting on me."

"Don't be so self-righteous. Just stop and ask yourself why you want to do what you are doing," Jackie said.

"That's just it, I don't know what I'm doing!"

"Listen, you need to calm down. The weight of the world is not resting on your shoulders."

"Hey, that's not fair," I said. "You have said it's hard to be aware too, and there is a lot of responsibility with caring, even when it's super stressful."

Jackie just looked at me. I was waiting to hear more from her, but she didn't say a word. Was the world waiting for me? Oh no, I'm really going to screw this up. I should have never ever started any of this. I am literally the worst person for the position. What am I going to say to everyone? Celia is going to think I'm an idiot. Ms. Morgan will be so disappointed in me. All of my classmates will go back to thinking I'm the airhead again.

"I'm the wrong person for this conversation," Jackie finally said.

"What? Why?" I said.

"I feel the same way, every day. Like everyone is expecting something out of me, and I can't stop." She looked at me. She grabbed a few blades of grass and ripped them from the dirt, immediately tossing them to the side. "I don't want to stop. I love what I am doing, and I think it's important."

"What's the problem?" I asked.

"There is no problem," she said. "I just know how you feel."

"This is not helping," I said.

"There is no good answer," she said. "You are either going to keep going and your direction will become clearer, or you are going to go back to your old, simple life. It's not a big deal what you choose."

Jackie sounded like she had more to add, so I waited. She looked up at the sky, and then laid back down on the grass with her hands interlaced behind her head. Was the answer in the sky? I decided to lay down next to her and look up as well. We laid like this for a good five minutes, just looking up. We didn't share our thoughts, but I'm sure like me Jackie had a thousand thoughts running through her mind.

I could choose to move forward. Or, I could choose to slowly back out and let others more qualified to take on the art show and the filming. I wasn't the important part of the puzzle, I was simply a piece. Lola had good ideas, so did Celia and Jaime, and even Brian.

Jackie interrupted the silence by standing up. She stretched her arms up over her head. I sat upright. She didn't look at me when she said, "I sort of think you have a good thing going. You may just want to see what unfolds."

She walked away, completely disinterested in what else I had to say. Jackie went right into the house, leaving me alone again with my doubts. This time, though I didn't sit with them long. There was work to be done.

BEESWAX BAGS
AND PLASTIC TREES

Actually, there was a lot of work that needed to be done. It was endless. I think I even got Ms. Morgan worried. She announced that the classroom would be thought of as a workshop. What she meant was that we would be working on our projects, and she was not giving any formal lessons. We were to come in and get started without her direction.

Celia had a group working on the beeswax bags. Lola was working with others to figure out how to raise money for the reusable plates and utensils for the school. Others were working on posters about the plastic ban to put around campus, and still others were perfecting their art pieces.

I was documenting.

I never knew how much fun it could be to have a camera in my hand and film what I regularly saw. It was taking a back seat and just witnessing the moment through a lens. Nothing was scripted, no one hammed it up, well except Brian who managed to get into almost all the shots somehow.

I wanted Dad to be there to film, but he said he couldn't make it, and reassured me that I had a steady hand, and a keen eye to capture the moment.

"Please be careful," shouted Ms. Morgan from across the room. Celia was melting the beeswax with a hot plate on the back counter. She was spinning it around with a wooden chopstick and she accidentally touched the side of the tin bowl, which caused her to immediately retract her hand and shake it out like she was fanning out a polaroid picture.

"I'm fine, it's ok," she shouted back.

Ms. Morgan ran over anyway, and decided her presence was best near the danger than the fundraising efforts with Lola's group.

Last week I told Lola that I was surprised by her sudden motivation. She said, "I have always been interested in this stuff."

"Sorry, that's not what I meant," I said. "It's just cool to see us all coming together."

Celia had overheard our brief conversation, and when we were at lunch she told me that Lola's dad was suffering from the same thing as her dad.

When Lola moved out of the neighborhood, it wasn't because she was moving on to something bigger, like my parents had, she was moving in with her mom's sister and her family. The house was actually bigger than the house from our old neighborhood, but now she shared a bedroom with her parents, and her little brother. Her mom said it was temporary, but they had been there for almost a year.

Finding out that her dad had the same kidney issue as Celia's dad made me so sad. They were both sick and couldn't work. Celia's mom had a good enough job that enabled them to keep their home, but Lola's mom had always been a stay-at-home mom, so they had no choice but to move out.

"Why has Lola never mentioned this?" I asked.

"Sometimes we don't want to talk about it," said Celia. "If we don't say it out loud maybe it will go away."

The problem I was seeing was that nothing was going to go away. The only thing we could do was something.

Ms. Morgan was now taking the reins on the beeswax, and Celia was back on cutting fabric into squares. She had put out the call to the rest of the class to bring in an old shirt, or pants, or bandana to be used to make the bags. The beeswax and the jojoba oil was donated by a few parents in our class. "My mom said that stuff isn't cheap," said Joshua.

When I told Eve about the progress we were making in our class, she immediately donated buttons from her classroom and string to fasten the bags closed.

Ms. Morgan had hung a long piece of twine that stretched from one side of the room to the other. After soaking the fabric in the beeswax and letting the temperature simmer down, Ms. Morgan passed us the piece to be hung on the clothesline. While minutes ago she had been over protective about the heat, she suddenly cooled down to let us climb the ladder and hang our piece of waxed fabric.

Looking at the fabric strung up across the front of the

classroom, it was clear we needed more precision with our cuts. Our supposed rectangles and squares looked more like a shirt that got caught in a vacuum cleaner and was ripped out. Celia kept saying, "It's not about looking perfect, it's for the cause." We laughed because they looked horrible hanging there for the rest of the school to see through the windows when they passed our classroom.

"We can make the edges straight with a paper cutter. Don't worry," said Ms. Morgan. "But, in the future let's be more careful with our cuts."

"How long will these need to hang up here?" Brian asked.

"Not too long," said Ms. Morgan. "We just want them to dry while flat. I'll remove them when our period is over to make room for the others."

That's when I found out that Ms. Morgan's other classes were catching on and interested in being a part of the project. We hadn't even begun our campaign with the rest of the school, but it seemed our small efforts in class were having the kind of effect we were hoping for.

Lola was working on the perfect letter to the Parent Teacher Organization. She was planning on attending one of their monthly meetings in order to ask for the funding for the reusable plates and forks. "I mean, they are the ones that will be using them a lot more than us, right?" Lola said.

I nodded in agreement.

"We should make the effort for others," Lola said. "Especially if they won't do it for themselves."

Lola was right. This was more than making the personal effort to exchange a reusable cup instead of buying another one at the coffee shop just to throw it away

30 minutes later. It was making the option available to others so they could make better decisions without having to think.

"Plus, in the long run it saves them money," Lola added.

"You're right," I said.

We worked on our projects for the entire week. Every day, we put more effort into the art, the letters, the baggies, the flyers. And, whenever anyone said they had nothing to do, Ms. Morgan handed them another web quest to research more about plastics. It was an eventful week, and we accomplished a lot. The classroom already looked like an art show.

Jackie took me to her newspaper meeting again. This time it was to show me what she and her friends had been working on.

Theo, one of her friends, pulled up the website and displayed it on the whiteboard for everyone to see, as Jackie had done with my unfinished video the week before.

There were ocean waves in the background, and sand-colored lettering. Across the top was a banner that read: *We Have Something to Say!* Just below the words, were three boxes, one holding a photo of trash at the beach, another was a graphic they had created I'm assuming, and the third one said DONATE.

Theo scrolled down a bit further, to show the video I had made. It still wasn't complete, which was bogging me down. The work was so tedious and long, and with everything else going on it was hard to stay on top. I needed to work with Dad a bit more on the music.

"Here, you can press anywhere to have the video play,"

said Theo.

I really didn't want to be reminded of my incomplete work yet again.

This time however, when Theo pressed play music came pouring out. *Huh?* What did they do? As I watched and listened I noticed that the lyrics Arjun had written were coming through. What was going on? My eyes wandered around the room searching for Jackie. She was in the back, leaning against the wall looking straight at me.

I mouthed, "How?"

She mouthed back, "Dad."

Dad had said that he was going to have a friend make music, and I *had* passed on the lyrics, but he never said another word. That's probably what he had been working on last week when he said he was busy. Who was singing, I wondered?

The video played on, and I couldn't believe I was watching my classmates in action. It looked so well done, and it got polished up without me.

"Up here in the menu bar is where you can write in your mission statement, and the *about,* like who you are, what you are doing, and what's up with this website," said Theo.

I didn't know where to begin, or what to say.

"Over here is the *donate* button. You will need to link in some bank information there. You might want to ask your Mom about that. She helped us with ours."

I looked at Jackie again in the back of the room. She just smiled.

While I was standing in awe, I was also met with those familiar anxious feelings again. *Mission statement? Bank information?* I don't know anything about that stuff.

"What do you think of the graphic?" someone asked me from the back of the room.

I turned around to see who it was, but my eyes were still adjusting from the bright screen. "Uh, um," I started. "Uh, it's really cool."

"Yeah, we thought maybe you would like it for your logo?" she said.

Logo?

"On this page, is where you can post up an article, or another video," said Theo. "The three recent posts will pop up on the home page, but we can change that if you want."

I had no opinion. It was all way over my head. Again, I was in too deep. Having it look so good was scary. Maybe if it had been more disorganized I would have felt at ease.

"If you ever want to start selling anything, like clothing for example to give something to those who donate, we can build that up as well," Theo said.

Jackie turned on the lights, and it shook me back into the room. Everyone was staring at me.

"Well, that was super amazing!" All the stupid words I am trying to banish from my vocabulary were all I could bring to the surface. "Super awesome. Wow, thanks."

"Do you have time to sit down, and I can teach you how everything works?" Theo asked me.

I wanted to admit that there was no way I could ever remember any of this. Even if I took notes, all of this might as well be a completely different language.

Jackie could sense my nerves. She spoke for me, "I think it would be best if we gathered a few of her classmates to teach as a group, so more of them know the ins and outs of the website."

"Good idea," said Theo. He turned to me, "Maybe you

can organize something at your house, and I can come over to teach you and your friends."

"Yeah, that would be super awesome!" I said. I had no idea what I was saying anymore.

When dinner came around, Jackie couldn't stop talking about the website, and the logo, and setting up a bank account.

"Well, this is all very exciting," Mom said to me.

I smiled in her direction, but brought my head back down to my plate.

"Can I show you two the website?" Jackie asked Mom and Dad.

"Isn't it your rule that there are no devices at the dinner table?" Mom said.

"You're right," said Jackie. "But also, I really don't want to wait." She ran out of the room to grab her laptop.

"Everything ok, Jenny?" Mom asked.

"Yeah, yes," I said. "Of course."

"I have to say I am very proud of you. Just a few months ago you were barely interested in talking at the dinner table, and now you are really reaching outside your comfort zone."

"Hey Dad," I said, stopping the onslaught of compliments that I couldn't handle at that moment. "Who is singing in the video?"

"Did you like it?" he asked.

"Yeah, it was kind of amazing. I didn't even know you were working on it. Well, I knew you were working on it, but I didn't know it was done. And, the song! Seriously, who is singing?"

"Brian," he said. "From your class."

"*Brian?* Brian can sing?" I said, more to myself than to Mom and Dad. "Wait. How did you get him to sing? Or know, or I don't even know any more."

"It's all good," Dad said. "I emailed Ms. Morgan, and she arranged it."

"She did? You did?"

I didn't understand how this was all happening.

"Yes. She is quite a remarkable teacher," he said.

"That is so weird that Brian sang," I laughed to myself.

Jackie came back into the room. "Ok, here it is," she said. She fanned open the screen, then flipped it around for the rest of us to see.

Jackie went through all the parts in the same order that Theo had done earlier that day. She clicked on everything, and explained what each button meant. Then we watched the video.

It was really good. Even the second time. Almost better, because now my nerves were put to rest. Watching my friends come alive on the screen, and seeing the work we were doing. It looked bigger somehow on screen. Were we really doing all this? It wasn't made up, it was real. Nothing was choreographed or prompted, it just was. Yet, somehow it felt fake, like it didn't actually happen.

"Wow!" Mom said. "You made this video?"

"Well, without the music, it's not that good," I said.

"But, you filmed all these parts, and edited it?" Mom asked.

"Well, kind of. It's more of a combined effort. Dad filmed the letter writing part. I did the rest. Jackie helped me edit the footage, and make it more of a story. So, really, it's not mine at all."

"Of course it is," Dad said patting me on the back.

"This is wonderful!" Mom said. "Can we watch it again?"

Jackie pressed the play button. I was more than happy to watch it a third time, and a fourth, and many more times after. I couldn't believe how it came out. I wondered if I was dreaming. Was this real? I looked at Mom and Dad who were glued to the screen, and Jackie who couldn't wipe the smile off her face.

"So, what now?" Dad asked.

"Now, Jenny and her little friends have to learn how to use the website," Jackie said. "That's easy, though. It seems difficult at first, but you get familiar with the buttons, and soon enough you'll be updating like a pro."

PICKING UP TRASH

I felt like my head was going to explode. Celia had been asking to go to the beach again, and it couldn't have come at a better time. I needed to get to the water where all my fears had a chance to fade. Conchita had to work all day, but I somehow convinced Mom that the best thing she could do all day was take us to the beach. Mom had to work in the morning, but was off after noon, and she promised she would drive us to the coast after.

I asked Jolene if she wanted to join us, but she was busy with her family. She desperately wanted to get out of her obligation, but it was no use, she had to stay back. Even though Jolene and Celia had become better acquainted, I could sense a sigh of relief from Celia when she found out it would just be the two of us.

"I brought a few garbage bags," Celia told me as we sat

in the back seat of my mom's car on the way out to the coast.

"Garbage bags?" I asked. "For what?"

"To pick up trash on the beach, of course." She pulled them out to show me. They were the typical big, black garbage bags. In other words, huge.

"Oh, right," I said. I sat there for a minute, and then immediately felt terrible. This feeling of guilt was a constant companion these days. Jackie had been telling me that it was part of the program, but it did absolutely no good. Jackie said the best way to combat it was to admit the guilt, and then do something to counteract that feeling, as in doing something good. If there were moments when that wasn't possible, she said to go for a walk or journal.

"Is it bad that I didn't think about picking up trash?" I finally asked Celia. "I mean of course I would pick up trash, but I didn't think about bringing a bag." I admitted my guilty feelings.

"Remember last time we came, and I picked up all that plastic?" Celia asked.

"Yeah."

"There was way more I left behind, because I didn't have a place to carry it. So I had to leave it there," said Celia. "I felt really bad. I saw it, and I didn't do anything about it."

"You did more than me that day," I said. I looked down at my hands. The embarrassment was too much.

"I figured if I were to bring a bag then I had no excuse, and I wouldn't have to feel so bad."

Celia had guilty feelings too.

"Are you hungry?" I asked.

"Kind of, but I can wait." She folded up the bags and

put them back into her backpack.

When we arrived on the beach, Celia and I took off our clothes and exposed our bathing suits, while Mom settled in for a nap.

"Here you go," Celia said to me, handing over the trash bag.

I looked it over. "I was thinking we could play in the water first, then go hunting for trash."

"I was kind of thinking the opposite," she said. "It would be more fun in the water, if we cleaned up first. Right?"

Again, I was left feeling guilty. I really wanted to play in the waves and not think about trash. Does that make me a bad person? But, what I told Celia was, "I like that idea."

Internally reluctant, but with a smile on my face I grabbed the bag from Celia, and we said bye to Mom, and went walking down the beach.

We didn't say anything to each other for a few moments. Celia knew I would rather hang in the water first, but she was adamant about doing the right thing before having fun. She wasn't mean about it, just direct.

"What did you do with the plastic pieces you found last time?" I asked Celia.

"I kept them," she said.

"For what?"

"Remember when we went on the field trip last year to the garbage and recycling place?"

"Yeah."

"I can't get it out of my head that there is almost 2 million pounds of trash per day in our county. Because, you know, most things aren't recyclable," she said.

"Yeah, that was crazy," I said. I remembered walking through the facility with neon vests and clear, plastic glasses. The smell was so intense when we were in the compost area we had to hold our noses. It just smacked you in the face, and made your eyes water. We didn't stay long in that area. What I remember vividly was a small green plant growing from the huge compost pile. The lady leading the tour had said, "Yup. Pretty cool, huh? That's why we should compost as much as possible. It's a closed-looped system." We were then led into where the trash and recycling ended up. Way less smelly, and way more interesting with the conveyor belts moving things around like highway ramps going in all directions. It was so loud, we needed headphones to hear the tour guide.

"I figured that those pieces of plastic can't be recycled, so they would just end up in the trash," said Celia.

"Better than the ocean," I said.

"Totally!" Celia said.

We both bent down to pick up the same piece of trash. It was a broken sand toy, a sand sifter, like a strainer used for boiled pasta. When I saw Celia's hand reaching down I pulled back. She looked it over. It was yellow and sharp at the edges.

"Take this piece for example," said Celia. "This is just trash. And, yeah it's better than in the ocean, but it just goes into the landfill."

Celia put the broken plastic in her bag, and we kept walking.

"It makes you wonder if someone legitimately forgot it, or did they see that it was of no use and left it behind only pretending to forget. Or, even worse did they leave it behind knowingly." She immediately reached down for another piece of the sand toy. "It's like no one understands tides. Like, duh, the tide is going to come up and wash this thing away."

I was learning that Celia was way more conscientious than me. Where did this all come from? She didn't have a Jackie at home telling her about everything, or an Eve teaching Jolene about the environment. Where did she get it from?

"So, what are you going to do with it?" I asked.

"The art thing is cool," she said. "I could make something for the art show."

"That would be really cool," I said.

"But, like, after the art show, then what?"

"What do you mean?"

"I have been thinking about that a lot lately," said Celia. "Sometimes I think about how wasteful the art is," she said. "Sorry."

"It's ok," I said. "I'm not offended." I wanted to hear what more she had to say.

"What I mean is that when we put all that glue or tape, then it all becomes garbage, if it wasn't already. Unless someone keeps the art, it just goes into the trash after a month or so."

Everything she was saying were things *I* had also been thinking about. The difference between us was that I let those thoughts eat away at me in private. Everything seemed so much bigger than I could handle. More and more I wanted to hide away in one of the caves at the beach, letting the tide enter, and just close off the rest of the world and all the terrible things that humans are doing to it.

"Listen, I think the art show is a great idea, and I think

you got a lot of our classmates to become more aware. We actually got all of Ms. Morgan's students to care," Celia said. "So, please don't take what I said the wrong way."

"No, not at all," I said.

We kept walking.

I continued to find pieces of plastic and other trash. Most of them were really small, and annoyingly hard to pull up without throwing handfuls of sand into the bag. Some of the pieces were so small and insignificant, I didn't even want to bend down. However, that is exactly what everyone thinks.

"Do you have other ideas on what to do with the plastic?" I asked Celia.

"I was thinking, what if we made something with the plastic," she said. "Like, something that is useful."

"Like what?"

"I really don't know. I keep thinking about it," said Celia. She bent down and picked up yet another piece of trash on the beach. "For now, I'm just going to collect, then sort the pieces at home."

I was jealous of Celia's passion. I felt all the same things she did, but for some reason she seemed more genuine. She could take action without worry.

"Can I ask you something?" I said.

Celia nodded her head.

"When did you get so interested in the environment?"

She stopped walking, and stared at me. "I told you already, it's not just for white people or wealthy people. There are others that care."

"Hey, I'm brown too! So is Jackie, and my parents," I said. "I get it."

She didn't say anything. We started walking again. I

dug my bare feet into the sand like a shovel, making silent but deliberate movements. When I felt enough time had gone by, I asked my question again. "What I meant was, where did you first hear about this stuff, and why do you care. I mean, most people don't care or want to care. Like, they say they want a cleaner planet, but then you see them ordering a ton of stuff that comes in plastic packaging, or they order drinks that come in plastic containers they just toss out later."

Celia started to dig her feet into the sand like me. Her bag dragged a bit. She was so quick to pick up trash. Really, we should have separated and taken different areas of the beach if we were going to do this well.

"Ms. Morgan," she said.

"Ms. Morgan?"

"Yeah. Earlier in the year she asked about my Dad. I don't know how she knew, maybe the office found out and told her. I don't know. When she asked me about him, she also told me that I could get help with his medical bills."

"Really?" I said.

"Yeah. She helped Lola too."

"What did she do?"

"She helped my mom get into contact with the city, who had been sued because of the VOCs in the soil," said Celia. "We started talking about environmental justice, and from there it seemed like everything was connected. Like even plastics in the ocean had to do with my Dad's situation."

"Does your Mom know about all the work we're doing at school?" I asked.

"Yeah, of course," said Celia. "She says she doesn't know how I can keep so much information in my head.

When I talk to her I always have to say things twice, because she has no idea what any of it means. She said all the stuff I am talking about is a first world problem."

"What does she mean by that?"

"I told her it wasn't. But what she means is that when you are starving or you don't have access to clean water, then single use plastics are not on your mind."

"She has a point," I said. "It's just that some of us have to do the work for others. Like when Lola was talking about the reusable plates and who would use them. I bet most people won't even give the plate much thought, but it helps to buy them for the school."

"Totally," she said.

We kept walking and picking up trash, and filling up our bags. My gaze had been at my feet and about a foot in front of me the whole time. I finally looked up from the sand to stretch my neck. The ocean was incredible. It went on forever, and there was no way any of us would see all of it in our lifetime. There is no way any of us are going to dive into all the parts and see all the animals and the plants that live under water. Most of us won't ever see the plastic pieces swimming around in the Pacific Ocean. We are never going to get on a boat and move through the junk we throw out there. We will only see it in footage or documentaries, or hear about it in stories and articles, and essays. It was an entirely different world, completely unexplored, and taken for granted.

TRASH TRAVELER

"Ok, so we know there is a ton of debris that finds its way into the ocean, right?" said Ms. Morgan.

We nodded our heads. It was all we had talked about for months. Sometimes I wondered if it was my doing that we were discussing plastics in the ocean, or if Ms. Morgan had this planned the whole time?

"What you are all getting really good at is refusing single-use plastics, and finding reusable alternatives," she said. Again, we nodded our heads, patiently waiting to see where this would lead. "You are also getting really good at saying 'other people.'"

She waited to see our reaction. Most of our faces looked confused. "Other people" always sounded condescending, like when Jackie talks about how ignorant people are.

"What do you mean?" I finally asked.

"What I mean is that as we are gaining more awareness, we see the fault in others," said Ms. Morgan. "This is kind of a good thing."

Again, we were confused. Finding the fault in others sounded as if we thought we were better somehow. How could that be good?

"Alright, I don't get it," said Jaime, throwing his arms up in the air waving an invisible white flag. Everyone was relieved when he let it out.

"When we see something that is not right, we can detect it right away, right? Like stealing, or lying. Now that you have built an awareness of single-use plastics, you are hyper sensitive when you see someone using a plastic bag when ordering to-go, or using a plastic straw or utensils, or ordering packages that are wrapped in plastic, only to be wrapped in plastic again."

"Are you saying we are judging people?" asked Brian.

"No, that is not what I am saying," said Ms. Morgan. "Let's look at it differently."

She turned around and wrote across the board: How Does Trash Get Into Our Oceans? Then she turned back around to face us, waiting to hear our responses.

"Carelessness," I said.

Ms. Morgan circled the title, and then wrote carelessness below, drawing a line to connect the two, like a web. Then she turned around and asked us, "How? What do you mean by carelessness? What does that look like?"

I felt obligated to answer, so I said, "Like when you throw something in the trash, but not deep enough and it blows away and out of the trash can."

"Okay, I like that," said Ms. Morgan. She wrote it on

the board and drew another line of connection. "What are other examples of carelessness?"

"This is kind of the same thing," said Lola. "But when garbage cans or recycling bins are overflowing with trash and it blows away, or when people just put their garbage on top or to the side of the can instead of finding another trash can that has space."

Ms. Morgan wrote down what Lola said and connected it to my thought. "What else?"

"How about when things blow off a garbage truck?" said Brian. "Or, is that the same thing?"

"They are similar, but different instances," said Ms. Morgan. "Thank you for sharing, Brian." She then wrote down what he said.

"People also leave stuff on the beach," said Celia.

"Yes!" said Ms. Morgan. "What kind of stuff?"

"Things like broken sand toys, bottle caps, small bits of trash, pencils and pens," said Celia.

"What about when people drop their cigarette butts on the ground to smash them, but then don't pick them up," said Lola.

"That is one of the worst problems," said Ms. Morgan. "Cigarettes are made of plastic, and as we know they will not disintegrate, just break down."

"What about concerts or big outdoor events where there is no way people can pick up all that trash and it just blows away?" said Brian.

"Seems like we have a common culprit," said Ms. Morgan.

"The wind?" said Lola.

We all laughed.

"Well, the wind moves it around, sure. But, the wind

is not to blame."

"Humans," I said. "Humans are doing this."

Ms. Morgan turned to me, looking for more.

"But we know this, Ms. Morgan," I said. "We have been talking about it, and we know that humans are the reason there is trash in the ocean, and that our air is polluted." I sounded rude, which is the last thing I want to be towards Ms. Morgan. It just seemed like we were talking about the same thing, over and over again. We are the problem. We are trying, but we are not succeeding.

"We are the reasons for overflowing garbage cans, and when trash flies out of garbage trucks," I said. "We are the reasons for dumping items we don't want on the side of the road because we think no one is looking, or that someone else will pick it up. We are the reason there is plastic in the first place because we buy it and we throw it wherever we want, because we don't think we matter. We are just one person and what we do doesn't make a difference, so why try? Why even care?"

"I care," said Celia.

I looked at her. "I know you do," I said.

"I care," said Lola.

"Me too," said Jaime.

"I'm not going to stop picking up trash on the beach, because tomorrow there will be more," said Celia.

"I didn't mean that *we* don't care, I mean that there are so many more people, people we don't even know, that could care less," I said.

"I get it now," said Jaime. "You were saying that we are 'aware' and we look at others who aren't doing what we are now doing, but what you meant is that we need to do more and get others to care more. Am I right?"

"We are," said Lola. "I don't understand, what more do we have to do?"

"You are all doing great work," said Ms. Morgan. "You truly are. Jaime, what I was saying is that it is important not to point the finger at others. None of us are perfect. Many of us don't know where to start and what to do to help a *very big problem*. How can we be kinder to others who are learning?"

"Have we been rude?" Brian asked.

"Not at all," she said.

I had an idea. "I think we need to get more people involved, but not just by telling them about it," I said. "I think there are more people doing environmental work than we know of. Wouldn't it be cool if we connected people together and allowed others to show what they are doing. It might actually motivate others to do more, as well as let others who are afraid come out."

"I think that is fantastic!" said Ms. Morgan.

"I was thinking the other day about how big the ocean is. I mean, I think about it a lot," I said. "But, this time I thought about how the majority of us will never really get to see all of the ocean. We will never get to see 10 percent of it! Most of us are not going to be able to see the garbage island we are working to clean. It just won't happen." I paused because I was starting to get that nervous feeling, where I realized that everyone is listening and I'm actually just saying whatever pops up in my mind, not something I rehearsed. Like, I could really screw it up and say the wrong thing.

"Can I show something to the class, Ms. Morgan?" I asked.

"Of course, what is it?"

"It's a video."

"Go ahead," she said.

I walked to where Ms. Morgan had her computer setup. Ms. Morgan has always let us use her computer for anything, and she gave us plenty of space without hovering over us assuming we would break something. I plugged in the projector, and waited for the white board to light up in blue. I typed in the right keys to pull up our website. It felt like I was taking an eternity to get it going, anticipating the impatience in others.

Finally I got to where I wanted to be, and pressed play.

Just as we all entered the screen, Jaime yelled, "What!? That's us!"

"That's my voice!" said Brian. I could see his cheeks turning red.

"That's your voice?" said Jaime.

"Uh, yeah."

"I didn't know you could sing."

"That's my song!" said Arjun. "I wrote that."

"You can write songs?" asked Jaime. "How come I don't know about any of this. Like, everyone is super talented."

"Can you start it over? And, can no one talk over it," said Celia, looking at Jaime.

"What?" said Jaime, folding his arms across his chest. "I just think it's cool."

I started it over, and we watched in silence the second time around. The video was about five minutes, which is the perfect amount of time to keep their attention, but stops just when the attention gives up. And I thought ten minutes was the right amount.

Watching the video for like the twentieth time still

made me really happy. It was a weird sort of happiness, very different from other times. I'm not sure how, but I really liked the feeling.

When the video ended, I showed the class the rest of the website, just like Theo had done for me. "Let me be clear," I said. "I don't really know how to do anything."

"That's our website?" Lola asked.

"What do you think?" I asked.

"That was us doing what we have been doing," she said. "It looks so good. It almost seems like that isn't us."

"Doesn't it!" I said. "That's what I thought!"

"I can't believe it," said Celia. "Seriously, what the heck! This is like so cool!"

"So Arjun wrote a song about how everyone can help the earth, Brian sang it, and you made a video, that is on a website with a donate button," said Jaime. "Whoa!"

"This is rather remarkable, Jenny," said Ms. Morgan. I knew that she had seen it before.

"Well, this is not all my work. My dad and my sister helped out a lot. Her friends built the website, and my dad's friend made the music. They also helped me with the editing to make more of a story," I said. "It's all our combined work in one place."

"Dude, this is rad!" Arjun said. "I'm going to be famous." He leaned back into his chair with his arms interlaced behind his head.

"So what are we going to do with it?" Lola asked.

"I was thinking," I started. I took a deep breath. Be brave, I told myself. "Like I was saying before, most people aren't going to see the middle of the ocean."

"Well, maybe when they fly to Hawaii," said Brian.

"Yes, but most people are not going to be on a boat.

We see things through documentation. Like what we did," I said, pointing to the screen that still held up our website. "We know what we have done in class. We have shared our personal stories with our parents and friends, and others at this school. But! We also captured it so now we can share it with way more people."

"Ok, so we are going to share our video?" Lola asked.

"I was thinking, what if we created the website to showcase what others are doing in their schools," I said. "What if we have a place where people could share their stories on how they are helping the planet. Then we could see how similar we all are, therefore making it more comfortable for people to get involved. It would be led by students and the stories would be told by students."

"Like, Jolene could put up a video of her class?" said Celia.

"Yeah!" I said, so thankful that Celia was helping me out while I hung out on a weak limb pitching this adventurous idea.

"Who's Jolene?" Jaime asked.

"She's a friend of ours that goes to a different school," Celia said.

"Ok, so how do we get others to want to share their stories on our website?" Jaime said.

"I'm not sure," I said. "But, we could start with Jolene. Or people we know."

"What about that donate button?" Lola asked. "What are people donating to?"

"I don't know yet," I said. "But I have thought that maybe if we raised money it could fund others' projects in their schools, like getting new garbage cans, or building a compost pile. I don't know."

The room burst into conversations about what to do with the website, the money, and video, being *famous*. Lola thought about the reusable plates she wanted to purchase for the school. Celia was saying we could buy more beeswax, and Arjun was thinking about his music career. I wondered if this is what Ms. Morgan was referring to when she said to be kinder to those who don't know what they are doing or where to start. I'm not exactly sure, but for a brief moment I looked in her direction and I could see her wiping away tears from her eyes.

"Hey, so what is up with the title?" Jaime asked.

"*We Have Something to Say*?" I asked, wondering if maybe I overstepped. Though, they weren't actually my words. I'm not sure who in Jackie's newspaper group thought of it.

"I have something to say!" said Lola.

"I have something to say!" yelled Brian.

"I have something to say!" screamed Celia.

"Whoa, take it easy," said Jaime, fanning his hands to the side like he was cooling a fire. "We *all* have something to say."

ARCHEOLOGISTS

I biked over to Jolene's house after school that day, while the idea was fresh in my mind.

"Hey," said Jolene. "I'll go get my bike, be back in a second."

"Can we ride in a little bit," I said. "There is something I want to talk to you and your mom about."

"Oh no, are you getting serious again?" she laughed.

"Hey!"

"Just kidding," she said. "What's it about?"

"Let's find your mom first."

"This sounds really serious now," Jolene said. She opened the front door and walked in, leaving it open for me to follow behind. I shut it, and immediately heard Eve's voice, "Hi girls."

"Mom, Jenny has something really important to tell

us," Jolene announced.

"I'm in the kitchen," said Eve.

"Jolene, it's not like that," I said. "You make me sound like I'm crazy."

"Well, lately you have had a bunch of new ideas," she said. "Don't get mad, I like it! Really!"

I jokingly squinted my eyes in her direction letting her know that I was mildly upset, but offset it with a smile, also letting her know that I wasn't going to let this end our friendship.

"Hi Jenny," said Eve. "What's the news all about?"

I sat down on the counter stool and brought my hands to the counter. "Remember when I came here a month ago and said I had an idea?" I asked.

"Yes," said Eve.

"I don't remember," said Jolene.

I looked at Jolene. "That's because I was still mad at you."

"Oh, ok," she said. Jolene reached over to the fruit bowl and grabbed a green apple. She spun it around to find the sticker, then bit into it. "Go on," she said.

"Eve, you told me to really think about what I was doing, and take manageable steps," I said.

"Yes, I remember that," Eve said. "I know about the beeswax bags. What came of your project?"

"Well, let me show you," I said. "Jolene, can I use your laptop?"

"Sure." She reached across the counter to where it was plugged into the wall. I then launched into everything that I had been doing with my class that they didn't already know. I showed them the website and the video I helped create, and my plan to create a platform for other students to showcase what they are doing in their schools.

Eve had taken a seat next to me on the stools, and Jolene sat on the other side of me. Eve had brought her hand to her face and was slowly squeezing her chin with her thumb and index finger. "This is your website?" Eve asked me.

I nodded my head.

"These are your classmates?" she asked pointing to the screen that was paused on a scene from our classroom deep in projects.

I nodded my head.

"And you put this together?" she said.

"Not alone, and really I barely did anything," I said. "This is the work of many. Like, Jackie's friends at the school newspaper put together the website and made the logo."

"Seriously, you did this?" Jolene asked.

"What? Are you surprised?" I said.

"Kind of," she said. "But, like in a really good way. Not that I didn't think you could do something like this. Don't take me the wrong way. What I mean is that this is like a ton of work!"

"Well," I said, looking at Eve. "I took small steps."

Eve smiled. "So you want to document my class working on a project for the environment?"

"That's what I'm thinking," I said. "If we can get more classes to join in then it could really gain momentum, and then we could actually start raising money to fund environmental projects."

"Enough said," Eve said. "We're in."

"Oh, ok, great!" I clapped my hands in excitement.

"I'll let you know when there is a good day to come

into my classroom," said Eve. "Most likely next week. That will give me enough time to get video permission forms from parents."

"Yes, of course," I said. "My teacher had to do the same thing."

Eve's class looked a lot like Ms. Morgan's class, and not at all. She had a lot more motivational posters on her walls, but she held the similar vibe of exploration. Her classroom, like Ms. Morgan's, wasn't just a place to learn, but a lab where things could be discovered, invented, and brought to life.

I knew I was only going to get one shot, and I really didn't want to mess it up, so I brought Dad with me. He was thrilled to help.

I watched as he set up quietly. Dad was like a jungle cat hunting prey, silent and purposeful. He melted into the background, never taking the focus off the others, simply reading the room and discovering the stories that may unfold, but also the best place for his equipment. It was equal parts artistry and professionalism. I was taking notes.

Eve and Jolene's class had collected trash from multiple beach-clean-ups together on field trips, and were in the process of sorting the found items. Before they got started Eve spoke to them, "Think about all that we have collected, like an archeologist. Archeologists dig up ancient remains, right? Then they study what they have found. Each item they uncover tells a story." She held up a broken plastic fork. One of the prongs was broken off, and it was hardly the white color it once was. "What will archeologists of the future say about us?"

The class first weighed what they had collected, which was nearly twenty pounds of trash. Then they sorted everything into three piles. The class recycled what could be recycled, which made up a very small pile. The trash pile was much bigger, unfortunately, but could work as a strong message nonetheless. The third pile consisted of items they would repurpose for projects throughout the school year.

"Part of understanding human behavior is to study it," said Eve. "What causes us to want to buy what we do not have a need for? What causes us to discard it wherever we please?"

The students continued to work through the piles. "Document everything," said Eve.

I knew she was talking to the class, but I felt ever more compelled to get the story they were telling. I pulled a few students aside to ask them a few questions.

"We really enjoy doing the beach clean-ups," said one of the girls. "Ms. Eve is really inspiring us to take the time to pick up even the smallest pieces off the sand."

Another student spoke up saying they had plans for a monthly beach clean-up throughout the rest of the school year. "We really want to keep it going in the summer, which is more important because there are more people going to the beach at that time, which means more trash will be left behind."

"We are hoping to purchase buckets and grabbers for the whole class," said Jolene. "And, maybe have extras available for others who want to participate in the clean-ups."

I loved hearing the stories. They were genuine, and the work being done came from a place of interest and a demand for a cleaner world. Before I knew it I had a ton of footage, and great interviews.

"What will this trash say about us that is different from ancient remains?" Eve asked her class.

"That our plastic is never really going to go away," someone said.

THE GREEN TEAM

I was happy to have so much footage to work with, but editing, I quickly remembered, was tedious work. I knew that I would get help from Jackie and Dad, but I needed to get the first draft completed on my own. Hours and hours passed, and my neck was stiff and my fingers cramped. There had to be an easier way to edit an hour of footage into five minutes.

I got up out of my seat off the floor to take a break and get some water. I passed by Jackie's room. She was working on something at her desk. She was hunched over her computer, looking intently at the screen, like Dad does when editing. Like I had just been doing. I stood in her doorway.

Without looking up she asked me, "When are you going to take the time to learn more about the website?

It's been over a week."

"I know, I'm sorry. I got right into filming Eve's class, and this editing takes up so much time."

"You have to delegate," she said, still fixated on the screen. "Remember you can't do everything on your own. You'll burn out."

"I know. You're right."

I left her room and continued into the kitchen.

I thought maybe I could ask Ms. Morgan for more time where we could work together during class. There never seemed to be enough time to get everything done.

"I'm sorry, Jenny, I cannot take up more class time," said Ms. Morgan apologetically. I met her at lunch, outside. She was eating cold leftovers. She wiped her mouth. "But I have an idea for you."

"What is it?"

"Why don't you set up a club where you and your friends who are interested in the project can meet and work on the details of the project."

It sounded like she was trying to move on from the art show and the website. It always seemed that way with teachers. Right when there was something cool happening we had to go back to tests and boring lectures where we just sat in our seats. Why couldn't school be 70 percent fun and 30 percent boring, not the other way around. Or, even 100 percent fun?

"I'm happy to be the advisor," she said. She closed up her container and wiped her fork clean before putting it back into her lunch bag. "We can meet in my room once a week either before school or during lunch."

"Really?" I said.

"Of course. I am more than happy to see this work continue."

Well, I underestimated her.

"Listen, Jenny, I would love to spend every day doing environmental work, but there are a few other things we need to study before the end of the year," Ms. Morgan confided. "Having a *green team* would be a great way to incorporate more students outside of your class and grade. The more the merrier," she said.

She made a great point. Jackie kept saying I couldn't do it alone. Even though I knew I wasn't doing this alone, there were times when it felt that way. More people could make it grow faster.

"The *green team*?" I said with a chuckle.

"You can call it whatever you want," said Ms. Morgan.

"It's not bad, just a little corny. Like we're super heroes."

"You know what they say?"

"So, how do I get started?"

"There are applications for starting a club in the office. Fill it out, then give it to me and I'll sign off and commit to being the advisor."

"Thanks, Ms. Morgan. I'll go do that right now."

I ran from where we were seated, and down the outdoor hallway. I managed to find the form in the office, just like she said. The questions were fairly simple to answer, and all I needed was Ms. Morgan's signature and commitment. I went right back to Ms. Morgan's classroom after school, she signed the form, and I had it back in the office for approval before the school day was done. Mr. Porter, the office administrator, said I would find out the next day.

"Do most clubs get approved?" I asked.

"Oh yeah," he said. "Pretty much all of them get approved."

"Is it really that easy?"

"Well, if you are interested in creating a place where people can come together, and you can manage to find a teacher that is willing to advise, then who are we to stop you?" He smiled encouragingly.

"Are there a bunch of clubs at our school?"

"Oh yeah, all kinds. Pretty much anything you can think of has been made into a club," he said. "However, most clubs dismantle after about six weeks. That is usually the time when people get tired of meeting, and either doing the same thing, or feeling it's pointless and they have other things they would rather be doing. Especially if you are meeting at lunch. It doesn't take long before people are disinterested in giving up their lunchtime."

"Thank you," I said. "I'll keep that in mind."

"Good luck," he said.

When I found out that my club had been accepted, I immediately told Celia and Lola.

"So, what does this mean?" asked Lola.

"It is a place where we can continue the project," I said. "Ms. Morgan was saying that we can't always use class time for our project."

"That makes sense," said Celia. "So, is it just us?"

"At this point," I said. "But, I think we can tell others in our class, and we could advertise around school to let people know."

"I could make a flyer?" Lola suggested.

"That would be awesome," I said. "We would meet in

Ms. Morgan's class every Wednesday at lunch."

"When is our first meeting?" Lola asked.

"We could get it going next week?" I said. "What do you think?"

"Might as well as get it going this week," said Celia. "We have no time to lose."

"Do you think people will want to join us?" Lola said.

"I mean, there are people like Brian and Jaime, right?" I said. "But, Mr. Porter in the office said most clubs give up after six weeks."

"Not ours!" Celia shouted. "We are different. We always have been, and we can do something better."

"Yeah!" said Lola.

Ms. Morgan announced the club in class the next day.

"Are you saying that we can't work on the art show anymore in class?" Jaime asked.

"Of course we will continue the conversation," said Ms. Morgan. "You are all doing incredible work! But now it's time for you to go further, and we don't have very much time in class. I am always here to help. I'm not leaving, just repositioning."

"Ok, cool," said Jaime, then turned to me. "When are you meeting?"

"Wednesdays," I said.

"I'm in," he said.

"Cool," I said.

"I'll check it out," said Brian.

"Me too," said Arjun.

Just like that, there was another wave of momentum.

WE NEED A NAME

Our first meeting took place as planned the following week. I had put myself on a strict deadline to finish the edit from Eve's class so that I could show it to everyone and they could see and feel the momentum we were building. I made sure there was music, and I have to admit Dad helped a lot. The editing was painful, but for some crazy reason I really like doing the work.

Lola had made the posters she suggested, and put them around campus the very next day. With her push and creativity, we had a turnout of 14 people. If what Mr. Porter said about a general waning of interest was true, I needed to keep things exciting.

I invited Theo to our first meeting to help us with the website.

We met in Ms. Morgan's classroom at lunch. I had no

idea how many people were going to show up, but I gave everyone five minutes before I started talking. Every minute that passed was causing an avalanche of nerves in my body. It was getting harder to breathe with my heart racing a marathon in my chest. Ms. Morgan looked in my direction and with her eyes she nudged me to begin.

"Hello everyone," I announced, immediately feeling the need to clear my throat. "Thank you for coming to our first meeting."

No one said anything. I'm not sure exactly what I was thinking, but I assumed that people would just start talking so I wouldn't have to do it all. Instead they all waited for what was next. Even Celia and Lola were looking to me to keep going.

Ms. Morgan could sense my nerves, so she spoke out. "I'm so glad you are all here, and I'm very excited to work with you all. I am impressed so far with the work being done in class, and I think that this club will take that work even further."

Again the haunting silence of a room full of people creeped in. Ms. Morgan looked at me to take the lead once again. I had to start. "Ok, well. Again, thanks for being here. Let's get started. I want to begin by introducing Theo."

I used both arms to point at him and everyone looked in his direction. He waved enthusiastically. "Hey," he started. "I'm Theo, and if you don't know me I'm a senior at Bayshore High School, where many of you will probably attend. I work with Jenny's sister, Jackie, at the newspaper, and I'm here to help you all with your website."

I was so thankful that everyone who showed up were Ms. Morgan's students. They had all been doing similar work as what we had been doing in class, and were familiar with the art show and the website.

"Should I get started?" Theo asked me.

"Um, yeah," I said, though I had no idea what I was doing. Again, I looked at Ms. Morgan for guidance. She smiled and gave me two thumbs up. *Is this how meetings go? Do we just jump in?* I wondered.

Theo pulled up the website. He went through all the buttons and showed us what each item from the menu meant. Everyone listened. Did they feel as clueless as I had that first day, I wondered. "Jenny," Theo said. "You said you made another video to add to the website?"

"Um, yeah. I wanted to show you all today, but it's not actually ready to put up on the website," I said.

"That's ok," said Theo. "Why don't we play around with it. I can use the video to show everyone how to upload it onto the website for future videos."

"Sure," I said. Though I was hesitant for others to see my work half done.

"Your website isn't live, so no one is going to see the video yet, just you all," Theo told us. "When you feel your work is ready, then we will publish."

Theo walked us through the uploading process, and then had a couple of us actually click the buttons for practice. Ms. Morgan then pulled out a few more laptops and we worked simultaneously while Theo displayed his screen on the projector for all of us to see.

Ms. Morgan came over to me and whispered, "Great job, Jenny. This is going well."

"Thanks," I said. "I just hope everyone else thinks so too."

"Don't worry," she said. "You are doing fantastic!"

I could hear everyone watching the video. Once they pressed play, they immediately turned down the volume with embarrassment. I'm not sure what it is, but it felt so good to see my work out there. It's a weird feeling, almost like I was bragging, but I know that I wasn't.

"How much time do we have?" Theo asked.

Ms. Morgan answered, "We have another five minutes until lunch is over."

"That's it?" said Celia. "That went by so fast. There was so much more we had to talk about."

"That's ok," said Ms. Morgan. "You all worked on something very important today."

"We got through most of the basic stuff," said Theo. "Play with it at home and pretty soon it will all make sense, and soon you'll be adding and changing stuff on your website like pros."

"Thanks, Theo," I said.

"No problem. If you need anything else, I'm happy to help," he said. "Now I have to head back to school as well."

He closed up his station with ease and slipped out with a wave.

"Ok, everyone," said Ms. Morgan, getting our attention. "Great first meeting. You really jumped right in and got to work. I am very impressed. Thank you, Jenny for bringing in Theo and having him teach us. That was very helpful."

"Is there a name for this club?" Jaime asked.

"Not yet," I said. "I didn't know what to call it, so I left it blank on the club application. Mr. Porter said we should come up with a name within a week. Any ideas?"

Everyone in the room sat puzzled, looked at one another for suggestions.

"Well, we don't need to decide today, right?" I said.

"Give it some time," said Ms. Morgan. "The name will come. For now, please clean up and we will all see each other next week."

We got up from our seats and started packing away the laptops, and plugging them in to the charging station.

"That was cool," said Lola.

I passed my laptop to her to plug in. "Yeah," I said. "Time really flew by."

"It sure did," said Celia.

We grabbed our backpacks and walked outside to go to our next class.

"Ms. Morgan said it was good, but do you think that is the way the meeting is supposed to go?" I asked them.

"I have never been in a club," said Celia. She heaved her heavy bag back up on her shoulder. "I have no idea."

"I have been in clubs," said Lola. "They never go like that."

"What do you mean?" I asked.

"In other clubs we sit around and talk about what we want to do, and make lists of things that never actually get done," said Lola. "Clubs are more of a place to get together."

"Was it boring?" I asked Lola.

"No way! This was big time stuff," Lola said. "We were actually getting things done, and not just talking about it."

"Right," I said. "I guess it's because we aren't starting from scratch. We have already been working on the art show and the overall project."

"How did the filming go with Jolene's class?" Celia asked.

"Did you watch the video?" I asked.

"Yeah, kind of."

"It was really cool," I said. "You would love her class. They did a bunch of beach clean-ups and sorted out all the trash they picked up. It reminded me a lot of you."

Celia just nodded her head.

"Have you figured out what you are going to do with the trash you collected?" I asked her.

"Still working on it," she said.

SOMETHING GOOD GOING HERE

I had showed the video of Jolene's class to what seemed like everyone except Jolene and Eve. So I invited myself over for dinner. I told Jolene I finished the video—well, that Dad and I had finished the video—and I wanted to show her and her mom. Since we kept it on the website from our practice session, it made it look official when I opened it up to show them.

They watched with intent, and laughed. Jolene pointed at the screen and said everyone's name when they appeared. She covered her face when she appeared, pretending to be embarrassed but reveling in the 15-second fame.

"I seriously can't believe you are doing this," said Jolene. "This looks really good."

"You thought I could never do this kind of stuff," I

laughed.

"You know what I mean," she said.

"Jenny, you should be very proud of yourself," said Eve.

"Thank you," I said. "We started a club at school to keep it going."

"We have something similar at our school," said Jolene. "To be honest, it's kind of boring though."

"I'm afraid our club will get boring too," I said. "We have only met once, so I shouldn't get too negative."

"Can I show the video to my class?" Eve asked me. "And send it out to their parents and the rest of the school?"

"Uh, yeah, of course. That's what it's there for, right?" I said. My nerves rippled through my body. "This site isn't live, so maybe I'll just send you the file."

"Ok. I'm sure they will love to see what their kids are doing," said Eve. "When do you plan to go *live*, as you say?"

"We need to get some writing on there, explaining things, and I need to figure out the donate button thingy, and maybe get a blog post or something," I said.

"Well, if I have learned anything from experience, don't let this sit. When momentum is lost, it is difficult to get it back. Soon enough, any little thing will become more important and you will lose interest," Eve told me.

"I keep hearing that," I said.

"It's human nature," she said. "We get really excited at first, filled of a lot of energy, and then it wears off when things get hard, or when you have to do the not-so-fun-stuff. So far though, you have kept up with your ideas. It's been a few months, right?"

"Surprisingly," I said. "It's been about four months."

"Well, keep up the good work," said Eve. "When are you going to have your art show?"

"It's really up in the air," I said. "We are thinking about the end of April."

"That gives you about two months to really get it polished," she said. "Plenty of time."

The very next night, Jolene called me. "Dude! Everyone loved the video. I mean, of course, everyone loves to see themselves on the screen, but they really thought it was awesome."

"Oh, wow, cool," I said. I felt my face getting hot just hearing it through the phone.

"You are really good at this," said Jolene. "I was talking to my mom, and she said the parents are stoked! They are asking how they can help."

"Help with what?" I asked.

"You'll have to talk to my mom. Once she sent the video out in the morning, she kept getting emails from parents all day saying how great it is, and, like I said, they want to know how they can help you."

"*Me?*"

"Yeah, my mom told them what you are doing," said Jolene. "She didn't share your website, don't worry. She did mention the art show. One parent said they would host it!"

"Wait, what!? Host the art show? Where?"

"Their house. Remember when we passed by that house when we went to the beach?"

"Yeah, but I didn't think they were interested," I said. "Actually, I never pursued it. I just figured they wouldn't want to."

"I guess that doesn't matter, because they are happy to do it. My mom must have said a lot more. I really don't know. Like I said, you'll have to talk to her. But, it's pretty cool, right?"

Jolene was excited for me, and instead of jumping on her hype train I felt nervous again. What was wrong with me? Why was my first reaction to be scared? The rest of the club would be thrilled. This is what we needed.

"What do you think?" Jolene asked me.

"What do I think?" I said. "I think it's really cool."

"You don't sound too excited."

"I am, really, I am. It's just that I don't even know this girl."

"Melanie, remember? Her dad is some techy guy. He works at Apple. His job is to make sure their products are eco-friendly."

"Really? That's crazy. Like, he gets paid to be an environmentalist?" I said.

"Kind of? I don't know exactly," said Jolene. "Anyway, don't get scared all of a sudden. This is a good thing. Plus you have all those people in your club and at your school to help. Jackie is good at this stuff, and I know my mom is psyched now, which means she will stop at nothing to keep this going!"

My nerves were getting even more unsettled. I really didn't know what I was doing, and now more people were involved. It was getting to be too much.

"I know what you're thinking," Jolene said to me.

"What?"

"I know you so well. You are totally scared."

"No, I'm not," I said.

"You are totally scared. That's what you do," she said. "You're afraid you can't do it."

"Not exactly."

"Actually, it is exactly that. Do me a favor will ya?"

I nodded my head, though Jolene wouldn't see that on the other side of the receiver.

"Don't sit back on this. My mom was saying you are going to do great things. She sees kids all the time. She has taught for, like, ever, and she says you are unique."

"She said that?"

"Ok, no," said Jolene. "Just kidding, she totally said that. She thinks you are onto something. She wants to help. Me too. I bet my whole school wants to help, and when they get going on a fundraiser, there is no stopping them."

BOOTS ON THE GROUND

I think I was officially tired of worrying about everything. It was getting old thinking I had to do it all. I am still a kid! While I felt incredibly empowered, I also finally realized I really couldn't do it on my own, and I rather enjoyed working with other people. I think I was finally ok with asking for help.

"Jackie?"

"Yeah?"

"Can you help me with something?" I asked.

"You know I will."

We had been sitting side by side at the dinner table working on separate projects.

"Can you come with me to check out a place for the art show?"

"When?"

"Um, today?"

"Today? Really, Jenny?" She threw down her pen. "You really didn't give me much notice."

"Are you busy?"

"I'm always busy." She went back to her notebook.

"With what?"

"Saving the planet, duh." She was scribbling away at something that didn't look that crucial.

"I don't know what I'm doing," I whispered.

"I know," she whispered back, without looking up from the page.

"I just figured I would go and get it done." I was baiting her a bit, trying to see if there was an ounce of interest.

"Get it done?" she asked.

"You know."

"Nope." Then she drew a straight line across a set of words, crossing them out.

"I mean, meet these people."

"Alright, fine Jenny. You have my attention," she said. "Do they even know you are coming?"

"Yeah."

"So, you had this planned?" she asked. "But you don't have a ride? I get it now."

"Yeah."

"What were you thinking?" she lightly punched my shoulder.

"I was thinking you could take me."

"Ugh."

"Please."

"Fine."

"Can we pick up Celia and Lola?"

"Whatever."

Eve had spoken with Melanie's parents, then she started an email chain where I was supposed to act professional and mature, even though I still don't really ever know what I am doing. Like I said, I'm just a kid. I desperately needed Jackie to be there with me. Not Mom, or Eve. It needed to come from me, not a parent. Jackie wasn't a parent, *and* she was good at this kind of stuff. So if it all went wrong, she could jump in. I think?

Jackie agreed to pick up Lola and Celia. I also needed them. "So what are you going to say?" Jackie asked us.

"Well," I started. I looked around the front seat and then out the window. I knew what I wanted to say, I just didn't think it was going to come out right. I pulled down the visor and looked back at Lola and Celia in the mirror.

"Don't tell me you were just going to knock on their door and say, 'Cool, thanks for letting us use your house for our little art show,'" Jackie said. She slammed her hands onto the steering wheel, then stared at me.

"Not exactly," I said.

"I wrote something," said Celia.

"Are you going to read it from the page, like you're giving a speech?" Jackie said.

"Nope," said Celia. "I have it memorized."

"Is this a pitch? Or, is this venue secured?" Jackie asked.

"What does that mean?" asked Lola.

"What I mean is are you asking these people to use their home for your art show, or have they already agreed?"

"It was their idea," I said.

"Their idea?" Jackie said. "How did that happen?"

"Eve showed the parents the video Dad and I put together of her class, and then told the parents what we are doing," I said.

"And they just said, 'We'll do it!'"

"Kind of," I said. "I mean I wasn't there, but it sounds like they really want to host it."

"Have you thought of the fact that most of the people from your school live 30 minutes away from this place, and getting people to show up is going to be difficult," Jackie asked.

"I thought about that," said Celia.

"And?" said Jackie.

"Jeez, why are you being so negative," I asked Jackie.

"I'm just asking questions," she said. She looked intently at the road, holding the wheel with both hands at the top.

We drove out to the coast, on the windy road, staring out at the grassy hills and farm land that separated the ocean from the city. I think we were all afraid to say anything more. Afraid that Jackie would attack again.

Jackie had been incredibly helpful. I don't know if anything would have lifted off the ground without her. She was a boots-on-the-ground type of person. Jackie wasn't afraid of jumping in and getting to work. She wasn't afraid of asking hard questions or getting into someone's face. She was also really good at living the life she wanted for the world. She was a vegetarian, she shopped at second-hand stores, she stood up for animals. She rode her bike whenever she could. Jackie reached out and found people to connect with and get the ball rolling. I didn't have that kind of courage.

"So, what do we know about these people, and what

do they know about you?" Jackie finally broke the silence.

"The dad works for Apple, and the daughter, her name is Melanie, she is in Jolene's class," I said. "Well, Eve's class."

"So, they know Eve and Jolene?" Jackie asked.

"It's the same person that Jolene had mentioned a month ago," I said.

"The one you have been too afraid to ask," Jackie said.

"That's the one."

"And, now they are reaching out to you?"

"Appears so," I said.

"Well aren't you lucky," Jackie said. "This kind of stuff doesn't often happen like this."

We pulled up to the house. It was right off the street. No sidewalk. It stood tall looking out to the ocean that was on the other side of the street. The house was large with two stories, maybe three, it was hard to tell from the car. The first floor was made up of glass walls that wrapped around. You could see right into the house, though there was nothing inside the first floor. It was like an empty parking garage with a few stone pillars holding up the ceiling.

"This is it?" Jackie asked.

"This is it," I said.

"Wow, this is amazing," said Lola.

"This doesn't even look like a house," said Celia.

"Jolene said it is. She said she's been inside," I said.

"Where is the front door?" Lola asked.

"Maybe over there," I said pointed at the path ahead.

"Well, let's go," said Jackie.

We piled out of the car, dusted off our clothes, and waited for someone else to lead.

"Go ahead," said Lola.

"After you," said Celia.

"Just go," said Jackie.

"Why me?" I asked.

"They are expecting *you*, right?" said Jackie.

"Ok! Fine!" I yelled.

I took the first step, and then another. The three of them were behind me, going as slow as I was going.

"Do I knock on the fence?" I asked.

"No one is going to hear that," said Jackie. "You go in past the fence."

"Really?" I said. "Why have a fence?"

"To keep people like us out," said Celia.

We all looked at her.

"What? You know what I mean," she said.

I pressed down the latch with my thumb and pushed the wooden door open. Inside was a beautiful garden. The grass was so green, and the stones leading up the house were so clean. There were purple flowers that blanketed the perimeter of the grass, like moss, and a flowing fountain in the corner with four tiers where the water dropped down into the next bowl.

"This place is unreal," said Lola.

"I know, right?" I said. "I'm not sure if they know what they said yes to."

We reached the front door. It had a long, rectangular glass window that ran all the way down from the top to the bottom. You could see right into the house.

"Stop snooping around," Jackie said.

"I'm not!" I said.

"Then ring the doorbell," she said.

"Do you ring the doorbell, or it is better to knock?" I

said.

"Knock," said Celia.

"No, they won't hear you," said Lola. "Ring the doorbell."

"What do I do?" I said.

Jackie reached over and let the doorbell ring long and loud.

"Oh my gosh!" I said.

"What?!" Jackie said. "One of us needed to get this going."

"I know, it's just that—" Someone was coming to the door. "Shhh!"

Just breathe, I told myself.

A tall man, with graying brownish hair walked toward the door. "Hello there," he said. "One of you must be Jenny."

When I didn't say anything, Jackie nudged me forward.

"Um, hi, that's me. I'm Jenny."

He reached his hand out, "Nice to meet you. I'm Frank."

I met him in a hand shake. "Hi."

"And, who is everyone else?" Frank asked.

"This is my sister Jackie."

"Hello," he said, reaching his hand out to Jackie.

"This is Celia, and this is Lola," I said.

"Hello there." He shook their hands as well. "Please, come on in."

He stepped aside, holding the door open for us to pass through. We then followed him to the living room. "Please, have a seat. Would you like something to drink?" Frank asked us.

"Sure, what do you have?" Lola asked.

We all looked at her.

"What?" Lola said.

Celia leaned in and whispered, "You don't say it like that."

"We have cranberry juice, water, sparkling water, and I think we have some apple juice," Frank said.

"I'll have apple juice," said Lola.

"Anyone else?" Frank asked.

"I'll take one," said Jackie. "Thank you."

"Me too," said Celia.

"Should I make it four?" Frank asked me.

"Sure, why not," I said.

"Alright, I'll be right back with four apple juices."

When he walked out of the room, Celia jumped at Lola. "What are you thinking asking him what he's got?"

"What? Is that bad?" Lola asked.

"Dude, this guy is seriously rich. He doesn't need us in here talking like we have no manners," Celia said.

"Celia, don't worry," said Jackie. "Relax. He's like anyone else."

"Except that he isn't," Celia said.

"Ok, here we are," said Frank, passing out the drinks to each of us.

When we were all given a drink, he sat down on the couch. "My wife will join us shortly. She is just finishing up a call," Frank told us. He took a sip of his drink and then set it down on the coffee table. "So, sounds like you are doing some very cool things, Jenny."

"Oh, thank you," I said. "It's not just me. It's all of us, and more of us at our school."

"Tell me more about this art show," he said.

People talk about elevator pitches. Is that what I need

to have? Where would I start? What are the most important things to say?

"I can talk about it," said Lola. "If that's ok?"

"Sure, go ahead," I said, relieved.

"We have been studying plastics in the ocean in our class with our teacher, Ms. Morgan," said Lola. "We looked at how that plastic is having a serious effect on the health of our oceans, and the marine life that lives in and around the ocean. At first we thought we needed to figure out a way to clean up the ocean, but then we realized that we needed to stop using single-use plastics. We wrote letters urging our representative to vote yes on the plastic ban. Then we thought if we told more people around our school to write letters it would become more effective. We cleaned up our school, and are in the process of making alternatives to single-use plastics and other unnecessary trash."

Lola paused to see if she should continue. She was doing great and I was not going to stop her. She smiled.

"Jenny, here, decided that if we documented the work we were doing we could inspire more people. With her Dad, who is a producer, she made a short video on our work in class, as well as areas in our school where trash seems to pile up. Then her sister, Jackie here, who is the editor for the Bayshore High School newspaper, helped us to make a website, where we could put the video and more information. That's when we realized there are more people who were doing this kind of environmental work in their schools, and if we shared our stories it might make the movement stronger."

"Well, well. What a great story," said Frank. "That's going to be hard to repeat to my wife, but I'll do my best."

I looked at Lola, who laughed along with Frank and the others. How did she do all that? Jackie looked at me and mouthed, *Whoa!*

I then mouthed back, *Right?*

"Hello everyone." Frank's wife stepped into the room. "Sorry I'm late. I'm Virginia, but you can call me Ginny. What did I miss?"

"Well, this young lady said it all," Frank said pointing at Lola. "These girls are on a mission to end single-use plastics, and they want to get others involved."

"Which one of you made that video?" Ginny asked.

"That was me," I said. "But I had a lot of help."

"Tell us about this art show you are planning," said Ginny.

I turned toward Lola to see if she wanted to do the talking again. Then Celia jumped in, "The art show is a place to showcase the artwork we have made from trash we found around school, and from plastics we found at the beach. We want to bring more awareness to plastics, and for trash that doesn't get put into the right place and ends up in our waterways and ultimately in our oceans. This is also a way to bring more people together, and to show others what we want to do with our website."

"What do you want to do with the website?" Ginny asked.

"We want to show what sustainable solutions students are doing in their school, and out of school," Celia said. "We are doing this through videos. We hope to raise money to provide resources for school projects. Like your daughter's school. With donations, we can give them the money to buy buckets and grabbers for their beach clean-ups. We could do this for others."

"How old are you?" said Ginny. "I'm kidding. Ms. Eve said wonderful things about you and others at your school. I have also seen what Melanie does in her class with Ms. Eve. I wish we had teachers like that when I was young."

"Yeah, they are great teachers," I said.

"Have you met my daughter, Melanie?" said Ginny.

We shook our heads.

"I thought maybe you would have through Jolene," she said. "Since we live so close to the water she picks up trash daily. We have fairly clean beaches around here, but you would be surprised what you find."

"I love doing beach clean-ups," said Celia.

"It sure would be great if there were more of you regularly doing that," she said.

"It's hard to get over here," said Celia. "We can't drive, and we don't always have a ride."

"It is interesting that you all have so much passion when you aren't even close to the water," said Ginny.

"The ocean is for everyone," Celia said.

"Of course, of course," said Ginny. "What I meant is that it's tough to care about something you don't see often."

"That's for sure," said Celia.

"Actually," interrupted Jackie. "A lot of marine debris comes from places that are not on the coast."

"Very true," said Ginny. "Well then, if hosting an art show here at our house can help your cause and get more of you out here keeping our oceans clean and healthy, we would love to be a part of your project."

"Thank you," I said.

"Now, have any of you ever planned an event?" Ginny asked us.

HIDDEN TALENTS

I appreciated that Ginny took us so seriously as to think we have ever hosted a fundraiser. Once we let on that we really had no idea, she was more than happy to take the reins. This was a great talking point for our next *green team* meeting, of which we saw returning faces. We did lose a few people, but we surprisingly gained a few more.

There were so many items to announce and a ton of work to be done, it was overwhelming. Lola, Celia, and I got together with Jackie that night after we met with Frank and Ginny. The drive home was full of *oh-my-gawds, holy-toledos, what-is-happenings*. With the information fresh in our minds, we sat down and hashed out what we were actually getting ourselves into, and listened to Jackie who had a lot to say. Mom made tacos with nopales in them, and she kept filling our plates at the table, warming tortillas on the stove, and making sure we were nourished.

"You have the possibility of putting together a really great event," said Jackie. "I don't know how you all did it, but this kind of opportunity doesn't just fall into your lap like this."

"Well, we did a lot of work, and Jenny made those videos," said Celia. "It's not like we sat around and Frank and Ginny fell from the sky."

"They kind of did," said Jackie. "But, you're right. You have all earned this. So don't blow it."

"Thanks," I said. I was on my third taco with no stopping.

"Ok, so let's get going," said Lola. "What are the important things that need to get done?"

"What works in your favor is that Ginny is going to get the word out to people you don't know and she is going to put together the event," said Celia. "All we have to do is bring in the art work and set up the website."

"Are you kidding me?" Jackie yelled. Her taco fell from her hand onto the plate, splattering cactus juice. "First of all, that is not as simple as you make it out to be, and there is way more that you need to do."

We stopped eating our tacos. Mom had come back into the room to add more tortillas to the pile we had on the table. "What's wrong?" she asked, looking around at our faces. "Is someone sick?"

"What do you mean?" I asked Jackie.

"You are hosting an event," said Jackie. "You need to have a schedule, speakers, activities of some sort to keep the interest in the room. Just because Ginny is organizing the food and some outreach, doesn't mean you are off the hook."

"Is everything ok?" Mom asked. She set down the tortillas carefully on the table.

"Yeah, we're fine," said Jackie. She grabbed one from the pile and started making another taco, filling it up with nopales, quest fresco, and Mom's homemade salsa.

"Can I say something?" I spoke up. "I have been really scared this whole time."

"We know," said Jackie, stuffing her face.

"Listen," I said. "I didn't know what I was thinking all those months ago, but I really just wanted to help out. I wanted to do something more than just refusing plastic bottles, and to-go containers."

"Me too," Lola smiled.

"I'm not good at talking in front of people, or organizing events," I said. "All of this stuff is actually frightening. I get really nervous, and I feel like I'm going to throw up when I have to speak. My heart races and sometimes I swear I'm going to faint."

"Well, then you just won't speak at the art show," said Jackie. "Simple."

"I would love to speak," said Celia. "I really enjoy being in front of people, and I think I have a lot to say."

"I get nervous too," said Lola. "But sometimes, I don't. It sort of comes and goes."

When we met for our next *green team* meeting, Celia led the show. It was that easy. I sat back, with a camera in hand, and documented the process.

"Hey everyone!" Celia announced. "We are going to get started right away today."

Celia had their attention quickly, and she was ready to take charge. She made it seem so easy.

"Our plans for the art show are underway," she started. "We have a venue, and the hosts are taking care of adult outreach and food. Which is awesome!"

"No way," said Brian. "How did you do that?"

"It's through a friend of a friend," said Celia. "Anyway, this leaves us in charge of reaching out to students and their families, we need more art to showcase from as many students as we can, our website has to be up and running with a lot more content, and we need to find people that are willing to speak at the event."

"What!?" yelled Jaime. "Dude, what is going on? Are you serious?"

"Totally," Lola chimed in.

"So this is really happening?" Jaime said.

"Yup," I said.

"How long do we have?" he asked.

"We have two months," I said. "But, it's going to go by quickly."

"At least we have some time, you girls are scaring me," Jaime said, holding on to his chest like his heart was about to explode.

We laughed.

"Basically, we need to break up into groups and get going," said Celia.

"I'm happy to help with student outreach," said Lola. "I'll make more posters, and I can have a booth at lunch to see if people want to sign up their art."

"That's great," said Celia. "We also need to put the call out to other schools."

"Uh," said Lola. I guess this is where she got nervous.

"We can get someone else on that," said Celia. "What about the website? Anyone want to start writing?"

"I'll do it," said Brian.

"I think we also need some social media, what do you all think?" Celia asked the group.

A group from the back shot their hands up and enthusiastically agreed to get an Instagram and TikTok account running.

"Theo said we can link that to the site, right?" Arjun whispered to me.

"Yeah," I said.

"I have been playing around with it," he said. "Did you see what I have added?"

I hadn't looked at the website for a couple days. The thought of pulling it up scared me because I knew that I needed to do something about it and I didn't know what to do. I pulled out a laptop from the charging case and looked it up. It appeared Arjun played around with fonts, and added photos. He also uploaded the lyrics to his song.

"This looks great Arjun," I said.

"Thanks."

Everyone broke off into groups, joining others, and getting right to work.

"Hey Jenny, what do we need written on the website?" Brian asked.

"Maybe we can start with a blog post?" I suggested.

"Ok, I can do that," he said. He started to walk away, then turned around. "About what, though?"

I laughed. "Maybe about something you are interested in that has to do with environmental sustainability, or plastics in the ocean?"

"So, I could write about anything? It doesn't have to be about the group?"

"What are you thinking?" I asked him.

"I have been thinking about writing what others do at home with plastic. Like, maybe people are doing more, or less, than we think," Brian said.

"I think that's a great idea," I said.

"Ok, cool. I'll go for it," he said.

That night, I started putting together little videos that we could post on social media. I was taking snippets from our class and also Eve's class. While the editing did take hours, I was finding it was fun, and it didn't make me as nervous as I felt when around people. It took up a lot of my time, and I was happy to give it, but it made me wonder what else would I have been doing all these months had I not found something worth working toward?

This work on the project, the art show, or whatever it was that we were doing, the whole thing, consumed me. I was constantly researching online, reading whatever I could about climate change. It was scary at times when I read about millions of people who would become climate refugees when the sea level rises so much so that they can no longer sustain their way of life, or when places get so hot it is unbearable and food can no longer grow. I thought about our very own fire season. It was like spring or summer, except that instead of bringing life and renewal it brought about destruction.

However, like Eve said a couple months ago, I found plenty of people and organizations doing a lot to mitigate or at least adapt to climate change, and all it took was a simple Google search. It wasn't hopeless, in other words. I just didn't want to stand up in front of people and talk. I was finding my strengths were behind the scenes, especially the documentation.

I watched Dad slumped over a computer for as long as I could remember, making his movies that I had no interest in whatsoever. Now, all of a sudden, it was the greatest thing that had happened to me. Filming and making videos was like a hidden talent I didn't know existed, and it gave me a way to be a part of something that I desperately wanted to shy away from. I was still scared, but I now had a way of helping out. My own way. I did have something to say, but I was finding that most of the time I wanted to encourage what others had to say.

COMMUNITY OUT-REACH

Lola had made posters that she plastered around campus. I'm not sure where she got the money for the supplies, but she didn't say a word. I told her I would reimburse her when we started getting money from our website.

"Can you do that?" she asked.

"I'm really not sure," I said. "I finally asked my mom to help us set up the bank account. She said we would eventually need to become a non-profit."

"Wow, a non-profit," Lola said. "That's like a dream. Of course my parents would have no idea what that is all about, but I think they would be proud."

"Jackie said it's a lot of paperwork, and we need to get a board of directors," I had to mention.

"I'll let you handle that," she laughed.

Like she had promised, Lola set out a table at lunch to

try to get people interested in the art show. We had all finally agreed on a name for our club: Standing Together. It went perfectly with our logo, which was a circular earth from a marine animal point of view, all blue. Around the blue circle was a golden ring, almost like a halo. Like we were angels helping to save the ocean. It represented the closed-loop feedback system we were promoting.

"Will you help me with this?" Lola asked. She handed me the poster and the tape she would use to display it. I tucked it under my arm, then picked up a chair for myself. She grabbed the folding table and another chair, and together we walked out to the picnic tables where people were eating.

Lola taped the poster on to the table, and we set out the chairs. "I need to grab one more thing," said Lola. "I'll be right back."

"Ok, I'll be here," I said.

I looked around at all the people eating, laughing and joking with their friends. I pulled out my lunch to eat as well. Things had been moving slowly along, and while there were days where I felt pressure, I also knew there were many others helping and the work would get done. For better or worse, we were going to hold the event.

"How is it going?" Ms. Morgan had walked up to the table.

"Oh, hi," I said. "Well, we just set up, so not too much action. I figure when people are done eating a few may come up with questions."

"Keep it up," she said. She walked off toward wherever she went. She generally helped someone on her lunch break. Who would it be today?

Lola was walking back with a colorful item in her

hands. I couldn't tell what it was from afar. As she got closer it still didn't look like anything.

"What is that?" I asked.

"Can't you tell?" Lola said.

"Sorry," I said.

"I'm just kidding. It's nothing really, but it got your attention, right?"

"It's very colorful," I mentioned.

"I wanted to bring out something that could be considered art, made out of plastic," Lola said. She set it down on the table without a sound. It was light in weight, and rolled a bit finding a landing spot. "Maybe someone will want to check it out."

"Do you make that?" I asked. I picked it up and spun it around.

"I did," Lola smiled. "I basically wanted to make something that was bright."

"Are you going to display it at the art show?"

"Maybe? I didn't think about that."

We sat together that day and not one person walked up, or were even curious about that colorful piece of whatever that was sitting on the table. We closed up shop with five minutes to spare.

"Do you think it's my art?" Lola asked.

"No, I just think it's difficult to walk up to something you don't know," I said. "Plus, I'm sure we look scary."

We laughed.

We returned the table and chairs to Ms. Morgan's room. "See you later," I said.

"See ya," Lola said.

The next day, we set up again. This time Lola had two colorful contraptions sitting on the table.

"Two now?" I asked. I really had no idea what they were, and I was afraid to ask. I didn't want to hurt her feelings. She seemed very proud of them.

"Yup," Lola said.

No one came up to talk to us that day.

The third day, we set up again. This time Lola had three of those things.

"Ok, so what is up with these things?" I finally asked.

"What? These art pieces?" Lola said.

"Yeah. There are three of them now," I said. "Don't take offense, but they look dirty."

"They are," she said. "I pulled them out of the trash."

"Oh," I said.

That day someone came up to our booth. He didn't say anything, just looked, smiled and walked away.

We closed up, put everything away, and hoped for a better day. Lola was determined to get someone interested.

The fourth day we were out, Lola had four art pieces. The fourth one was a bit smaller than the rest. They were taking up a lot of space on the table. It looked messy, but Lola didn't seem to mind.

That day a group of girls walked up to us. "So what are these things?" one of them asked. She had a face full of disgust and curiosity all at the same time.

"This one is the collection of all the recyclable items that were thrown into the trash can yesterday. This one is from the day before, and this one is from Monday," Lola was going down the line. "The one here is from last Friday."

"I don't get it," the girl said.

"All of these items can be recycled, but people threw them into the trash," Lola clarified.

"Oh," she said.

"Wow," said another girl. "So, you pulled all this stuff out of the trash cans?"

"Exactly," said Lola.

"What are you two doing here with this booth, anyway?" the girl asked.

"We are part of the Standing Together club. We are here to raise awareness of plastics in the ocean," said Lola.

"Yeah, it's bad," the girl said. She picked up one of the pieces and turned it around in her hands. "I mean, I was watching a video the other day, and there is a river in Cameroon where the river is so thick with plastic bottles you can't even see the water."

"Did you know there are over five trillion pieces of plastic in the ocean?" Lola said.

"That's a lot," said the girl.

"Those pieces get so small from the sun, and the water and the wind, that animals eat them, and get sick and can die," Lola added. "Or, it messes with their reproduction."

"So, are you two here to tell people this?" she asked.

"We are putting together an event, where there will be others there that will hopefully donate to our cause."

"What do you mean donate to the cause?" she asked. Her friends had walked away at this point, no longer interested in the fact that Lola was rummaging through trash.

"We are hoping to showcase students doing environmental work in their schools, and raise money to fund their environmental projects," I said. I had to say something eventually. I had been sitting there listening like I had nothing to do there but offer moral support.

"That's interesting," she said. "By the way, my name is

275

Lucy."

"Hi Lucy, I'm Lola, and this is Jenny."

"So you two are really going to get people to donate to your *cause*?" Lucy asked.

"We sure hope so," said Lola. "We have a website, if you want to check it out. It's we-have-something-to-say-dot-com."

Lucy pulled out her phone and typed it in. She stared down at her phone and with her thumb scrolling through.

Brian had written a few blog posts, interviewing students what they were doing in their homes to recycle, ways to reuse items, as well as a story from someone who does none of the above. He got Joshua to help him find a bunch of facts about plastic pollution, and together they compiled a list that was added on a sidebar. Brian was really good at making it look fun and enticing. We had all worked on our "about" section and our mission statement. It's pretty good, but we may need to tweak some of the words. Mom said it sounded great, but she was happy about everything that was going on. It was like I could do no wrong.

"Who made the video?" Lucy asked.

"I did," I said raising my hand.

"Really? That's cool. Do you do this for other people?" Lucy asked.

"What do you mean?" I said.

"I mean, like would you make me a video?"

"Uh, for what?" It was a weird question.

"Our art club," Lucy said. "It kind of goes along with what you have going on here." She tapped at Lola's creations that were starting to smell. "We only work with materials we find. Like, we don't buy anything new. I mean except for glue and stuff. We mostly try to use string. In fact we find a ton of fishing nets on the beaches all the time. Those work really well to hold things together."

"A big part of the event is the art show!" Lola said. "We are displaying art made from plastics and other trash from our school and the beach. You and your club could show off your art work there."

From that moment the Standing Together club was collaborating with the Heart from the Art club. Lucy and the rest of the club came to our meetings and we went to theirs. Well, not all of them, but we reminded each other of when it might be important to attend.

Heart from the Art was all about what we were doing, only they accidentally fell into environmentalism. They didn't have money for supplies. They wanted to form a group to get together to make art and talk about art, and just be in their own world. At first they gathered what they could from the trash cans, but then they started to look on different websites where free stuff was given away, and they managed to get their parents to drive them and pick up whatever it was they thought would be useful.

I told Lucy I was happy to make a video about what they were doing. The day I showed up they had an old roll-top desk they found on the side of the road and were smashing it to pieces with hammers. Talk about moving footage. Shards of wood were spewing out like fireworks. I shot some of it in slow motion, which made for some great artsy footage.

They all agreed to focus on plastics for the next month, and were more than happy to have their work displayed at the art show.

Jackie couldn't believe my luck. We managed to get 11

high school students who were interested in showcasing their art work, after Jackie got her friends at the paper to write a story about us, which was more about the art show and opening it up to others who wanted to showcase their work. Everything helped.

Eve's class was knee deep in art work, and a few other classes at her school were excited to make plastic art. She said it was a lot of fun, and the kids never wanted to stop.

We all stayed in touch with Ginny, though Eve was spearheading that portion. Ginny said to expect 200 people.

I couldn't make sense of what was happening, but either way it was happening. For the record I was making mistakes left and right, but there were people all around me that cared, wanted to help, and actually helped. We were making mistakes together, and sharing in the small victories as well.

LUCK

"Hey Ms. Morgan," said Jaime. "Do you ever think we will hear back about the letters we wrote on the plastic ban?"

"That's a great question," she said. She pulled her hair behind her ears. "I want to say no, which I understand is not very encouraging."

"So, they'll read the letters, and just toss them?" he asked.

"I don't think they just toss them," she said. "They consider them. You have to understand that if people show an interest in something, politically, they will be considered."

"I don't really believe that," said Jaime. "Our letters won't make a difference."

"It's not that your letter alone will make a difference, it is every single person that supports the plastic ban. With more voices and action things happen," said Ms. Morgan. She rolled a chair to the center of the class. "Take for example, Standing Rock. Thousands of people camped out along the way of the proposed pipeline. They stayed out in the cold, even when dogs attacked them, or when police cleared them out, and even when police doused them using water cannons. They stood strong."

"That all happened?" Brian asked.

"It did," said Ms. Morgan nodding her head furiously.

"Water cannons?" Brian said. "That sounds crazy."

"They stood strong, even when the decision they desired was actually granted but then reversed. Eventually the court shut it down a couple years after saying that the people of Standing Rock were not told of the potential hazards."

"So, you're saying it's not just our letters," said Jaime. "It's going further and doing more work."

"Yes, and it is getting more people aware and involved," Celia chimed in.

"That's right," said Ms. Morgan. "It's about not giving up. If you think this cause is worthy you will find a way."

"No offense Jenny, but will this art show really make a difference?" Jaime asked.

I wasn't offended, just embarrassed. I looked at Celia and Lola who had also done so much work. I looked at Brian and Arjun, and Ms. Morgan.

"I think it will," I finally said. "It's more than getting people to switch out a plastic straw or bottle, or lid, it's taking on a bigger issue that gets heard. If I have learned anything this school year it's that I cannot do anything great on my own." I took a moment to pause. Even with all my nerves, I wanted to say something to everyone out loud. So I pushed through. "We need each other, and that is how the movement is built. We can't do everything in the classroom, but it needs to start somewhere." My face was getting hot. "To answer your question, Jaime, I think all the work we are doing leads to something, and along the way we are making connections. Like Standing Rock, when those people were camped out, they were actually learning from one another. Indigenous people were teaching non-indigenous people their ways of taking care of and living off the land in a regenerative way. We may not move mountains at our age or our school, but with all this work, we just might when we get older."

"Are you sure you don't want to speak at the art show?" Celia laughed. "That was good."

"I really wasn't trying to make you mad," said Jaime. "But, that was amazing. You're right. I was never interested in plastics before. Seriously, my Mom buys coffee on the way to school every morning. She orders it online then we pick it up. After all this, I managed to get her to walk into the coffee shop with her own cup. It's so easy now, that I don't even know why we thought we were saving time."

"We don't buy paper towels anymore," said Lola. "It actually wasn't that hard either."

"We don't eat meat in our home," said Arjun. "Well, we didn't really eat meat to begin with, but now instead of it just being for cultural or religious reasons, I see the environmental benefits of promoting vegetarianism. It makes me feel more a part of something instead of an outcast."

"I have been researching ways to reuse plastic," said Celia. "Since finding all the plastic at the beach and wanting to do something with it but not knowing what, I found an organization in Canada called Ocean Legacy that collects trash off the beach, grinds it up and then sends it off to places that use it to make products. I found that I wanted to be a part of something bigger that was closely related to water and specifically the ocean. I want to join groups where I can do more in the ocean. So, I started taking swimming lessons a couple weeks ago, so that when I get the chance, I'm ready."

"You can't swim?" said Jaime.

"Not yet," said Celia.

"That's cool," Jaime said. "I can swim, but I'm afraid of the water."

We laughed.

Listening was a big part of this journey. It was speaking up, and it was also really listening to what others had to say. Had I only heard myself, I wouldn't have been a part of so much growth and greatness. There was so much going on around me. Each time I opened my eyes and looked at my surroundings and the people in it, I found others who were equally interested, if not more. I am still in awe. I never saw this work being done before, and was equally amazed it was all available and right in front of my nose.

Each time we posted something on social media, our account grew. It was of course people we knew, but somehow there were a small number who had discovered us all on their own. Through these social connections we found more young people doing environmental work in their schools, or in different organizations. I and others reached out to them to see if they were interested in being a part of our website. Most everyone said yes, because it was another way to connect and promote. They would send their videos, and we would post them on our site.

I am making it sound easy; it's not. There were so many of us helping. It was our class, it was others at our school, it was the Standing Together club, it was the Heart from the Art club. It was Eve's class and others at her school, it was the parents of Eve's students, and it was high school students. It was Jackie, my parents, and everyone else's families that were supporting them to not only create an event, but also encouraging us to be stronger.

Everyone around me gave me a chance. Jackie kept pushing me, and Celia and Lola were pushing themselves. Everything that had happened up until this point was an effort by so many. There is no one person that can take credit, and there is no way we would be where we are now without everyone's involvement.

I'm lucky, and I don't take it for granted.

STAY HUMBLE

It was a week before the art show. There were so many things happening. We needed to check in with things at Ginny's house that we couldn't do over an email. Mom and Dad drove us out to the coast, and Jolene and Eve joined us. Plus Dad wanted to get the lay of the land so he knew what he was getting into when he was filming the event.

None of the rented furniture was set up, and wouldn't be until the day of the show, Ginny said. She walked us through where it would all go, and where the podium would stand.

"Let's pray for good weather," said Ginny. "April can be tricky."

She had a plan to open up the glass doors out onto the lawn in order to invite more people in. Ginny had lights strung up across the yard. "We rarely use them. It will be nice to turn them on," she laughed. "Actually I'm hoping a few bystanders will walk by and want to join in."

She wasn't charging for admission, which made me feel uncomfortable because I knew all of the rentals and food would come from her and Frank's pocket. Ginny didn't say a word.

"Eve," I whispered. "Is she really paying for all of this?"

"Not all of it," Eve said.

"Then who is?" I asked.

"A lot of the parents from my class have chipped in."

"Why?"

"Well, they are proud of their children's work," said Eve. "Also, they have the ability to fund this kind of event. So they did."

"Are they all coming?" I asked.

"I don't think everyone can make it. People have busy lives. I believe many of them will show up, though."

Ginny asked about the art. "So, tell me how many pieces are we looking at, and how big are the pieces? I know that many of the students will bring their art with them when they arrive, but I want to have a general idea so I can plan as best I can."

"Right, um," I said. "There's a lot."

"That's wonderful. I'm thinking about having the pieces all around the room. Almost as if they are in the way, forcing people to go around them and therefore looking at the art with more intention," said Ginny.

"We have about 35 students showcasing work," I said.

"Oh, wow," said Ginny. She stepped back with a dramatic flair. "Well then, um, some of them will be set on tables together. I don't know if we have enough room to have them all on their own stand."

"There's an art club at our school that has some big pieces," I told Ginny.

"Maybe we can put those larger pieces on the lawn?" Ginny wondered.

"I mean, they are all made of plastic, so water isn't going to hurt them," I said. "You know, in case the weather is bad."

"They just might break down," Lola laughed.

"Not completely, though," said Celia, matter of factly.

Ginny's daughter Melanie had just come home. She walked in through the fence barefoot and in her wetsuit. Her friend was behind her. They skipped around to the side yard where there was an outdoor shower.

"That is so cool," Lola whispered to me.

"Totally," I said.

"I really want to learn how to surf," said Celia.

"How are the swimming lessons going?" I asked her.

"I can totally swim," said Celia. "Not great. I don't think I'm ever going to be a good swimmer, but at least I feel safer in the water."

The Standing Together club met again at lunch the day of the art show. Heart from the Art showed up with their art work. It was bold! There was a six-foot water bottle they constructed using clear plastic packaging. They also made a boat using plastic bottles and fishing nets. It was incredible. I still had no idea what Eve's class was planning, but she had said it was going to be big. She told Ginny she might need to put it outside the event space. It had something to do with the kelp forest.

"Tonight is the night!" Celia announced. She was getting

really good at leading the meetings. It was like she born for the role.

"Seriously, I'm so nervous," I said.

"We know," a few people said. It was a joke now. I developed a behavior where I would braid a piece of my hair from the back of my head and then let it unravel, then braid it again. I'm not sure where I got it from. When I started doing it my friends would laugh and announce, "Jenny's getting nervous."

"Everyone have their speeches ready?" Celia asked.

Those who were going to speak nodded their heads.

"Jenny, you called the local paper to cover the story, and they are going to be there, right?" Celia asked.

"Yeah, and Jackie called the local paper in their town and they are excited to run the story," I said. "Though, I think they are going at the angle of local philanthropists helping underfunded schools. Jackie told them it wasn't quite like that. Hopefully their paper will get more of the story tonight."

"Can I interrupt for a second?" Ms. Morgan said. "I am so proud of all of your efforts. I have never had students who were so passionate and driven. You have inspired me to be a better educator."

We collectively blushed.

"It's because of you," said Jaime. "You taught us so much this year."

"Yeah, and you helped us all out in some way," said Celia.

"You kind of made us believe in ourselves," said Lola.

"Ok, ok," said Ms. Morgan, wiping her eyes. "You are all great on your own, already."

***

"Are you ready for tonight?" Dad asked when he picked me up from school.

"Everything seems ready to go. The art, the speeches, the music," I said. "It's not too complicated."

"Well, not when you have someone who is funding the party, taking care of the venue, the food, and inviting other people you don't even know who might possibly donate to your cause," said Dad. "Yeah, I would say for you it's not too complicated."

"It has been lot of work, Dad."

"I know, I'm just giving you a hard time, and keeping you humble."

THE ART SHOW

The four of us, Mom, Dad, Jackie and myself, drove together to Ginny and Frank's house. Of course we arrived early. Dad needed to set up; I had a few art pieces to bring from classmates that wouldn't be able to make it, including the huge salt dough map of the ocean floor, that was technically not made of plastic, but I felt it was appropriate.

Lola had already arrived and was busy hanging the large poster she made in the entryway. It said, *We Have Something to Say!* written across in bold lettering, and just below she wrote *Plastic Art Show*. She clearly had put a lot of time and effort into it, and it was beautiful. It was rectangular, nearly five-feet in length, and was clearly visible from the street. There was no missing it.

In the walkway, before reaching the fence, she had

placed all the balls of recycling bits that she rummaged for in the trash. Since she started this little art project, she had made 15 trash balls. Again, hard to miss. It looked like she just tossed them around the path, making it hard to walk around them. Ms. Morgan had suggested making a sign with a title for our art pieces. Lola made hers out of plastic, of course, and she titled it, *I didn't see a recycling bin, sorry?*

There were so many creative sides to Lola that came out over the school year. For as long as I had known her she had always been nervous and shy, and all the while we all had no idea how incredibly talented she is. Her posters were a huge factor in the school community outreach. Lola saved each poster she ever made, refusing to throw them away.

I had to ask her where she was storing them, since she lived in a single bedroom with her family.

"Oh, I tack them up on the walls," she told me.

I laughed. "Like, where you all sleep?"

"Yup."

My mother would have never let me put up posters in her bedroom or anywhere in the house that wasn't my own bedroom. Even if I was allowed, Jackie would have humiliated me for sure.

"This is already so beautiful," Mom said as she was walking past the trash balls. Mom wore a simple black dress, with purple wedge heels. "I know we saw the house last week, but seeing it with the sun starting to go down is even more incredible."

Dad was shuffling about. "What's wrong?" I asked.

"I think I left my mic in the car," he said. "At least I hope."

He started running back to the car shouting, "See what I told you, you can never be too prepared, and you'll never be prepared enough."

When he said that my nerves started acting up. I felt prepared for the night, and I think everyone from our club and our school that were participating were prepared, but what if it all went terrible. What if we weren't prepared enough?

Jackie opened the gate and let Mom walk in first. Before I could get in, Mom blocked the walkway. She brought her hand to her mouth and stood stunned.

"What's wrong?" I shouted. "What happened?" I pushed her aside and forced myself in.

It was like nothing I had ever seen.

The lights were strung up, and while the sun was still hanging above the horizon, it shined bright across the front yard. It felt like we were entering a secret garden of sorts. A garden of plastic trees. There must have been 20 trees constructed to look like a forest. Hanging on the lights above were waves of blue plastic. Each tree was built with a simple piece of wood and a small base. They were no more than four-feet in height and very thin. Each little tree was covered in green plastic, or plastic that was painted in green. It was an underwater kelp forest, engulfed in plastic. It was greater than I could have imagined.

"Jenny, did you make this?" Mom asked. She walked up to the little trees, like she was standing in a forest. Jackie took a picture.

"I think this is Eve's class," I said.

Jackie had been taking a bunch of photos. "This is going to make a great story!" she yelped.

I honestly couldn't remember Jackie that genuinely excited about anything, without putting it down first.

I joined Mom among the trees and looked at the details in the work. "Oh, Jenny, this is very cool," she said.

"Hey you two!" Eve said. She walked out to the grass from inside.

"Is this the art from your class?" I asked.

"It is," she said. "What do you think?"

"Eve, this is amazing," Mom said. "How did you get them to do this?"

"They did it, I swear," Eve said. "We brainstormed on a bunch of ideas, and they decided they wanted to make one big art piece."

"I can't believe it," I said.

"Wait until you see what the high school kids dropped off earlier," said Eve. "Come check it out inside."

I decided at that moment that I was going to leave the ocean floor map in the car.

"Eve, what do you call this?" I asked.

"Oh, is the sign not visible?" she said.

"I didn't see it, sorry."

She walked around to where it was. The little wooden sign had fallen over. She picked it up and put a few more rocks over the base. It was titled: "*Dynamic (PET) Ecosystem.*"

"All right, let's go inside," said Eve.

Dad was running up the steps. "I have it," he said. Waving the mic bag.

"Cool, Dad."

"Whoa, wow, look at this," he said. He pulled out his camera and started filming the kelp forest.

We left Dad outside, as we walked through the glass

doors. In the middle of the room was a large whale made of plastic straws, bottle caps, and plastic packaging, swimming in a kiddy pool of even more plastic pieces. On the ceiling hung seagulls with their guts exposed showing plastic in their bellies. It was kind of gross, to be honest, but I think it was going to get the point across.

Ginny had rented a bunch of the tables that were tall and small. There were other tables set out that didn't have tablecloths on top, that I could only assume were for the art work from my class. I placed the few little pieces I had. They weren't as big or glamorous as the others, but they looked like they had a seat at the table.

"Hello, hello," said Ginny, walking in the room. She was wearing a dress full of flowers that reached her calves and tall skinny heels that made her three inches taller. "What do you think so far?" She opened her arms wide like she was about to turn a letter on Wheel of Fortune.

"I don't know what to say," I said.

Mom had pulled out her phone and was taking pictures of everything. She took a picture, looked at it, then laughed. "Jenny, do you see this."

"Yeah, Mom, I see everything. I'm standing right next to you."

"Everything looks great," I said to Ginny. "Are you really expecting 200 people?"

"Well, I am expecting 200 people because I don't want anyone to go home hungry," said Ginny. "So, as you know the podium is up there, so when we are ready to start, just give me the thumbs up. Of course, I know more artwork is coming. I heard something about a six-foot water bottle?"

"Yeah, that's from the art club. They also have a boat," I said. "It's pretty cool."

"Everything is fabulous," said Ginny. "It is way beyond what I thought." She looked intently at the whale at the center of the room, and ran her fingers across the straws. "Did you take in the trees outside?"

"Yeah, wow, those are incredible," I said.

"And, the seagulls," she said pointing to the ceiling.

"It's all pretty remarkable," I said. I didn't know what else to say. It was overwhelming. I had a mix of emotions. I was happy that everything looked great, and also nervous for when people were to show up. Would they think it was as cool as I thought? I guess if Ginny thought so, then others would?

"Well, I have a few things to do. If you need anything, come hollering through the house." She walked off in perfect fashion, like a boss.

Mom looked at me like who the heck was that, even though she met her the other day, here at this house. After many emails, I came to the conclusion that this was what Ginny loved to do, and she was really good at throwing parties. She would make sure it went well. No worries, right?

There wasn't much for me to do. I wasn't filming that night, except what I could capture on my phone for our social media. Dad had it covered, and he was taking it very seriously. Almost like he thought he was auditioning for those attending.

I walked outside to the kelp forest. I knew I wasn't going to speak in front of others, but there was a feeling I was still very nervous about. I knew people would pick me out and ask me questions. I felt comfortable talking about what we were all about, but to people I didn't know, that was different.

"Hey," said Jackie. "Come over." She signaled me over to where she was standing by the fountain. "What do you think of all this?"

"Jeez, it's way more than I thought, but in a good way," I said. "It's almost as if this isn't our event."

"It is still your event. You have to understand, a lot of the parents are here supporting their children," said Jackie. "Having all these other people is a good thing, because they are interested in what you are doing."

"Oh, the impoverished kids?" I laughed.

"Oh, yeah, that reporter," Jackie said. "Let them write it. It's all good."

"You think?"

"You can correct them," she said. Jackie placed her hand into the fountain and let the water wash over her. She flipped her hand back to front. "Can I tell you something?"

"Yeah, of course."

"This is all pretty unique, you know. Like, no one I know gets this kind of attention, so quickly," she said.

"I know, I keep hearing that, especially from you. But, we did do a lot of work. It just seems like there are a lot of people that have the same interests."

"When I started, just like you, at your age, climate change was considered, but no one really cared. That was *only* six years ago. Think about how much has changed. People are willing to listen more. It's not to say they are all going to change their ways, but they will actually listen," said Jackie. "Jenny, you have their ear, you and your friends. Tonight is your night. Enjoy it, and tell them all the truth."

I knew what Jackie meant. It was easy to give the soft

truths. The truths that made people feel comfortable. "We are just kids, Jackie."

"You and I have to live with the consequences of inaction," Jackie said. She walked away.

Soon the glass house was filled.

Mom had found Conchita and they linked arms the rest of the night. Lola's parents couldn't make it, but she made sure to take a lot of pictures and videos to share with them later.

Jolene introduced me to her friends at school, and I introduced them to mine. We gathered around one another, and shared in the same nothingness that comes from initial conversation.

Celia leaned in, "I think I'm actually getting nervous."

"Oh yeah, I thought you don't get nervous," I said.

"I didn't think I did," she said.

It had been about an hour since the night officially started. It was time to begin. I found Ginny to let her know.

Ginny went to the podium and began the introductions. While she was busy naming and thanking everyone, I stood with Brian, Arjun, Jaime, Joshua, Lola, and Celia.

"This is it," I said. "Are we ready?"

"Dude, I'm ready!" said Jaime.

"Lola?"

"Ready!"

"Ok, Brian and Arjun, you're up first."

Once they heard their names announced they walked to the podium. Arjun had his guitar, and Brian had his vocal chords ready. They were going to sing their song.

The two of them played, and it felt like time stopped. The art stood out, the people watched politely, and the lights outside on the kelp garden were luminous, like snorkeling at night with a head lamp.

It was weird because they were just kids. We were all just kids.

Applause erupted, and Arjun and Brian took a bow.

Jaime and Joshua looked at one another. "You ready?" Jaime asked Joshua.

"No, but we have to do it anyway."

"Let's do this!"

They walked up in style. Their own style.

"Hello everyone, I'm Jaime."

"And I'm Josh."

Celia and I looked at each other, "*Josh?*" Then we laughed. It was good for our nerves.

"I hope you are enjoying the art," said Jaime into the microphone.

Everyone in the audience seemed to nod their heads.

"The reason we are here today is to talk to you about plastics," said Joshua.

"But, both us aren't any good at long speeches," said Jaime.

"So, we decided to write you a kind of poem," Joshua said.

That's when I pressed play and music came pouring out. It was probably a little rougher than what the audience was used to, but that's what Jaime wanted. I had watched them practice at school many times. They took turns speaking with each new line.

To the beat, they started:

"This is called 2050," said Jaime.

"That plastic cup you chose," Joshua said.

"The plastic bottle you bought at the gas station."

"The time you didn't bring your own cup."

"No, it's the time you forgot to say, *no utensils*."

"And, the time again."

"And, the time after that."

"Did you think about the albatross, who ate the spoon?"

"And the other sea bird who swallowed five bottle caps."

"And the lid, that broke into smaller pieces in the ocean."

"That looked like food."

"Was the island of trash not enough?"

"Did you have to swim through it?"

"To feel the plastic in your fingers."

"Would it be the loss of the coral reefs?"

"Or, the thousands of marine animals."

"Will it matter that the ocean became a dead zone?"

"Or, will it be when you can no longer look out."

"At the horizon and see a whale spout in the distance?"

"What will it be that makes you say, 'Enough?'"

"What will it be that makes you decide to say no to the plastic packaging?"

"The bag."

"I have my own."

"I won't buy that."

"Will you look back?"

"In 2050."

"And, say I knew."

"And, I did nothing."

"Or, will you dive deep in the ocean?"

"See the beauty for all that is it supposed to be."

"And say you refused plastic."

Their hip hop riff was complete, and the crowd loved it. The applause was loud and long. They were so good!

"I guess they liked their flow better than our song," said Brian.

"Nah, it's just different," I said. "They're both great."

I looked at Celia and Lola. "Your turn!"

"Bring it on," said Celia.

The two of them walked up to the podium.

Celia took ahold of the microphone. "Hello everyone. Thank you for coming tonight. I'm Celia."

"And I'm Lola." She waved to the audience.

"We are so happy to have you all here," Celia started. "We never thought our little class could have ever been part of something so big. When we started we never had the intention to have a big event, or build a website and connect with other schools and organizations."

"It has been a great experience, and we are forever thankful," said Lola.

Celia took in a deep breath, letting her shoulder drop low. She looked at me, and I gave her the thumbs up, like Ms. Morgan had given me so many times before.

"My whole life I have learned about climate change in class. Well, somewhat. I heard words like global warming and greenhouse gases casually thrown into our lesson on the water cycle. I imagined a green plant wilting and dying in a windowed-hall. Well, I said to myself, just plant more? That was my first-grade self. When I was in second grade my teacher told us about how to reuse packaging for our lunch instead of plastic baggies. Then it was looking at endangered species because of habitat loss. All of a sudden nobody was saying global warming anymore, it was climate change because not everyone or everywhere was going to get super hot. Well, at least that was what I thought."

Lola took the microphone. "None of our teachers really wanted to talk about it, though. They threw in some vocabulary, and we discussed trash and recycling. We all said things like eco-friendly, but most of us didn't even know what *eco* meant, and nobody cared to ask. Of course this was all before Ms. Morgan came to our school. She was the first teacher to talk about the climate crisis, which really took hold of my attention. *Climate Crisis!* It was frightening the way it came out. I went from making sure items went into the proper bins to melting polar ices caps and sea level rise. I listened to every word. I couldn't be the only one shaken?"

Lola passed the microphone back to Celia. "Of course I had been keeping my thoughts to myself. I wasn't ready to share. It's frightening raising your hand. I thought that people who are passionate were people that were older. People who read a lot of books, or even wrote books. They are the kind of people who speak their mind. The kind of people who aren't afraid."

Celia passed the mic back to Lola. "But, if I continued to feel intimidated, I asked myself, 'What do I gain by being silent?' I decided that I didn't want to live a life where I was afraid to stand up for what I want, and what I believe everyone deserves. I said to myself, we have to have more people that care, otherwise before we know it there won't be a planet to live in."

Celia took the mic once again. "So we got together. We studied our oceans. We studied human behavior at our school. We wrote letters to our congresswoman, and we cleaned up trash at our school. Individually we cleaned up trash at the beach. We reached out to others and we shared our stories. Then others started sharing their stories with us. And, we found out that we have a lot of similarities. One of them is that we want a healthy planet to live on. We found out we have more in common than what we disagree about."

Lola took the mic for the last time. "We are gathered here today to show how much plastic is out there in the ocean. We also came here to demonstrate what students are capable of. We want to show you that we care, and we are begging you all to care as well. We are told that in just ten years there will be more plastic than fish. We are told that ice shelves are melting. We are told Florida and many other islands outside of the United States will be underwater. We are told that the air will be toxic, and that our home, here in California, will have constant severe fires that will burn throughout the state. We are asking for a better way of life. It's not just plastics, but we needed to start somewhere."

Lola passed Celia the mic. "When we got together and started talking we found so many others that wanted a better way of life. There are students all over the world that have great ideas. We want to be able to support those great ideas. Thank you for coming tonight, thank you for listening to our speeches and songs. Thank you to everyone who made incredible artwork. Thank you, Ms. Morgan. Thank you, everyone."

They received a loud round of applause. They were incredible. I had heard them practice so many times before, but there was nothing like a microphone and a room full of people listening to you what you have to say.

There was a new feeling that came through my body.

It wasn't the familiar nervousness. It warmed me up and made my skin tingle. I think it was hope.

COURAGE

We packed the car with food, water, a blanket, and sunscreen. We were headed to the beach. Both Mom and Dad drove so we could fit Celia, Lola, Jolene, and I. Jackie came as well. We were going to have a picnic at the beach, do a beach clean-up, and Celia and Lola were going to learn how to surf.

When Jolene had introduced us to Melanie at the art show Celia couldn't wait a second longer and blurted out, "Can you teach me to surf?" Melanie seemed more than happy, and she actually answered her phone when Celia called the following week.

Mom and Dad helped Lola and Celia rent wetsuits at one of the local surf shops on our way to the beach below Melanie's house. Jolene had brought her own.

"Aren't you going to surf with us?" Celia asked me.

"Maybe another time," I said. I wasn't scared or worried, I just knew they wanted it more than I did, and I didn't want to get in their way.

While they went out with Melanie and her friend, I sat back with my family on the sand.

"I have an announcement," said Jackie.

"Did you finally pick a college?" Mom asked.

"Actually, yes," Jackie said.

"Oh, I can't wait!" Mom squealed. She straightened the blanket, readying herself for the news.

"Drum roll," Dad said, tapping his index fingers on his knees.

"UC San Diego," Jackie announced. "To study marine biology."

"That's wonderful, Jackie," Dad said.

"Oh, I'm so happy you aren't going to be too far away," Mom said, pulling Jackie in for a hug.

"I didn't know you wanted to study the ocean?" I said.

"I didn't at first, but something inspired me in the last few months." She smiled at me.

There was so much that inspired me in the last few months. When the art show ended, we were all relieved it went well, and were soon taken aback with the money we raised that night. There was so much I had to learn about the financial side, donations and the rest, but it was a strong first start.

Brian wrote a piece the next day discussing the event, and we posted on our website. A week later we posted more stories from the two newspapers who ran an article about our event. Those, and the videos we put on our social media, grew our following by a couple hundred new people.

We were able to buy buckets and grabbers for Jolene's class, who had set up three beach clean-ups over the summer. Lola got her reusable plates and utensils for school events. We held a school assembly after Dad and I finished the final edit from the art show, and Celia passed out her beeswax bags to as many people who wanted one.

I often wondered if Ms. Morgan had this plan all along.

Remembering Jackie on the newspaper panel felt so long ago. She was ready with information, she knew what she wanted to say, she was passionate, and she was not in the least bit nervous to speak her mind. Jackie was up against others who had an equal and opposite reaction, and yet she held her cool and kept fighting back. I realize now, we need more Jackies speaking for the planet's health.

I also realized that I'm not the type of person who wants to speak in front of crowds. I'm terrified, but I still have ideas and I find that when I stand behind the camera, I am able to share more.

I looked up from the sand just in time to see Celia catch a wave. She fell off her board almost as soon as she stood up, but when her head popped up out of the water she threw her hands up and shouted, "I did it!"

She walked to the shore and picked up her board, tucking it in under her right arm. If you were to look at a live map, I wonder if you could see a human that stood at the very intersection of the land and the water. A tiny dot on the map, where the blue meets the green.

At one time we all seemed so small. The problems we discovered at the beginning of the school year were too big for us. Yet here we are, with solutions at our fingertips, and ready to face what comes next. Maybe we are still small, but we found out we're not insignificant. We just eliminated fear and found out we had crazy amounts of courage.

The End

ACKNOWLEDGEMENTS

Nothing great is easy, and nothing is done all on your own. For this single book to have been written there were generations of strong women and men who led courageous lives. I am grateful to stand here today because of the actions and bravery of those who came before.

Thank you to the team at Atmosphere Press, Nick, Alex, Erin, Ronaldo, Evan, and Cammie, and all the others behind the scenes. Everything looks so beautiful!

A special thank you to a class I taught (you know who you are), who inspired this book, and who made me realize we can all make a difference if we believe in ourselves.

A special thank you to all my friends and family, and to my wonderful Coastside community. Thank you to my parents Tim and Guadalupe Iverson for giving me the platform to be wild and whimsical. To my beautiful sister Erika for everything. A special thank you to my ever-supportive husband Curt, the producer. And, to the reason for it all, my daughter Coral. You are the sun that guides and warms my life. You are the greatest gift. Now, let's go travel the world.

RESOURCES
(you may find helpful on your journey):

Books:

How to Change Everything, Naomi Klein with Rebecca Stefoff

Youth to Power, Jamie Margolin

No One is Too Small To Make A Difference, Greta Thunberg

Drawdown The Most Comprehensive Plan Ever Proposed to Reduce Global Warming, Paul Hawkin

Documentaries:

A Plastic Ocean

Chasing Coral

Websites:

https://www.nationalgeographic.org/encyclopedia/ocean/

https://www.noaa.gov/ocean-coasts

http://www.savethebay.org

https://www.marine-ed.org/ocean-literacy/overview

https://www.epa.gov/

https://www.congress.gov/bill/116th-congress/house-bill/5845

ABOUT ATMOSPHERE PRESS

Atmosphere Press is an independent, full-service publisher for excellent books in all genres and for all audiences. Learn more about what we do at atmospherepress.com.

We encourage you to check out some of Atmosphere's latest releases, which are available at Amazon.com and via order from your local bookstore:

The Gingerbread Diva, by LaNesha Tabb
Gloppy, by Janice Laakko
Wildly Perfect, by Brooke McMahan
How Grizzly Found Gratitude, by Dennis Mathew
Do Lions Cry?, by Erina White
Sadie and Charley Finding Their Way, by Bonnie Griesemer
Silly Sam and the Invisible Jinni, by Shayla Emran Bajalia
Feeling My Feelings, by Shilpi Mahajan
Zombie Mombie Saves the Day, by Kelly Lucero
The Fable King, by Sarah Philpot
Blue Goggles for Lizzy, by Amanda Cumbey
Neville and the Adventure to Cricket Creek, by Juliana Houston
Peculiar Pets: A Collection of Exotic and Quixotic Animal Poems, by Kerry Cramer

ABOUT THE AUTHOR

Sonia Myers started her writing career at the Half Moon Bay Review Newspaper contributing articles and reporting on sports. She is currently a middle school science teacher, and a 2021 Grosvenor Teacher Fellow with National Geographic and Lindblad Expeditions. She lives on the California coast with her husband and daughter. *We Have Something to Say!* is her first novel.

Made in the USA
Middletown, DE
22 September 2021